Praise for
RONDA THOMPSON's
Previous Novels

THE UNTAMED ONE

"Thompson cleverly blends paranormal elements into a fine-tuned historical romance with well-crafted characters and a tender, blossoming romance."

—*RT BOOKclub* magazine

"*The Untamed One* . . . is compelling and sexy. It's also smart and well-written."

—*Romance Reader at Heart*

THE DARK ONE

"Gripping, intriguing, and sexy. Engaging characters and edge-of-the-seat action—this book has it all."

—Christine Feehan

"*The Dark One* grabbed me and wouldn't let me go. Sensual and engaging, Thompson redefines the werewolf story even as her characters redefine for themselves the meaning of love."

—Susan Squires

"This story hooked me from page one and never let me go. I can't wait for the next one!"

—Amanda Ashley

"A deliciously dark world . . . [illegible]es of humor, great passion, and exceptional chara[illegible]

[illegible]*OOKclub* magazine

"This well-written [illegible] characters, utterly romantic lo[illegible]y captivated me from the very b[illegible] ending."

[illegible]*Paranormal Romance Writers*

MORE . . .

"Completely, utterly, absolutely engaging. I was swept away by the story of Armond Wulf and Rosalind Rutherford. *The Dark One* is one of the most wonderful tales I've gotten my hands on in a long time. I'm so thankful Ms. Thompson decided to make this a series. The Wild Wulfs of London will definitely be on my 'must buy' list!"

—*Romance Divas*

"Ronda Thompson delivers a fresh and everlasting Regency romance with a touch of magic and evil that will stand the test of time. Oh, and the smokin' hero helps!"

—*Romance Reader at Heart*

"I love paranormals, and this one is one of the best!"

—*Romance Junkies*

"Readers will believe in the existence of the werewolf . . . sub-genre fans will fully treasure the first Wild Wulfs of London thriller. 5 stars!"

—Harriet Klausner

ST. MARTIN'S PAPERBACKS TITLES
BY RONDA THOMPSON

The Dark One
The Untamed One
The Cursed One

THE CURSED ONE

Book Three in the Wild Wulfs of London series

RONDA THOMPSON

St. Martin's Paperbacks

This is a work of fiction. All of the characters, organizations and events portrayed in this novel are either products of the author's imagination or are used fictitiously.

THE CURSED ONE

ISBN: 0-312-93575-7
EAN: 978-0312-93575-7

Printed in the United States of America

St. Martin's Paperbacks edition / December 2006

St. Martin's Paperbacks are published by St. Martin's Press, 175 Fifth Avenue, New York, NY 10010.

10 9 8 7 6 5 4 3 2 1

TO MARLEY AND SHANE. *I wish you both all the joy and romance years of marriage and reading have given to me. Hold hands through your life jouney together. Be happy.*

Love, MOM

THE CURSED ONE

Damn the witch who cursed me.
I thought her heart was pure.
Alas, no woman understands duty,
be it to family, name, or war.
I found no way to break it,
no potion, chant, or deed.
From the day she cast the spell,
it will pass from seed to seed.

Betrayed by love, my own false tongue,
she bade the moon transform me.
The family name, once my pride,
becomes the beast that haunts me.
And in the witch's passing hour
she called me to her side.
Forgiveness lost, of mercy none,
she spoke before she died:

"Seek you and find your worst enemy;
stand brave and do not flee.
Love is the curse that binds you,
but 'tis also the key to set you free."

Her curse and riddle my bane,
this witch I loved yet could not wed.
Battles I have fought and won,
and still defeat I leave in my stead.
To the Wulfs who suffer my sins,
the sons who are neither man nor beast,
solve the conundrum I could not,
and be from this curse released.

IVAN WULF,
In the year of our Lord seventeen hundred and fifteen

CHAPTER ONE

COLLINGSWORTH MANOR, ENGLAND, 1821

Her husband was going to kill her. The thought struck Lady Amelia Sinclair Collingsworth about the time Lord Collingsworth's hands closed around her throat. But his usually soft hands did not feel like hands in the darkness. They felt like . . . claws. It was her wedding night, and Amelia's shy husband was acting neither shy nor like the gentleman she had married early that morning in London. What had gotten into him?

"Robert, you're hurting me!" she gasped, pinned beneath him on the marriage bed where she had planned to lose her innocence, not her life.

Her bridegroom laughed. Not a normal-sounding one. His voice was deep and garbled, as if he had a throat full of rocks. The feel of his clawlike fingers moved down her neck, ripped the nightgown she wore open from neckline to waist. Amelia screamed, struggling beneath his weight, which was surprisingly heavy for a man her father had once referred to as "frail looking."

"Robert, please!" she begged. "You are frightening me!"

The laugh again. The one that rose hackles on the back of her neck. "Robert is not here," he rasped.

What did he mean by that? Was Amelia having a nightmare? Maybe she would wake in a moment and find herself in her parents' home in London. Maybe she had not married that morning in front of a great number of London's upper crust. Maybe she had not journeyed to Robert's country estate with him for a short honeymoon before they were to travel abroad for an extended celebration of their nuptials.

"I'm dreaming," Amelia whispered, trying to reassure herself. "I will wake in a moment."

Robert barked a short laugh and rolled off of her. Amelia could breathe again. There were sounds of ripping cloth and she thought Robert might now be tearing at his own nightshirt. Dream or not, the hammering of Amelia's heart inside of her chest, the sting of scratches upon her neck, felt real. Every instinct she possessed cried out for her to run . . . while she still could.

She rolled toward the edge of the bed, thinking to make her escape. Bony fingers yanked her back, then Robert was on top of her . . . only he was naked . . . and his skin did not feel like skin. It felt like fur.

Amelia formed her nails into claws and raked his eyes. Robert howled like a wounded animal. She pushed with all her strength and scrambled from beneath him. Rolling, Amelia landed with a thud upon the floor. She quickly crawled away from the bed. For modesty's sake, which she didn't have much of, Robert had insisted the lamps remain unlit. The darkness was as heavy as a blanket. Where was the door?

"Bitch!"

The garbled hiss sent chills up Amelia's spine and froze her in her tracks. She was afraid to move. Afraid he'd know her location. Groping around on the floor, her hand met with the leg of a piece of furniture. A secretary, she recalled, having only seen Robert's adjoining room earlier when she'd come upstairs for a short nap before dinner.

Slowly Amelia rose to her knees. She searched the desktop until her fingers grasped something cold and thin. Before she had time to identify the object, she was jerked back and slammed against the hardwood floor.

"You are mine now."

Although she couldn't see Robert in the darkness, Amelia felt him looming over her. His breath was fetid, like the breath of an animal that ate raw meat. Her head hurt where she had struck the floor. Her neck stung from the scratches. Robert shoved her gown up and forced her knees apart. The feel of his smooth, sharp claws against her thighs churned the bile in her stomach.

Now this man, this thing, who couldn't be Robert, would defile her. Amelia's mother had told her that she must meekly submit to Robert on their wedding night. That she must do all that he asked of her. Like hell she would. Clutching the thin, cold object in her hand, she brought it up and struck out.

There was a sound, a sound that reminded her of Cook stabbing a knife into raw mutton. Robert suddenly howled again, then toppled backward off of her. Heart still hammering, Amelia flipped onto her belly and crawled away. She expected the clawlike hands to grab her foot at any moment, expected Robert would kill her in his wounded rage. Instead, the door to her adjoining suite suddenly crashed open.

Amelia had left a candle burning in her room. The soft glow outlined the silhouette of a man—a man nearly as tall as a tree and built like one. Candlelight danced within the strands of his golden hair. Now Amelia knew she must be dreaming. She'd dreamed of this man often.

"What the bloody hell is going on?" he demanded.

Odd. He had never spoken in her dreams before. If he had, she would have conjured just the voice he spoke with now. Deep, low, disturbingly sensual. Only Lord Gabriel Wulf would have a voice like that. Only he would come crashing through her nightmares to save her. But of course he couldn't really be here. This couldn't really be happening. She giggled at her own imagination, but she couldn't ignore the hysterical edge it held.

"Who's there?" he asked.

Would he converse with her if she answered? Her dream had grown more absurd by the moment. "Lady Amelia," she answered. "Collingsworth," she added, then stifled another giggle. "Or I was. I've just killed my husband."

An awkward pause followed her statement. The silhouette stepped farther into the room. Amelia noticed the dark shape of a pistol clutched in his hand. Oh, good grief. Would he shoot her now? Would the nightmare turn from Robert trying to kill her to Gabriel Wulf becoming the murderer?

"Where is Lord Collingsworth?"

Amelia supposed even in a dream she should answer a man carrying a weapon. "There, on the floor beside the bed." If she was dreaming, and she must be, the nightmare was much too vivid. She swore she felt blood trickling down her neck. "Robert . . . he tried to hurt me. He is . . . not himself."

Why she bothered to explain anything when nothing about her dream made one whit of sense Amelia did not know. But perhaps on a deeper level she did understand why she would dream that her husband of one day had become a monster and why Lord Gabriel Wulf had appeared to save her. Society was the true monster.

Doing what had been expected of her came with a punishment. Gabriel Wulf represented the rebellious side of her nature. He represented freedom.

"Robert is not here."

That he would repeat the very words Robert had rasped raised the hair on her arms. More than a reminder of earlier events unnerved her. If Robert was not there, where was he?

A dark shape suddenly loomed up behind Amelia's blond angel. A flash of silver shone in the darkness. The object moved downward in a stabbing motion, straight into Gabriel Wulf's shoulder. There were sounds of a scuffle. A pistol fired. Amelia screamed and closed her eyes, covering her ears with her hands. She screamed again when someone touched her.

"Don't be afraid. I won't hurt you."

How could a man possess a voice that was darkly sensual and yet soothing at the same time? One couldn't. Not unless he was a figment of her imagination. Amelia grasped that tiny shred of sanity and held it to her. She should wake now. Wake before she threw herself into his arms. Before comfort became something else. But she did not wake, nor did she throw herself at Lord Gabriel Wulf. The door to Robert's room suddenly creaked open. A tiny flame flickered there.

"My lady?" a female voice called. "I heard a shot. What is happening?"

Eyes round with fright, a slim figure hovered in the doorway. Amelia couldn't recall the young servant's name. She had been the only one to greet Amelia and Robert when they'd arrived at Collingsworth Manor. The girl, willow thin and around Amelia's height, wore a worn dress, an apron, and a cap upon her head, covering the entirety of her hair. Amelia had judged her to be around fifteen and certainly too young to take on the responsibilities she had at Collingsworth Manor.

Robert had been more than a little distressed to learn all of his servants but this girl were gone. Only one man had been tending the stable. Her husband had told Amelia to go upstairs and rest while he got to the heart of the matter. But later, when the girl had come to fetch Amelia for supper, Robert had acted differently. He hadn't wanted to discuss what he had learned.

"My lady?" the girl called again.

"Bring the light over here, girl!" Gabriel Wulf ordered. "Quickly!"

As if from a long distance, Amelia saw the flicking flame of the candle move closer. The girl bent beside her, the candle casting an eerie glow around the dark room. Amelia's gaze sought out Gabriel Wulf. She'd once seen him riding down the streets of London with his older brother, Lord Armond Wulf. At the time she had thought Gabriel Wulf was the most handsome man she had ever seen . . . and he still was.

It was him all right. She might be gawking like a milkmaid, but he was busy studying her form, probably looking for signs of injury, possibly looking at her breasts, which had no doubt spilled from the front of her torn nightgown. He gently touched her neck, and Amelia winced. His gaze lifted and met hers. In the dim candlelight, his eyes widened a fraction.

"You," he said softly, although she had no idea what that meant.

Amelia's head began to spin. Her vision blurred. Darkness closed in on her, and Gabriel Wulf's face became farther and farther away. She had never fainted in her life, but she realized that was exactly what she was getting ready to do.

Lord Gabriel Wulf gathered the unconscious woman in his arms and rose. If he didn't have adrenaline racing through his blood like wildfire at the moment, he might have been more conscious of the stab wound to his shoulder and the even more serious bullet wound to his thigh. He carried the woman into the adjoining room and placed her upon the bed.

"Water," he called over his shoulder to the serving girl. "And clean cloths to wipe away the blood."

He touched the lady's neck again. Two deep scratches marred her pale skin. He glanced at her face, making sure she was, in fact, who he thought she was. Her skin was like white marble. Soft blond curls framed her face, and her eyes, when open, were heavy lashed and as blue as a robin's egg. Her face was oval shaped and she had a slight dimple in her chin.

She was beautiful, which he supposed was the reason she had caught his eye on the streets of London months ago to begin with. He'd never met her, but since that day he had dreamed of her. Often.

"The water, my lord."

Even while carrying a clean crock of water and washing cloths stuffed beneath her arm, the young servant moved as silently as night slipped into dawn. She settled the crock next to a basin on the stand beside the bed.

"Where are the other servants? The head housekeeper?" he asked the girl.

"Gone," she whispered. "Everyone is gone. Frightened away."

Gabriel poured the fresh water from the crock into the empty basin. "Frightened away by what?" He'd spent a good deal of his boyhood at Collingsworth Manor and never had thought there was anything to fear here.

For a moment, the girl did not answer. Gabriel glanced up at her. "I fear if I tell you, my lord, you will think I'm daft in the head."

"Give it a go," he said drily. Gabriel was trying like hell to ignore the pain in his shoulder, the throbbing in his leg, and the fact that he had just shot his boyhood friend.

"Beasts, my lord," the girl whispered. "The beasts in the woods surrounding the house. Sometimes they are wolves. But sometimes they are men."

A normal man would indeed think the girl was daft. Gabriel was not a normal man. "Have you seen these creatures, girl?"

Lowering her gaze, she nodded. "Yes, my lord."

Gabriel took the clean cloths the girl had brought and dipped one in the water. "And yet you stayed when everyone else fled? Are you so very brave?"

Her head jerked up and she shook it vigorously. "No, my lord. I had nowhere to go. Got no family except my brother, and he's off working God knows where. Was new to the staff and then this business began. No one offered for me to come along. It was every man for himself when they ran."

Gently dabbing at the unconscious woman's neck, Gabriel asked, "Why did you not answer my summons downstairs? I saw that there were still lamps burning in the house."

"Don't answer the door these days," she said. "Not with this strange business going on."

Gabriel still wasn't certain what "business" he had stumbled upon. What had gotten into Robert to attack his bride? To attack Gabriel, as well? He'd only stopped at Collingsworth Manor because of the throbbing wound to his thigh and his lame horse. No one had been in the stable when he'd stalled his horse.

He'd thought about simply stealing one of Robert's horses and forging ahead to Wulfglen, his own family estate, which bordered the lands of Collingsworth Manor, but he and Robert had been boyhood friends. Conscience dictated that Gabriel at least ask the man for the use of one of his horses.

When no one had answered Gabriel's summons earlier at the door, he'd resigned himself that he might indeed be forced to take one of Robert's horses and explain later. Then he'd heard screams. He'd tried the door again, but it was firmly bolted against him. Recalling a tree that he and his brothers had often scrambled down from Robert's room, when they would swim naked late at night in a pond not far from the house, Gabriel had climbed the tree to gain access to the house.

Once he'd slipped inside, the screams had led him to this room, where he realized they were actually coming from the adjoining suite. The lady moaned and he glanced back down at her. Her gown was torn open, and although he tried not to notice, her pale breasts were partly exposed to his eyes. He glanced away.

"Tend to her," he told the girl, placing the bloodied cloth aside. "Find something to cover her."

He rose, took the candle, and went into the next room. Gabriel half-expected Robert to come at him again, even though he was fairly certain a shot from a pistol at close range had killed the man. He still couldn't quite believe he had killed Robert or that his boyhood friend had stabbed him. The Robert he had known was a shy, frail boy.

Their friendship had ended years ago. All of Gabriel's prior friendships had ended once it was discovered that the Wulf family was cursed.

Moving the candle closer to the floor, although he had no need for the added light, Gabriel searched the area. He saw quite well in the darkness, but what he saw confused him. It was not Robert Collingsworth who lay dead on the floor from a bullet wound.

"Girl," he called. "Come here."

Quiet as a mouse, she appeared beside him.

"Who is this man?" Gabriel asked her.

The servant sucked in her breath sharply. " 'Tis Vincent. Stable help—the only one left who hadn't run away. What is he doing in the lord's bedchamber?"

A question Gabriel wanted answered, as well. What the man had been doing, or trying to do, was obvious. He was naked. Where was Robert? How had he let something like this happen?

"See to the lady," Gabriel said to the girl. "I will search for Lord Collingsworth."

"Don't go outside," she warned. "You may not come back."

Gabriel suspected the girl's imagination had gotten away with her, yet he knew such things existed as men who could shift their shapes. Years earlier, Gabriel's father had killed himself over just such a transformation. Gabriel's mother had followed his father shortly to the grave, a result of shock or madness. All of society believed the Wulfs were cursed by insanity, and they were therefore excluded from the social set. Gabriel had always thought the joke was on them. If only it were a mere case of madness.

Gabriel walked toward the door leading into the hallway. "Close that door." He indicated the adjoining one, although it hung precariously from its hinges. A result of Gabriel's foot.

"What about . . . about him?" The girl nodded toward the body on the floor.

"I'll deal with him later," he assured her.

After exiting Lord Collingsworth's bedchamber, Gabriel snuffed out the candle he held. He had unusually good eyesight in the dark. He had unusually good hearing. He had a good deal of unusual things about him. He decided to check the upstairs rooms first.

Nothing looked out of place upstairs. It was upon the stairs going down to the lower level that he again became aware of his injuries. For months he'd been searching for his younger brother Jackson. The fool had gone missing in London, and Gabriel had promised his older brother, Armond, that he would find Jackson. It hadn't been easy, tracking him.

Finally, Gabriel had trailed Jackson to a little village called Whit Hurch. Gabriel had ridden into the village to inquire as to whether or not anyone knew the whereabouts of his brother, only to be set upon by angry villagers carrying pitchforks and muskets. The villagers had obviously mistaken him for Jackson. Gabriel took a ball to the thigh before he'd been able to get his horse turned around and charge his way through the mob.

They'd given chase. He'd spent the better part of a week trying to lose them. He'd spent the better part of another making his way back to Wulfglen. For all he knew, his idiot younger brother had returned home. Now this.

The parlors downstairs were empty. The study, as well. In the kitchen, a pot of stew simmered on the stove. Gabriel limped toward the pantry. Not well stocked, and empty of anything save necessary staples. He found a door leading down to the root cellar.

The stairs creaked beneath his weight. His thigh throbbed. It was blacker than pitch, but still, he made out shapes. A scurrying mouse—supplies that needed the cooler temperature to keep from spoiling. The cellar smelled like damp dirt and . . . he stopped. Gabriel closed his eyes for a moment and inhaled. Death.

Gabriel moved farther into the cellar, already sure of what he would find. Robert lay upon the damp dirt floor, staring sightlessly upward, his face a mask of horror, one hand clutched to his heart. He was dead.

Chapter Two

That awful smell. Amelia came up from the darkness in a rush. She fought to remove the foul-smelling odor from beneath her nose.

"There now, my lady. It's only the smelling salts to bring you back."

Amelia coughed. She glanced around the room, confused. It was not her room in London. The nightmare came rushing back. Chill bumps rose on her flesh. Was she still dreaming? God, she hoped so.

"Pinch me," she whispered to the serving girl. "Pinch me so I can wake up."

The girl's large eyes softened. "You are not dreaming, my lady. You've had a terrible fright."

Amelia glanced toward the door joining her room with her bridegroom's. It was closed but hung oddly upon the hinges. Gabriel Wulf had kicked the door open. Or she thought it was Gabriel Wulf.

"There was a man. . . ."

"I know, my lady," the girl said. "From the stable, and I don't know how he got into the house, or into the young lord's room. He's dead now. The other man killed him."

Amelia's head began to reel again. "What? What man from the stable are you talking about?"

"Vincent," the girl answered. "He's the one dead in the next room. Don't know the other man. Tall as an oak and nearly as broad in the shoulders. Have no idea how either man came to be in the house. I bolted the doors myself."

"But." Amelia rubbed her pounding temples. "But it was Lord Collingsworth in the next room. I saw him in the candlelight when he rapped upon the door and bade me to join him."

The girl frowned. She shook her head again. "Not your husband in there. Vincent, from the stable. That's who tried to hurt you. The other man has gone in search of the lord."

Lying back against the pillows, Amelia tried to digest what the girl had told her. It had been Robert who bade Amelia to join him in their marriage bed. How could what the servant said possibly be true? But why would she lie to Amelia? And if this was not a nightmare, was it really Gabriel Wulf who'd gone in search of Robert? And if it was, whatever was Gabriel doing at Collingsworth Manor?

The door to her room opened. A blond giant of a man stepped inside. Lord Gabriel Wulf. He glanced at Amelia, then at the girl. "Will you fetch us something to drink? Something strong?"

The girl nodded. She moved toward the door but hesitated, her eyes round and frightened. "Are you sure it's safe?"

"It's all right," Wulf said. "There's no one else in the house. I made certain."

Reluctantly, the girl continued toward the door.

"Bring up some of that stew cooking on the stove," Wulf called to her. "The lady could probably use sustenance."

Amelia eyed Gabriel Wulf warily. It was a night to be wary, if she was not in fact dreaming. "What are you doing here?"

He swayed a bit on his feet and glanced around the room. "One of those dainty chairs would break beneath me." He indicated two Queen Anne chairs arranged before Amelia's hearth. "May I sit upon the bed? It's my leg."

She noticed a dark stain covered the thigh of his buckskin breeches. "Are you injured?"

Without waiting for her permission, he limped forward and settled his weight against the soft down of her mattress. "It's the reason I stopped. That and because my horse is lame. I planned to ask Lord Collingsworth to borrow one of his and push on to Wulfglen but . . ."

Still dazed, Amelia whispered, "The girl said the man in the next room is not Robert. I tell you it must be. It was he who knocked upon my door and bade me to join him."

Dark, thick lashes veiled Wulf's gaze until he glanced up at her. His eyes were vividly green, not hazel, no hint of brown—green, like springtime. Dark whiskers shadowed his strong jawline. His hair was dark blond with streaks so light they almost appeared silver in the candlelight. For a big man, his features were refined. Short, straight nose, dark brows, high cheekbones, and a mouth sculpted perfectly to fit the rest of his features. He was breathtaking.

"Lord Collingsworth is dead," Wulf said bluntly. "I found him in the root cellar."

Amelia stared blankly at him. She feared she was in shock and his words could not penetrate her mind. The events leading up to now could not penetrate. She hadn't loved Robert. She'd married him because he was a good match and her parents had approved of him. Amelia might have tried to fool herself into believing she would one day come to love him, but she did not believe in love. "Love" was a pretty word people used instead of "lust" or "duty."

"Dead," she repeated, stunned, although not a moment past she had thought he was dead in the next room. "Dead from what?"

Wulf ran a hand over his cheeks. "Near as I can tell, his heart. I didn't find a scratch on him."

Tears stung her eyes. Amelia blinked them back. It didn't matter whether she loved Robert or not; he was her husband. She wouldn't wish him dead. Spoiled and coddled all of her life, Amelia had expected her young husband to continue in that vein. Now he was supposedly dead. And the man in the next room supposedly was not her husband at all. It didn't make sense.

"This can't be happening," she whispered. "I swear to you, it was Robert in the next room with me earlier. There wasn't time for a switch to take place."

Wulf scooted closer to a basin that rested on the night table, grabbed a cloth, and wrung it out. "Your neck," he said. "It's bleeding again."

She still felt the sting of the scratches. He dabbed gently at the area. Amelia did have the presence of mind to glance down at herself, relieved to discover she'd been draped by a thin blanket. Her robe lay beside her on the bed.

Her nightgown was thin and a bit daring for a new bride, but Amelia had always been a bit daring. The gauze material had ripped easily beneath Robert's . . . claws. She shuddered.

"I'll light a fire." Lord Gabriel obviously mistook her reaction for one of being chilled. He put the cloth he'd used to wipe blood from her neck in the washbasin, rose, and limped toward the hearth.

The girl entered a moment later. A heavenly aroma wafted from two steaming bowls on the tray the servant carried. Amelia swore she could not eat at a time like this, but her stomach disagreed with a soft grumble.

"I've brought the stew," the girl called to Wulf. "And a bottle of brandy. Thought it might help warm the lady."

For all her youth, the girl seemed mature for her age. Amelia, however, knew she was on the verge of hysteria. The night's events seemed unreal. Like a dream or, rather, a nightmare. Collingsworth Manor had given her an uneasy feeling from the moment she and Robert first arrived.

The house wasn't as large as she had expected. It was constructed of crumbling white stone. Thorny, bare bushes surrounded the house. Dead. All the greenery that surrounded the house was dead and ill kept. There was a nice archway that led into the yard, but what ivy had managed to survive was sparse and unattractive. The shutters all needed paint. The house looked as if it was falling down. The condition of Robert's country home had surprised her. Surprised and distressed her.

Robert had assured Amelia's father that he would take proper care of her. That she would have the finest of everything, as she was accustomed to. Her bridegroom had laughed upon seeing her expression when they'd arrived at Collingsworth Manor. Robert told her she would have a free hand in making it presentable again.

As a bachelor, Robert admitted he had no flair for such things or any interest in them. His horses were what interested him most at Collingsworth Manor. The horses and the rich farmland . . . but the fields had looked neglected when they'd driven past them. Robert had said nothing, but she knew he'd been brooding about the matter for the remainder of their journey. To arrive and learn most of his servants had fled had only added to his bad humor.

"The coachman," Amelia suddenly recalled. "And a footman. They accompanied us from London. They should have been in the stable."

Now that a fire blazed behind him, Wulf limped back toward the bed. "There was no one in the stable," he assured her. "I called out so as not to be mistaken for a horse thief."

"Maybe they've run away like everyone else," the girl said softly.

By speaking, the servant drew Wulf's attention. "Put the tray over there," he instructed, pointing to a chest with a mirror. He winced and rubbed his shoulder. Blood stained his shirt as well as his dusty trousers.

Amelia recalled that Robert, or, rather, whoever had been in the next room with her, had stabbed Lord Gabriel. Here he was, fussing over a couple of scratches to her neck, and the man might be bleeding to death.

"Lord Gabriel," Amelia called. "Please come and sit. You need your own injuries seen to."

Instead of obeying, he walked to the chest, lifted a decanter of brandy, filled two glasses, downed the contents of one, and brought the other to her.

"Time enough for that later," he said, extending the glass toward her. "Drink this. It will burn at first, but it will strengthen you."

He didn't have to ask her twice. Amelia took the glass, brought it to her lips, and drank the contents without stopping. When she finished, she noted Wulf's raised brow. "I've had brandy before," she explained. "In fact, it was your sister-in-law Lady Wulf who introduced me to it."

"Rosalind?"

She nodded. "We are the best of friends."

Wulf did sit then, and upon the edge of her bed. "How do you know my name?"

How foolish Amelia now felt for all the hours she'd spent thinking of Gabriel Wulf when she should have been thinking of Robert, who'd at least paid her court. She'd only seen Lord Gabriel once, and yet he'd stayed in her thoughts. Even this morning, as she'd said her vows, his image had popped into her head.

"I saw you once in London. Later, I recognized you

from the portrait that hangs in your family town home. Rosalind told me your name." She lifted her empty glass. "Could I have another?"

Wulf glanced at the girl, who quickly fetched the decanter. While the servant poured, Amelia tried to gather her strength. Feeling Gabriel's eyes upon her, she forced herself to at least sip the liquor this time. "Would you look away while I slip into my robe? I wish to rise, and my gown is torn."

For the briefest of seconds, Wulf's eyes moved down her body and up again. "I noticed."

It was an odd thing to say in the face of everything else going on. He'd noticed her gown had been ripped, her breasts no doubt spilling forth. Odd as it was, it made her tingle a little that he'd noticed. Amelia wasn't by half the prude her young husband had been. She'd shocked Robert often during their courtship. Then he'd shocked her. Only, supposedly, it had not been Robert who attacked her.

"You should stay in bed," Wulf said. "I'm certain a lady of your sensibilities would only faint again, and truth be told, my shoulder stings to the point I'm not certain I could lift you a second time."

His response somewhat shocked her. It wasn't a very gentlemanly thing to say, but then, Amelia knew that Gabriel Wulf was no gentleman. It was, she supposed, part of his dark appeal to her. "I will not faint," she said evenly, and prayed that was true. "If you won't look away, I will simply bare my breasts to you."

His brows shot up. Now she had managed to shock him. Amelia might have smiled if circumstances hadn't robbed her of the ability.

"Perhaps you should go out for a moment, my lord, while I help the lady into her robe."

Amelia had almost forgotten the girl's presence.

"He can barely stand without swaying on his feet," Amelia dismissed the suggestion. "If he faints, I doubt the both of us together could lift him."

The corner of Gabriel's mouth turned up, just a hint of a smile. "I believe we have both been put in our place," he said to the girl.

The servant didn't smile, but she came forward to help Amelia into her robe.

"What is your name again?" Amelia asked her.

"Mora, my lady," she answered.

"Mora says there are beasts surrounding the house. Wolves that turn into men, and vice versa. Do you believe in such things, Lady Collingsworth?"

Wulf kept his gaze trained straight ahead while Mora helped Amelia into her thin robe. It felt odd to be addressed as "Lady Collingsworth." A bride for a day and now a widow. Amelia could hardly grasp her circumstance . . . but she wasn't insane.

"Of course not," she answered. "No offense to the girl, but such things are only folklore. Stories made up to frighten young village children so that they don't wander off into the woods and become lost."

Tying the ribbons of her robe, Amelia regarded the girl, hoping to display an emotion that said she didn't blame her for believing in things that did not exist. They came from very different backgrounds.

The girl, in response, merely lowered her gaze, ducking her head in a submissive manner.

"Mora, would you fetch items so that we may tend to Lord Gabriel's wounds?"

Mora slipped quietly from the room. Amelia moved past Wulf to the chest and mirror, lifting a bowl of stew and taking it to him. She had never served anyone before, well, except tea, but under current circumstances thought it best not to put on too many airs.

"I think you might also need fortification," she said. "Are you hungry?"

When he took the bowl, his fingers brushed against hers. His hands were not soft . . . not like Robert's, but an odd tingle ran the length of her arm. "I don't recall when I last ate anything decent," he admitted. "I've been on the run."

Amelia's legs suddenly felt wobbly beneath her torn gown. Afraid she might actually faint again, she sat beside him upon the bed, although she knew it was improper. "On the run?" she asked.

Despite the fact that Wulf was probably starving, he ate with manners. He chewed and swallowed before answering, "Looking for my brother Jackson. He went missing in London a few months past."

"Lord Jackson?" Amelia blinked at him. "I saw him just this morning at my wedding. Your brother and his lovely wife, Lady Lucinda."

Wulf had a bite poised at his lips. He lowered the spoon. "Wife?"

Assuming by his stunned expression that Lord Gabriel was not aware of his younger brother's recent nuptials, Amelia asked, "You did not know that your brother had married?"

He'd eaten only a couple of bites of his stew, but he placed the bowl aside on her night table. "I did not even know that he had returned home, much less that he had taken a wife."

Thankful for any distraction at the moment, Amelia said, "There is some scandal attached to that. Lady Lucinda is rumored to be a witch, but I like her. And the child is adorable."

Lord Gabriel's eyes, as green as spring's first blades of tender grass, widened. "A child?"

"A boy," she provided. "His name is Sebastian. Looks nothing like his father, mind you, but a very handsome babe all the same."

Wulf ran a hand through his hair and shook his head. "I need to go home."

Amelia felt more than a pang of homesickness, herself. She wanted to go home, as well. She longed to be there this very moment, safe beneath her parents' roof.

Mora entered, her arms loaded. Gabriel reached forward and took a pitcher of clean water and cloths from the girl. Mora dropped the rest of the items upon the bed. There were bandages, scissors, and a long pair of nasty-looking tweezers.

"Brought all I could think to bring," the girl said. "I've tended a scratch or two before."

Amelia hadn't a clue about tending to anything other than her personal hygiene and her society events. She felt rather useless and wondered if she could even stand to look at Gabriel's wounds, much less clean and bandage them.

"I'll see to the shoulder first," the girl said. "You'll need to remove your shirt, my lord."

He did so without thought, tugging his torn, soiled shirt from his snug trousers, then up over his head, although he winced again from having to move his shoulder. Amelia thought she couldn't stand to look, but to the opposite, she couldn't seem to look away.

His chest was smooth, a deep tawny color, and he had flat copper-colored nipples. His stomach had not an inch of fat. His shoulders were broad and muscular; then she saw the wound, the blood, and she had to glance away.

"Not too bad," the girl muttered. "Could have been worse. Don't think I'll have to stitch it closed."

Amelia's stomach rolled. She walked unsteadily back to the chest. The smell of stew had made her stomach grumble earlier; now it nauseated her. She reached for the brandy decanter instead.

"I wouldn't have too much of that. It might make you ill."

She glanced over her shoulder to see Wulf watching her while the girl bandaged his shoulder. Now that the wound was covered by a snow-white bandage, Amelia found she could look at him again without feeling queasy. "It doesn't affect me," she told him. "I drank a good deal of it one afternoon with Lady Wulf and never felt any ill effects."

"We need our wits about us," he cautioned despite her claim.

Amelia frowned at him. "If anything else bad is going to happen tonight, I'd just as soon be drunk as a loon."

He nearly smiled again, and she wondered what he might look like if he did. When he spoke, she saw that he had straight, white teeth. The girl recaptured his attention.

"Now the leg." Mora's cheeks flushed. "You'll have to shuck the trousers, my lord."

Just the thought of seeing Gabriel Wulf naked flooded Amelia with sudden heat. She eyed her brandy glass. Perhaps it was the liquor. A bride should not be having such thoughts about another man on her wedding night. She set the glass aside and turned toward him.

"You may use the blanket on the bed to cover yourself," she said. "Mora and I will turn our backs while you undress."

He shrugged in response. "It makes no difference to me one way or another." He rose and began unfastening his dusty, bloodstained trousers. Amelia realized neither she nor the young maid had turned from the sight until he was nearly finished.

"Mora, join me," she instructed. The girl obediently came to stand beside her. It took Amelia a minute more to actually turn from the sight of Gabriel Wulf about to shuck his trousers in front of God and anyone who cared to look.

Both she and Mora stood facing the chest and mirror. Amelia had a devil of a time not looking into the mirror in hopes of catching Wulf undressed. The liquor must have affected her for a fact, and still she reached for the decanter to fortify herself again.

"Best leave me some of that," Mora said. "I'll need it to clean his wound once I've dug the ball from him."

Curious, Amelia asked, "Did he tell you he'd been shot?"

The girl blushed. "No. Didn't have to. Seen such wounds before. Not a particularly good background I come from, my lady."

"All right, I'm covered," Wulf called behind them, interrupting the conversation. "Hurry, girl. I still have much to do tonight."

They turned to see Gabriel sitting upon the bed. The blanket was wrapped around his waist, parted so that his injured leg could be tended. Amelia had never seen a man's naked leg before. While men's fashions left little to the imagination these days, it was altogether different seeing a man's bare leg from simply seeing the shape of his leg outlined in snug-fitting trousers or tights.

Even injured, Gabriel Wulf's leg was quite something to behold. It was long and muscled and dusted with blond hair. Amelia stood gawking as Mora sprang into action. She supposed she watched the entire procedure, stood numbly by as the girl dug a ball from Gabriel Wulf's thigh with the long nasty-looking tweezers. He gritted his teeth and a sweat broke out upon his brow, but other than that, he complained little.

"The spirits, my lady," Mora called to her. "If you don't mind, would you fetch the decanter for me?"

Glad for something to do, Amelia lifted the decanter from the tray and brought it to the bed. She took another sip from the bottle before handing it to Mora. The girl, in turn, offered the brandy up to Gabriel.

"To fortify yourself," she said. "This will sting something fierce."

He nodded, took the decanter, took a swig, and handed it back. An odd thrill ran through Amelia at the thought of him placing his mouth where hers had been. As if he felt her regard, Wulf's green gaze lifted to her. He stared into her eyes while the girl poured the liquor over his bloody thigh.

He never so much as flinched.

"Now I've got to stitch you," Mora said. "Then I'll be finished. If you keep it clean like you've been doing, you should heal."

Wulf said nothing in response. He kept staring at Amelia, and she suspected he did so to distract himself from the pain. Bold as she was at times, she grew uncomfortable under his intense study. Amelia suspected he could nearly see through her thin robe. She wasn't as modest as a proper young woman should be. Once, she'd been bold enough to wet her gown at a social function. Her mother had nearly fainted dead away when Amelia emerged from an upstairs guest room, where several other ladies had been doing the same thing.

Still, something about the way he watched her . . . like a fox watched a rabbit, made her uneasy. And she was uneasy enough with all that had happened. She needed something to do to keep her mind off of it.

"I might find you something clean to wear," she offered. "Robert." Her voice caught and she took a moment to collect herself. "Robert was not nearly as big as you are, but perhaps I can find something."

"No need to trouble yourself with that," he said, and his gaze finally broke from her to stray to the closed door that separated her room from Robert's. "I won't ask you to go back in there."

In a way, Amelia needed to see the body. If for no other reason than to convince herself that the man was not Robert. How could her mind have been so confused? How had the man managed to trick her?

"I can do it," she whispered, not sure who she was trying to convince more, herself or Gabriel Wulf.

CHAPTER THREE

Amelia took a candle with her. She feared the door, barely hanging upon its hinges, would fall off when she opened it, but it held. She didn't want to look at the floor where she knew the impostor's body lay. She'd just as soon avoid it, but it had been her intent, besides finding something clean for Gabriel Wulf to wear. Taking a deep breath, she glanced down at the floor. No one was there.

She breathed a sigh of relief. Wulf had obviously removed the body during or after his search for Robert. Steadier now, Amelia walked to Robert's wardrobe and opened the doors. She thought a nightshirt would have to make do for Lord Gabriel as a shirt. Breeches or trousers of any sort she couldn't imagine fitting him. He was much taller than Robert had been, and his legs, well, his thighs were nearly the size of tree trunks.

Grabbing up a nightshirt, she turned and picked up the candle she had set aside. Something gleamed at her from the floor next to the bed. It appeared to be a silver letter opener. Blood tinged the tip. She shuddered; then she noticed something else there on the floor. Amelia tucked the nightshirt under one arm, bent, and picked it up. It looked like an animal claw. She quickly dropped it.

Upon entering the adjoining room, she saw Mora just rising from her position upon the floor next to her patient.

"Got him fixed up, I think," the girl said to her.

Amelia placed her candle on the stand next to the bed and unfolded the nightshirt. "This will have to do for the time being," she said.

Wulf took the garment from her and put his muscled arms through the sleeves first. Amelia was staring again.

"Thank you for taking . . . for removing the man. I thought I should look at him just to assure myself he wasn't Robert, but then—"

"What?" Wulf paused in his task of pulling the nightshirt over his head. "What did you just say?"

"The body, you moved it . . . didn't you?"

He pulled the nightshirt over his head and was off the bed in an instant. The broken door didn't survive his wrenching it open and fell partway off the hinges. Shocked, Amelia simply watched him. She heard him in the next room, heard him curse, then the sound of running feet in the hallway.

But wait, it was not running feet she heard in the hallway. It was the sound of horses running. The stable!

Amelia opened her door and ran into the hallway. She just caught a glimpse of the white nightshirt Gabriel wore moving down the stairs. She glanced around her room and spotted his pistol still lying on the chest.

"Stay here," she instructed Mora, rushing over to

grab the pistol. Amelia ran from the room and downstairs. Lord Gabriel had left the front doors standing wide, and how he managed to unbolt everything and still be ahead of her, Amelia had no idea. Dust coated the damp air outside, and she coughed. Someone grabbed her from behind.

"What are you doing out here?"

Amelia had almost screamed; now she sagged against him with relief. "The pistol. I thought you might need it."

Wulf reached around front of her and took the heavy pistol from her hand. Amelia wanted a moment longer to simply lean against him. He felt solid, strong, and represented safety.

"Someone's run the horses off," he said. "I intend to go to the stable and find out whom. Go back into the house. Bolt the doors."

Whatever else her mind would or would not accept tonight, Lord Gabriel represented safety to Amelia. He had rescued her from an impostor bent on defiling her. She didn't want Lord Gabriel out of her sight. "I'll go with you," she insisted.

When he sighed, his warm breath brushed her ear. She shivered. "I haven't time to watch your back and mine both," he argued. "Do as I say, woman."

In shock, half-inebriated, whatever she was, Amelia was not the sort to tolerate that kind of talk from a man. "Woman"? Had he called her "woman"? "I hardly do as I'm told by men who are related to me," she informed him. "I certainly don't take orders from complete strangers. I'll wager I'm safer tagging along with a big, strapping man such as yourself rather than cowering in the house with a frightened girl."

His hands were warm through the thin fabric of Amelia's robe when he turned her to face him. "That 'girl' is showing more sense than you are. She at least knows to stay put and not to argue with her . . ."

She blinked up at him. It was dark, but a half-moon made his features readable. "With her what?" she asked. "Her betters? Is that what you were going to say?"

Wulf didn't answer. He shook his head and muttered something along the lines of "God save us from independent women." He moved past her. "Do whatever you want then. It's your neck."

Amelia reconsidered now that he'd actually given her permission to follow him into possible danger. She glanced behind her at the house. All was dark except the candle burning in her upstairs bedroom. She saw Mora's pale face pressed against the glass. The girl hardly inspired confidence that she would be helpful in any way should Amelia be attacked again.

Gabriel was already halfway to the stable. Even in nothing but a nightshirt, his long legs bare, he was a formidable sight. She'd take her chances with him.

The lady baffled him. Gabriel knew she followed. She wasn't like any society miss he'd met before, not that he had met many. She wasn't like his perceived notions of a society miss. Perhaps the brandy had given her courage, for he expected hysteria and constant vapors would be more the norm after having been attacked and widowed in the same night. Instead, the woman stalked after him in the dark, wearing nothing but a thin robe that revealed more than it hid.

His shoulder and thigh hurt, but he tried to concentrate on the task at hand. The lady's scent distracted him. The lady in general distracted him. Everything about her baffled him. From the fact that he had seen her before and hadn't been able to forget her, to the way she stirred him as no other woman had stirred him to date. He'd been attracted to her from the moment he saw her upstairs, and in circumstances that made feeling anything besides worry for her safety and sorrow for her loss ridiculous.

Gabriel shouldn't be having such thoughts about a woman barely married and now widowed . . . one who had been wed to his childhood friend, Robert Collingsworth. If she was bent on following though, Gabriel wanted to know where she was. He paused before the stable doors, which were now thrown wide since the horses had been turned out of their stalls. Once Lady Collingsworth reached his side, he pressed a finger to his lips to warn her to keep quiet. Together, they crept into the stable. There were no lanterns lit and it was deathly quiet.

Gabriel glanced around, his hand trained upon the pistol he'd rushed off without. It embarrassed him that he hadn't thought to take the weapon, but then, he got on well enough with his fists in most confrontations. He heard the scurry of mice in the loft—the creak of leather as harnesses and bridles swung in the breeze of the open doorway. A coach sat inside. He'd noticed it earlier when he'd ridden inside but hadn't thought much of it.

Where were the coachman and the footman? Gabriel had a very strong feeling he knew. He turned to Lady Amelia. "Stay here," he said; then he walked to the coach and opened one of the side doors. Two bodies lay inside, both men's throats slit. He quickly closed the door and returned to Lady Collingsworth, took her arm, and steered her toward the open stable doors.

"What is it?" she whispered. "What did you see?"

He didn't answer. Something was terribly wrong at Collingsworth Manor. He had to get the lady back inside the house and bolt the doors again. He nearly had her there when the howling began. Both he and Lady Collingsworth froze in their tracks.

The noise came from the surrounding woods. Close. Too close. Wolves? To Gabriel's knowledge, wolves had long been extinct from England. And wolves did not open stalls and run horses off. They did not crawl into bed with a new bride and pretend to be her husband. They did not murder men for no good reason.

"It sounds as if there are a hundred of them," the lady whispered beside him.

Sound, Gabriel knew, traveled easily in the woods around Collingsworth Manor. He doubted if there were as many wolves as it sounded like. He also knew from listening to the direction each answering howl came from that they were surrounded.

CHAPTER FOUR

Amelia opened her eyes to a confusing sight. She wasn't in her bed at home in London. Across the room, a man stood with his back to her, staring out her window at the first rays of dawn. He wore a nightshirt and dusty buckskin trousers along with knee-high boots. His hair brushed the back of his collar, dark blond except for the lightning-colored streaks. Gabriel Wulf. And she was not safe and sound at her parents' home. She was caught in a nightmare.

"Have you slept at all?" she asked.

Lord Gabriel turned from the window. Amelia tried not to suck in her breath. Good lord, he was handsome, and it obviously took more than being terrified for a woman not to notice.

"I thought it best to stay awake."

She glanced around. "Where is Mora?"

He moved to the bed and stood staring down at Amelia. "Downstairs. She said she'd fix us a bite of breakfast. A very practical young woman, that one."

As opposed to a very impractical one, Amelia understood, such as herself. She let the statement pass.

There were more important things to worry over. “What are we going to do?” she asked him.

He raked his fingers through his hair. “We need to get to Wulfglen.”

Amelia frowned at him. “Do you mean walk? The horses are gone.”

Without being invited, he sat upon the edge of the bed. Amelia supposed it was a good thing for him that she wasn’t very practical, for she knew it was indecent of him to do so.

“Afoot, it might take us a few days,” he said. “But if we make it to the main road, we might find someone to give us a ride.”

Collingsworth Manor was a bit off the beaten path. Amelia knew that from her journey yesterday. The fields were some distance off, and the area around the house was completely wooded. “We’d have to travel through the woods,” she said. “All things considered, I don’t believe that is a wise idea.”

“Because of the wolves?”

Amelia considered his question. “Because of whatever or, rather, whoever is killing people around here. The coachman and the footman are dead, aren’t they?”

His green gaze slid away from her. He didn’t answer, which was answer enough for her. “I don’t believe the wolves we heard last night are normal wolves.”

Amelia remembered the feel of claws against her neck, the smell of fetid breath, the sensation of fur against her skin. She shivered. But she was being ridiculous, and so was he. “Of course they are wolves,” she said. "Don't tell me the girl has you spooked about such things."

"And after what happened to you last night, you are not afraid?" he challenged.

She didn't want to think about last night. Amelia couldn't wrap her mind around what had happened to her. "Last night, I was quite hysterical," she said. "I couldn't have heard and felt what I thought I did in the room next door. I must have imagined it."

He lifted a dark brow. "What did you hear and feel?"

As if closing her eyes could block the memory, Amelia tried. Only the nightmare was there waiting for her. She quickly opened them again. "I was attacked by a man pretending to be Robert. He must have looked a great deal like him to have deceived me."

Wulf shrugged. "Not really. He might have been about the same height, the same build, same color of hair, but he did not resemble Robert otherwise. I saw him, remember?"

Amelia rose from the bed and began to pace. "There must be some logical explanation," she insisted.

Lord Gabriel rose and blocked her path. He reached out and gently touched her neck. "And is there a logical explanation for these scratches? Is there a logical explanation as to why a man I shot, and took for dead, somehow managed to escape the room next door and disappear? Is there a logical explanation as to why Robert is dead in the cellar and two other men are dead in the stable, their throats ripped out?"

Amelia's heart lurched. Tears stung her eyes. "Robert," she whispered. "I cannot believe he is gone.

I keep thinking this is a nightmare and I will wake in a moment, and everything will be as it was before."

Her words softened Wulf's gaze upon her. "Forgive me. It was insensitive to say that to you. I'm sure you cared deeply for Robert."

Did she? Amelia wouldn't try to fool herself into believing she had loved her husband. She was sorry he was dead, but to carry on too much would be hypocritical. "I cared for him," she admitted. "I thought he would make a fine husband. His death saddens me, but I will not pretend that he was the great love of my life. I do not believe in love."

A slight smile tugged at the corner of Wulf's sensuous mouth. "By all means, be forthright."

She raised her chin. "Would you have me lie?"

His slightly bemused expression faded. "I understand seldom is a match made in London that has anything to do with love, but you could have lied. Robert is no longer here to say otherwise."

She wouldn't be baited by him. "Lied for whose sake?" she challenged. "Yours?"

He stepped closer, towering over her. He was quite intimidating size-wise, and Amelia fought herself not to take a step back from him.

"He was once my friend."

Guilt rushed up to claim her. A flush burned her cheeks. "I'm sorry," she said. "You must think I'm terribly cold."

Wulf turned and walked back to the window. "I don't think you're terribly anything, Lady Collingsworth. I hardly know you."

Mora poked her head inside the room and startled

Amelia. "Breakfast is ready," Mora said. "I was wondering if I should bring it up or if you will both dine downstairs?"

Amelia couldn't say she wasn't glad for the distraction. Why would it sting her that Lord Gabriel Wulf had so casually dismissed her and her feelings? Perhaps because of the dreams she'd once had about him. On some level, she did feel as if she knew him. Which was silly. She did not know him at all.

"Downstairs will be fine," Wulf answered. "No point in you having to bring trays up. I'm sure you are as tired as the both of us."

Lord Gabriel was a more considerate person than Amelia. She'd just been thinking it would be nice to dine upstairs and return to bed, to escape from reality for a while longer. When Wulf glanced at her for confirmation, what else could she do but say, "Of course. If you will both retire there, I will join you as soon as I've dressed"?

Mora nodded and hurried back out. Wulf walked across the room. He gave Amelia a slightly curious look before exiting and closing the door behind him. Amelia supposed he thought she couldn't even dress herself, and she realized she never had, not completely on her own. She moved to her wardrobe, where her gowns had been unpacked the previous afternoon. The sight of her frilly garments brought her a measure of comfort. They reminded her of her old life, the one she'd lived only yesterday.

Choosing a light blue day frock with short puffed sleeves seemed a trifle cheery considering she was now a widow. Amelia supposed even taking consolation in the fact that she looked good in black with her fair coloring was also insensitive. But what choice did she have? It wasn't as if she'd thought she would need somber clothing on her honeymoon. She had no choice but to wear what she'd brought. Amelia stripped from her robe and her ripped gown. Being wed and widowed on the same day would certainly cause scandal.

Her parents would not be pleased. She had hardly done a thing in her life that pleased them, so years ago she'd decided she might as well be good at displeasing them. She'd once promised the Dowager Duchess of Brayberry, a friend of the notorious Wulf brothers, that she would someday become the most shocking woman in all of England. She supposed she was off to a good start.

Suddenly Amelia was angry. Angry at Robert for putting her in this awkward situation. Her life was supposed to improve with marriage; instead, it had all gone horribly wrong. She was supposed to wake this morning a woman, her past indiscretions with her parents forgotten, forgiven. Robert was supposed to make her happy. He had promised. He never said a word about dying. He never said a word about any of this. Not the creepiness of Collingsworth Manor or that she would be in danger here.

Certainly not that wolves weren't always what they appeared to be. Amelia immediately steered her thoughts in a different direction. She didn't want to think about that. She didn't want to think about last night. Instead, she tried to concentrate on getting dressed. Her corset was a problem. Amelia tried lacing it from the front with the intention of sliding it around to the back, but she laced it too tight and she couldn't tug it around like it should be. She broke a nail in the process of trying. It was the proverbial straw that broke the camel's back.

Her knees suddenly buckled and she went to the floor. A lump rose in her throat. Her eyes began to water. She squeezed them closed and fought down the despair gripping her. It was no use. First a slight sob escaped her throat, then a wail. Then the floodgates burst open. As shallow as she wanted to be, as much as she wanted to distance herself from pain, from fear, from facing up to what had happened last night, and the fact that Robert was dead, Amelia couldn't.

It was as if a lifetime of emotions had gathered against her in that one moment, in that dark hour. She completely broke down. How long she sat weeping or, rather, caterwauling like a kitten left out in the rain Amelia could not judge. She lost track of time and was only brought to the present when she felt a hand upon her shoulder. She nearly screamed. Her head jerked up and she was suddenly staring Lord Gabriel full in the face.

"I thought I'd come up and see what was keeping you," he said. "I didn't mean to startle you."

If he didn't mean to scare her, he shouldn't move so quietly. Amelia wiped her face with the edge of her petticoat. It occurred to her when his gaze lowered for a moment before lifting back to her face that she wore only her chemise, a petticoat, and her twisted corset.

"I couldn't get my corset turned around properly," she explained.

He lifted a brow. "All this over your corset?"

Amelia sniffed. "I also broke a nail," she added.

His gaze softened upon her again, and it did funny things to her insides. "I'll help you," he said; then he rose, wincing in the process. He pulled her to her feet and turned her to where her back faced him. His fingers were sure and steady upon the laces as he loosened her corset and pulled it around in the proper position, before he began lacing her up.

"I think you've had experience with this sort of thing before," she said in a dry tone.

Wulf laughed softly. "Not really. But I suppose I've watched enough women shimmy out of their clothes to understand a corset's workings."

Amelia wasn't certain how she felt about that. In her dreams of Gabriel Wulf, other women had never been involved.

"How tight do you want it?"

Considering all that had happened, perhaps she should leave it somewhat loose in case she was forced to run for her life. "Not too tight," she answered. "I think I should be able to breathe."

"I think you don't need it at all." His hands were warm around her waist, so warm she felt their heat. "Your waist is small enough without it."

Best to guide her thoughts from the direction they were headed. It wasn't right, and certainly not after she'd just broken down and actually grieved for poor Robert. She might be a shocking girl, but even she knew one did not grieve for one man one moment and lust for another the next.

"I'm glad I did not love him," she whispered. "I

don't think I could stand the pain. This is awful enough."

Gently, Gabriel turned her to face him. "He deserves at least a few tears from his wife, and my respect, for a friendship we once shared. Maybe a moment of silence between us, for poor Robert."

Amelia nodded and closed her eyes. She peeked beneath her lashes a second later to see if Gabriel had also closed his. His lashes made dark smudges against his high cheekbones. She wondered why he was blond but had darker facial hair. The contrast was very nice.

Everything about him was very nice, physically anyway. He made her feel quite dainty with his broad shoulders and his impressive height. He opened his eyes and suddenly they were staring at each other.

She knew she should look away, but she felt suddenly mesmerized. It was then that she noticed his scent. Her nostrils flared slightly in an effort to identify it, but she could not. She'd never smelled anything quite like it. But wait . . . she had. The day she first visited Lucinda Wulf and had met Lord Gabriel's younger brother Jackson.

Heat gathered in her belly and spread out in all directions—up her chest to her neck and face, down her legs, and most especially between them. Her nipples tightened. Her lips parted and she had trouble drawing a normal breath. He could do anything to her and she would not resist. The thought entered her mind even as she wanted to deny it. Body outranked mind and she took a step toward him. He drew in a shaky breath, but still his eyes bored into hers and he did not step away from her.

She wanted his hands on her. His mouth. She wanted to lie with him upon yonder bed and have him take what no new bride should still possess. Her innocence. As if he read her thoughts, Gabriel reached out and touched her. His hand was large and callused from work but warm against her skin. Slowly it traveled up her arm to her neck, then behind it as he pulled her closer. She still stared into his eyes when they suddenly glowed with a strange blue light.

Her mind was playing tricks on her, Amelia reasoned. Perhaps she was still dreaming. She must be, because regardless of how attracted she was to Gabriel Wulf, with all that had happened she wouldn't want him to kiss her. And she did. She wanted it desperately.

He slid his hand from behind her head, cupping her cheek before his thumb traced the shape of her mouth. "So tempting."

His lips were so close she nearly felt the sensation of them against hers without touch. Amelia closed her eyes and raised herself upon her tiptoes.

It was wrong, deliciously wrong, she knew that, but for months she had wondered what it would feel like to kiss Gabriel Wulf. Warm, firm, the first sensation that registered when his lips brushed hers. A mingling of breaths before his hand slid back behind her head again and he slanted his mouth against hers. He nudged her lips farther apart and then his tongue penetrated her, teased hers into a dance. It was as potent as any brandy, his kiss.

Amelia was helplessly lost. Lost in sensation, lost in the scent of him—the feel of him—the warmth spreading through her. Her heart hammered against her chest;

her blood coursed hot through her veins. Robert's chaste kisses were nothing compared to this, had made her feel nothing compared to this. It was like drowning in chocolate. It was like nothing she had experienced before.

He teased her lips, nibbled at them, sucked at them, then claimed them again, a master at seduction although she couldn't say he seemed to know that. It was as if he was at the mercy of his emotions, just as she was, and just as helpless to fight them.

Amelia leaned into his solid strength. He pushed her back, not away from him, but toward the bed behind them. She went with a willing heart. She went without thought or doubt. She went without guilt.

A moment later her knees met with the end of the bed and she tumbled backward. Scrambling up upon her elbows, she stared up at him. His eyes still glowed with blue light. His broad chest rose and fell inside a nightshirt that once belonged to her husband. He wanted her; there was no mistaking the desire in his eyes as they raked her from head to toe. He took a step toward her, looked as though he'd join her upon the bed, but suddenly he stopped himself.

As if night had slipped into day, darkness into light, he blinked and stepped back from her. "What in the hell am I doing?" he asked in a husky voice. He glanced around as if he tried to recall where he was, who he was, and perhaps who she was, as well. His gaze strayed to the broken door joining her room to the master suite. He closed his eyes for a moment before he glanced back at her.

"Forgive me. I had no right." That was all he said

before he stormed across the room, out, and closed the door firmly behind him.

Shaken, Amelia stared after him. Good lord, what *had* just happened? How could she have behaved so brazenly with him when her poor bridegroom wasn't even buried as of yet? True, Amelia understood that she was a sensual creature. She'd been much more interested in the wedding night than she thought poor Robert had been.

She'd shocked her intended once by putting her tongue into his mouth when he'd finally gotten up the nerve to kiss her, but even she had not behaved with him as she'd just done with Gabriel Wulf.

Amelia covered her face with her hands. Perhaps she was mad. She could no longer trick her mind into believing everything that had happened since last night was a dream. If she were dreaming of Gabriel Wulf just now, he would not have walked away from her. Instead he would have slipped into bed with her and made her a woman. What was she supposed to do now? Amelia couldn't hide upstairs all day. Decisions had to be made. Realities must be faced.

There was only one thing that she could do. Dress and go downstairs. The only thing worse than having to face Gabriel Wulf again would be forcing herself to go to the root cellar and view Robert's body. But she must. To accept that Lord Collingsworth was truly gone, she must see him for herself.

CHAPTER FIVE

Gabriel had made a halfhearted attempt to eat. Manners dictated that he wait for Lady Collingsworth to join them, but he sure as hell did not have manners. He'd thought he'd be starving, since he'd eaten little in the past week while making his way home, yet his hunger was not for food. It was for her. The woman upstairs. Damn, what was happening to him? He was a man used to having control of his emotions, control of his life. Suddenly he had control of neither.

He caught her scent before she appeared in the dining room. Her perfumed soaps masked it for the most part, but beneath the perfume, she smelled of woman's musk and hot promises a man could not ignore. Gabriel must ignore them.

The girl, Mora, sat across from him, looking out of place at the dining table. They had not conversed beyond general civilities. Once Lady Collingsworth entered the dining room, Gabriel rose, as had been taught him at one time when manners had still mattered. The lady looked lovely in a blue sprigged muslin gown. She'd swept her long hair up in some semblance of a fashionable hairstyle, if it looked a bit haphazard and portions of it were already falling down her back.

He had no idea what had happened upstairs. Why he'd behaved as he had. Why he had dreamed of this woman before. Why he had nearly lost control with her. Why he'd given into the impulse to kiss her—the widow of his childhood friend, not even buried as of yet. Gabriel had wanted to do more than kiss her. Much more.

"Sorry I'm late," the lady said, seating herself. "Have we decided anything?"

She was good at pretending as if nothing untoward had happened upstairs between them. She didn't even blush. Gabriel decided to follow her example. "No," he answered, reclaiming his chair. "I still think we must somehow forge ahead to Wulfglen, where the two of you will be safer."

"We can't leave," Mora whispered, lifting her big eyes to the both of them. "Not with the beasts waiting for us out in the woods. They're planning something, mark my words."

Lady Collingsworth placed a napkin in her lap and turned toward the girl. "Wolves do not plan," she said. "I have decided that our imaginations got the better of us last night. Today, we will approach our situation with rational thought. Perhaps it would be best if we left Collingsworth Manor and forged ahead to Wulfglen."

"Gives them the advantage," Mora mumbled softly. "Forgive my forwardness, my lady, but I believe we'd all be safer staying put. Maybe they will go away now."

Studying the girl, Gabriel picked up his spoon and contemplated the porridge sitting before him. "What makes you believe so, Mora? Why would they suddenly just go away?"

The girl was obviously uncomfortable being the center of attention. She squirmed a little in her chair and tugged her bonnet down around her face. "Because of Vincent," she answered. "I think he was one of them. Since he did not get whatever it was he wanted from the lady, maybe they will all go away now."

Gabriel glanced at Lady Collingsworth for a reaction. Her face paled and her hand strayed automatically to the scratches upon her neck. "What he wanted was obvious," she said. "He wanted me to believe that he was Lord Collingsworth so that I would submit to him."

Leaning forward, Gabriel rudely placed his elbows upon the table, although he knew better. "If you believed he was Robert, why did you not submit to him? Why did you scream? Why did you fight him?"

Lady Collingsworth's face bloomed with sudden color. So, she could blush after all. "The man was hurting me. He kept laughing . . . only, his voice did not sound . . . human."

"I told you so," Mora said softly. "I am convinced he was one of them."

Since Mora had spoken up, Gabriel had a few questions he wanted her to answer. "How did Vincent get into the house? I checked the locks myself while searching for Lord Collingsworth. Everything had been bolted up tight."

The girl shrugged. "I'm assuming through the root cellar. There's a door leading to the outside. I didn't think about anyone coming in that way. Truth is, I relaxed my guard a little since the young lord had returned. I was more than happy to let him decide how to keep both me and the lady safe."

What Mora said made sense. Robert was found in the root cellar. He'd probably heard something down there and gone to investigate. "Did you tell Lord Collingsworth that wolves that could turn into men had frightened the other staff and field workers away?"

Suddenly Mora's eyes filled with tears. She shook her head. "Was afraid he'd think I was touched and turn me out. I should have told him right away. I should have warned him. He's dead now because I didn't."

The girl seemed generally distraught over the situation. Gabriel had no idea how to comfort her. He wasn't used to dealing with women and their tendency to weep. To his surprise, it was Lady Collingsworth who rose from her chair and went around to the girl, placing a hand upon her shaking shoulder.

"It is not your fault, Mora," she said. "Lord Collingsworth, well, I'm sorry, but he wouldn't have believed that tale any more than I do. I don't know what is going on, but it isn't your fault."

The girl shyly touched Lady Collingsworth's hand. "Bless you for saying so, my lady." The servant looked as surprised by Lady Collingsworth's show of kindness as Gabriel felt.

He hadn't expected kindness toward a servant from Lady Collingsworth. He hadn't expected the passion she'd shown upstairs. She became more intriguing to him by the moment. She turned from offering the girl comfort and looked at Gabriel.

"I need to see him," she said softly. "I cannot believe Robert is gone if I do not see him."

The lady had acted as if she believed Robert was gone easily enough upstairs, but that was not her fault. Gabriel was the guilty party. His scent had been what attracted Lady Collingsworth—what had made her act irrationally with him. His younger brother Jackson had once told him of this particular "gift" all Wulf brothers possessed.

Gabriel had never to his knowledge used it upon a woman. Perhaps he couldn't help it upstairs. Perhaps the scent simply seeped from him when he was unreasonably attracted to a woman.

"I need to bury Robert," Gabriel said. "Him and the other two in the stable."

Lady Collingsworth took a steadying breath. "Robert deserves a proper burial. One with his friends around him to mourn his passing. And how will I explain . . . I mean, if he was murdered . . ."

"There is no proof that he was murdered," Gabriel reminded her. "I told you, there was not a scratch upon him. It was as if he'd been frightened to death."

The lady shuddered and he realized he had not taken care with her sensibilities. Gabriel wasn't a stranger to women, but he preferred them as jaded and world-wise as he was himself. He had no idea how to deal with a delicate butterfly pleasing enough to look at but rather useless when it came to the harsh realities of life.

"We cannot leave Robert and the others as they are," he said. "They deserve to be laid to rest."

The lady had steadied herself with a hand placed upon the back of Mora's chair. She put a brave face forward, but Gabriel noted that her hand shook. "I suppose you're right," she agreed. "But please at least bury Lord

Collingsworth in the family cemetery. I know it must be somewhere on the property close to the house."

"Not far from here," Gabriel said. When she lifted a brow, he explained, "We used to play there sometimes when we were boys. We'd hide behind the stones and jump out at one another."

Lady Collingsworth nodded. "Please, I'd like to see him now."

"But your breakfast, my lady," Mora said. "You need your strength."

The lady shook her head. "I find my appetite seems to diminish the moment food is placed before me. I'd rather get this behind me."

"Then I'll come along and offer you my support," the girl said.

Lady Collingsworth pressed a hand to the girl's shoulder gratefully. Gabriel placed his napkin aside and rose. He paused to pull Mora's chair out for her, a gesture that seemed to surprise the servant almost as much as Lady Collingsworth's comfort had earlier. Gabriel reasoned it probably was for the best that Lady Collingsworth viewed her husband's body. She needed some type of closure regarding what had happened last night.

Although Gabriel still wasn't certain what was going on at Collingsworth Manor, he could at least allow the lady to grieve. His leg throbbed, but the wound felt better than it had for the past two weeks. Gabriel tried not to limp as he led the way to the root cellar.

The root cellar reminded Amelia of a crypt in itself, with its damp smell and cool, dark confines. Her legs trembled beneath her gown, but she put one foot in front of the other and followed Gabriel Wulf down the creaky steps. Mora followed behind her, and she was glad for an extra body. Strength in numbers. As she moved farther down into the cellar, she tried to mentally prepare herself for the task of viewing Robert's body.

Although she'd attended viewings in the past, most had been old relatives. It seemed sacrilege that a young man would be cut down in his prime. But then, Robert had never looked the picture of youthful vitality. He hadn't liked to dance, she recalled. He always seemed winded afterward.

"He's over here," Wulf said, holding a lantern that did little to dispel the darkness. Amelia braced herself. When Lord Gabriel shone the lantern light to the floor, there was nothing there.

He frowned, then walked around the cellar, casting light in all the corners. All Amelia saw was a few sacks of potatoes, a basket of carrots, one of onions, but no body.

"He's gone," Wulf said.

"They must have taken him," Mora whispered.

"Damn," Wulf swore. "It never occurred to me that Robert's body would also come up missing, and it should have."

Amelia shivered in the damp, musty air. "Why would anyone take him?"

Wulf looked none too pleased by the development. "More important at the moment is how?"

Mora walked to a dark corner. "The root cellar door, my lord," she reminded. "Someone could have carried him out that way."

Lord Gabriel joined the girl and shone the lantern

light up earthen steps. "Mora, we need to block the door."

The servant nodded. "Yes, my lord, but we'll have to do it from outside. Should we leave the safety of the house?"

He considered. "It is at least daylight," he finally said. "And I do have a pistol. I think we'll be all right long enough for me to have a look at that door."

Amelia had visions of opening the cellar door from below only to be confronted by a killer waiting on the other side. "I think we should go back through the house and outside."

Wulf glanced back up the darkened stairs. "Probably a wise idea," he agreed. "I can look out of the windows before we go out and see if anyone might be lurking about."

The matter decided, Wulf led the way back to the stairs leading down from the house. Amelia and Mora followed. After checking the outside view from several vantage points, Wulf unbolted the front door and swung it wide. Amelia stood behind him while he removed the pistol from the waistband at the back of his trousers, unseen beneath the nightshirt that hit him midthigh.

"I'll warrant the bodies that were in the coach are also now missing," he said. "Whoever these people are, and I'm convinced there are more than one of them, they cover their tracks well."

"They are not people," Mora whispered behind them. "At least not normal people. Mark my words on that."

Amelia suppressed another shiver. It was ridiculous. To fear something that could not exist. Wolves were wolves, and men were men, and that was that. She tried to forget the claw she had picked up from the floor in Robert's bedchamber.

"I'll check the stable first." Wulf extended his pistol toward Mora. "Do you know how to use a weapon, Mora?"

The girl shrank back from him. "Won't touch one," she said. "Seen too many times firsthand what they can do to a body."

His gaze strayed to Amelia. He seemed to dismiss the possibility before even asking the question. That he would annoyed her. "I know how to use a pistol," she said. "I am, in fact, quite an accomplished marksman."

Her professed skill had him lifting a dark brow.

Amelia supposed she should explain. "When I was younger, I was determined to show my brother up at all things masculine. Mostly to upset my father," she added.

His lips turned up in the usual hint of a smile. "Why does that suddenly not surprise me," he remarked. Lord Gabriel handed Amelia the pistol. "Stay here on the porch until I return."

The pistol was heavy in her hand, but Amelia welcomed its weight. It represented a measure of safety. What, she wondered, as she watched Wulf walk away, did he plan to do if confronted in the stable? A thought occurred to her.

"Mora." She turned toward the girl. "Surely there are other weapons in the house. For hunting and such?"

"Not anymore," the girl said quietly. "The servants took what they could find when they fled. For protection."

"Shame on them for leaving you behind in the first

place, but defenseless as well, it is inexcusable," Amelia muttered. The truth of the matter was, Amelia might not have given the plight of a servant a second thought before she'd been sucked into her current nightmare. The girl was so young, looked so helpless, that Amelia couldn't help but be enraged on her behalf.

"Kind of you to care, my lady," Mora said. "But to be honest, not much had happened before. Not until last night. Not until he came."

Mora nodded toward Gabriel's retreating figure. Amelia suddenly wondered how Wulf had gotten into the house last night. She didn't remember him explaining that. But she was being silly to suspect him. Lord Gabriel might be from a family considered outcasts among the social set in London, a family said to be cursed by insanity, but his family still maintained wealth. Her best friend was married to his brother. There was nothing in the least suspicious about Gabriel Wulf. He'd saved her life last night.

Wulf disappeared into the stable a moment later. That's when Amelia noticed it. "Listen," she whispered to Mora.

The girl glanced at her. "I don't hear anything, my lady."

Amelia gripped the pistol tighter in her hand. "I know. There should be sounds. Birds chirping in the trees. Insects buzzing. It is totally quiet."

Mora rubbed her arms. "Do you feel it?" she asked. "Eyes watching us?"

Scanning the trees surrounding the manor house, Amelia saw nothing. But Mora was right. Amelia felt as if they were being watched. If Lord Gabriel didn't come out of the stable in a moment, she would take Mora back inside and bolt all the doors again.

Amelia breathed a sigh of relief when Wulf emerged from the stable. He was frowning. Even so, he was so handsome she couldn't help but stare at him. Just as she had done those months ago in London, her chaperone finally cuffing her on the back of the head for being so bold in public.

"The bodies are gone, just as I suspected," Gabriel said upon reaching them. "I saw no signs of tracks. Mora, show me where the outside cellar door is."

The girl nodded, although it was plain that she didn't care to be outside in the open. Gabriel took the pistol from Amelia's hand. Their fingers brushed and again an odd tingling raced up her arm. She thought by the slight tensing of his jaw that he felt it, too.

"Around the back of the house," Mora said. "This way."

The three of them moved away from the porch and walked around the side of the manor house. Luckily, the thorny shrubs that surrounded the house would also make gaining access to the many windows on the lower floor difficult, Amelia noted.

"They once bloomed with wild roses," Wulf said to her, as if noting her interest in the shrubs. "That was when Robert's mother was still alive. He's let them go since her passing."

"How did you get into the house last night?" There, she would ask and put her mind to rest over the matter.

Lord Gabriel nodded toward a tall oak that cast shade over one side of the house. "As boys, we all used to climb down that tree late at night and steal away and swim in a pond not far from here. I recalled that and climbed the tree. The window to Robert's boyhood room was not latched. We should make sure all windows are latched when we return to the house."

"Yes," she agreed.

"Here it is." Mora halted before a wooden door that lay upon the ground. "Look," she breathed, nodding toward the door.

Deep claw marks marred the old wood, as if something had been digging at it. Amelia shuddered again. Wulf studied the door.

"I see no way to secure it from the outside. I'll bring up whatever you think we will need, Mora; then I'll secure the door leading to the cellar closed from the house."

"You sound as if we must make the house a fortress," Amelia commented.

"Yes," he answered. "At least until we decide to do something different."

A thought occurred to Amelia. One that raised her hopes. "Surely someone will come along . . ."

Wulf glanced up at her. He seemed to weigh his words; finally he shook his head. "I feel I must be honest. Both Collingsworth Manor and Wulfglen are quite isolated. And with you being on your honeymoon, I doubt anyone would think to intrude upon your privacy."

Damn all considerate people, Amelia thought. "We weren't to return to London for a month. My parents expected us to stay with them until our ship set sail for abroad. An extended honeymoon. We won't even be missed for that long."

"Don't know that we have supplies to last us a month," Mora worried. "The servants took most with them when they fled."

"No need to worry just yet," Wulf warned the girl. "We are not even certain exactly what the threat is."

"Of course, my lord," Mora apologized.

Amelia had a nettling suspicion that Wulf was trying to protect her from the truth of their situation, even if he'd said he had to be honest with her earlier. The reason was obvious. He didn't believe she could handle the truth. And yet, upstairs, he had kissed her. He had wanted her. That, she supposed, made him no different from most men. Always looking at the outside of a woman and judging. Oddly, it had never bothered her before that her face and figure alone attracted men to her. It bothered her now.

Something bothered her worse. Staring out into the woods, she thought she saw a shadow move. And then another.

"Come, ladies," Wulf clipped, and glancing at him, Amelia saw that he had seen them, too. "We must return to the house and spend the day preparing."

He ushered Amelia and Mora toward the front of the house. One weapon. Very little in the way of food supplies. "Preparing for what exactly?" she asked.

He was silent for a moment. Then he answered, "For the night. And whatever it brings."

CHAPTER SIX

Amelia had checked and double-checked the windows upstairs. Mora and Gabriel had fetched necessities from the root cellar and Gabriel had barred the door. They all now sat in the parlor as day turned to night. A cheery fire burned in the grate. Gabriel had nodded off once Mora checked his wounds. Amelia imagined the man was exhausted. The girl, too, had leaned her head back and closed her eyes. Amelia was too keyed up to rest. Besides, someone needed to maintain a vigil, and it seemed she was the one.

Up until her marriage to Lord Robert Collingsworth, Amelia's duties in life had been rather nonexistent, with the exception of finding a suitable match. She'd never had to wonder if she might starve because the pantries were not well stocked or fear for her very life. She had never had to question what was real and what was imagined. She'd never looked in the shadows and felt threatened by what she saw or didn't see.

All of that had changed on her wedding day. The absurdity of her situation made her fidget nervously. She wished she'd been practicing her needlepoint when she'd been a gangly girl instead of trying to show her younger brother up at one masculine sport after another. Then she could possibly sit and stitch to give herself something to do.

Tea sounded heavenly and she almost leaned across the settee to nudge Mora awake and ask her to prepare her a cup. Amelia stopped herself, realizing that it was time she learned to do for herself. At least until they were safely away from Collingsworth Manor. Fixing tea wasn't so very difficult. Amelia felt certain she could manage.

She ignored the fact that earlier she thought she could dress herself without help, as well. Besides being humiliating, the memory was laced with thoughts of Lord Gabriel. The feel of his warm hands against her skin, the thrill of having him kiss her, of having him desire her. And as he had said, whatever happened in that brief moment of insanity, it was wrong. Wickedly, deliciously, wrong.

Amelia rose from the settee. She moved toward the parlor door but stopped before Gabriel. In sleep, his features relaxed, he resembled more the young man in the portrait that hung in the parlor of the Wulf townhome. A lock of hair hung over one eye and she was tempted to reach out and push it aside. Why these tender feelings for a stranger? Why couldn't she have felt them for poor Robert?

What she needed was a distraction. Tea, she recalled, and made her way through the house to the kitchen. The stove was still stoked from the modest dinner Mora had prepared earlier. A kettle already sat upon the stove. Amelia touched the lid and jerked her hand back. She stuck her burning finger into her mouth. She glanced outside and marveled at how bright the moon shone down and how well she could see in the darkness. As she recalled the shadows she'd seen earlier, her gaze scanned the tree line closest to the house.

A second later her heart nearly stopped beating. There, among the thick vegetation, she made out the shape of a man. A moment later he staggered forth into the yard. She saw him quite clearly in the moonlight.

"Robert," she breathed. "Wulf!" Amelia called. "Lord Gabriel!"

Gabriel was beside her in a heartbeat. "What?"

Amelia pointed. "Look, it's Robert."

Robert stumbled into the yard. He went to his knees, holding out a hand as if beseeching Amelia.

"Stay here," Lord Gabriel said, then he was gone.

Stay here? What if it really was Robert this time? Amelia had never seen his body. Maybe Lord Gabriel had been mistaken. Maybe Robert hadn't been dead. Amelia rushed after Gabriel. Mora had stirred and now stood at the door, her eyes wide.

"He told me to bolt the door behind him," she said. "What is happening?"

"Stay here," Amelia repeated Gabriel's instruction to her. "Keep watch for our return, but if you see anything or anyone else, bolt the door."

Amelia rushed out. She ran around the house to see Lord Gabriel standing a few feet from the man, his pistol drawn.

"No!" she screamed. Amelia ran to Lord Gabriel and placed a hand upon his arm. "I believe it truly is Robert. He needs our help!"

"Get back to the house!" Wulf growled. "It is not Robert, Amelia. Robert is dead."

How could he be so certain? The man looked like Robert to Amelia. Then he called to her.

"Amelia."

Hackles rose on the back of her neck. It was the same voice she'd heard in the darkness upon her wedding night. Amelia stumbled back a step.

Gabriel cocked the pistol. "Who are you?" he demanded.

The man with Robert's face did not answer. His eyes glittered strangely in the darkness. Then he did speak, or rather, he peeled back his lips and growled. His coat gaped open and Amelia saw the blood that stained his shirt. Blood, she suspected, that came from the wound where Gabriel Wulf had shot him.

Before Amelia's eyes, the man began to shift. His features changed into those of another man . . . she recognized him now. He'd been tending the stable when they arrived. Then he began to shift into something else. Something inhuman. His teeth grew longer; hair sprouted from his body. His form began to twist and turn, to shrink. That was when Lord Gabriel shot him for the second time. The man, thing, whatever it was, jerked backward.

The howls began. All around them the sound echoed in the night. "Damn," Wulf cursed. "He was meant to draw us out. Run, Amelia! Run to the house!"

She heard his instruction. She knew she must run, but it was if she were frozen. Frozen by fear and shock. Wulf cursed again; then he gathered her in his arms and raced toward the house.

Even in shock, Amelia heard the sound of tree branches snapping behind them. Whatever was in the woods, they were coming after her and Gabriel Wulf. She also realized how fast he moved, how effortlessly he carried her. How could a man with a wounded leg run so fast? How could any man run so fast?

They reached the door and he slammed against it with his shoulder, knocking Mora back in the process. He rushed inside and nearly threw Amelia at the startled girl. Amelia's knees were wobbly as a newborn foal, but she managed to stand, surprised that Mora had the strength to support her.

The girl looked like she'd weigh slightly more than a wet kitten. Wulf nearly had the door closed when something thudded against it. A hand reached inside. A hand that was neither human nor animal. A hand covered by thick fur, with long claws jutting from the fingertips.

Amelia screamed. Wulf slammed his body against the door, and whatever stood on the other side howled in pain, retracting its hand. Then Lord Gabriel had the door closed, throwing home the bolts. He stepped back and aimed his pistol at the door.

"Mora, get Lady Collingsworth into the parlor, away from any windows."

Together, Mora and Amelia moved to the front parlor, where a cherry fire still burned, making a mockery of the nightmare without end. Amelia was in shock; she knew that. Her hands and feet were freezing. Mora helped her sit upon the settee and crouched down beside her, the girl's eyes large and frightened.

Through the doorway, Amelia saw that lamps were being extinguished. Soon the house was plunged into total darkness.

She heard nothing, nothing except the pounding of her heart. How long they sat waiting she couldn't say, but finally Gabriel entered the parlor.

"They are gone . . . for now." He bent down before Amelia, took her cold hands in his, and began to rub.

"How do you know they are gone, my lord?" Mora whispered, her voice frightened.

Yes, Amelia's mind screamed, although she couldn't seem to speak. How did he know?

"Trust me," he answered. "They've slunk back off into the woods. I don't see them anymore."

"It's dark outside," Mora said. "Maybe you just can't see them. Maybe they're still there."

Gabriel glanced away from Amelia. He turned a stern look upon the girl. "No need to upset the lady further, Mora. They are gone. We are safe. I will make certain we remain safe. Understand?"

The girl ducked her head and nodded. Wulf's voice was gentler when he said, "Take a candle and light it from the fire. Go into the kitchen and fix Lady Collingsworth a cup of warm tea."

Amelia's throat finally relaxed enough to allow her to speak. "Something stronger would be better," she said.

"We've used all the brandy," Mora responded softly.

Gabriel continued to rub Amelia's hands between his, and she felt his warmth spreading to her. "See what you can find," he said to Mora. "Even cooking sherry will suffice, but bring the tea, too."

The girl rose from her crouching position, took up a candle and lit it with the fire, then moved quietly as a mouse from the parlor.

"What are those things?" Amelia asked him. "How can they do what they do? How can they become beasts? How can they become someone else?"

Gabriel wasn't certain how to answer. Could men turn into wolves? Yes, he knew that for a fact. He'd seen his father turn into one at dinner one night years ago. The Wulfs were cursed by a witch in a time long ago. The transformation had to do with a full moon and with a man's heart. But Gabriel had never heard of a creature taking on the likeness of another person.

"Gabriel?" Amelia repeated.

Her wide blue eyes held shock and fear, as they should. The same expression he would see in them if she knew that Gabriel was not a normal man, either. He was also part of the shadows.

"I don't know what they are," he finally answered her. "But I do know that Robert is dead, Amelia. You must plant that fact firmly into your mind lest one of them tries to fool you again."

Her perfect brows furrowed. "How do you know the man in the cellar was Robert at all? Maybe it was another impostor. Maybe Robert is still alive. Maybe he has gone for help."

Explaining would be difficult, but Gabriel knew that he must. Amelia must understand once and for all her husband was dead and help would not be coming.

"All people have a scent. One that marks them," he said. "I have an unusual ability to identify a person by their scent. I knew it was Robert in the cellar. When we were boys, his scent had a certain . . . ill smell to it. He still carried it as a man."

Amelia blinked down at him. "Do I have a scent that marks me?"

"Yes," he answered, reaching down to pull her dainty slippers off. Just as he suspected, her feet were as chilled as her hands had been. He began rubbing them. "Although you mask it with sweet-smelling soaps and perfumes. Because of that, it is harder for me to pick up a woman's natural scent."

"You have some rather extraordinary abilities," she remarked. "Outside, I've never seen a man run as fast as you did, and carrying another person at the same time."

Circumstances had forced him to rely on his odd abilities, and he wondered what else Amelia Collingsworth would discover about him. "I was scared," he said.

When she didn't respond, he glanced up at her. Her blue eyes held his stare boldly. "I don't believe that you're afraid of anything," she said.

Mora chose that moment to enter with a glass of red liquid. "Cooking sherry," she proclaimed, and brought it to Gabriel.

"I'll fetch the tea now," the girl said, and moved on.

Gabriel lifted the glass to Amelia's sweet lips. She drank the sherry down just as easily as she had the brandy the night before.

"I like brandy better," she proclaimed. "Sherry is too sweet."

He could not help but smile up at her. Lady Amelia was a most unconventional young woman. The more time he spent with her, the more he became aware of her uniqueness. Still, this was no place for her. She belonged in London, in a ballroom, wearing a pretty dress and turning heads with a smile.

"What you said about people having particular scents," she said, placing her glass aside. "I believe you're right. I might not have noticed that until today."

He glanced up at her. "Why today and not yesterday?"

She moistened her lips. They were pink and plump and made him think of things best left alone. "Because you have one. A scent," she clarified. "Upstairs earlier, when we, when you came to check on me, I smelled it. It made me feel odd."

Gabriel glanced back down at her dainty feet. Any true explanation would make her distrust him, and he needed her to trust him right now. He needed to keep her safe. "I've heard that men can put off a scent at times that attracts women. Something in the sweat. At least that is what my brother Jackson told me once."

"You were not sweating."

He glanced back up at her. "Nor am I particularly clean right now," he pointed out. "I haven't had a decent bath in a while." He decided to try to lighten the mood, although that seemed rather impossible given the circumstances. "It must be the reason you were attracted to me upstairs earlier. I'm the ugly duckling of my family."

"That is obviously a matter of opinion," she said. "And what happened earlier is just as obviously something we should both forget about."

It was hard to forget when they were so close to each other, when he had his hands on her soft skin. Her feet were dainty and he wanted see if her legs were as smooth and soft as the rest of her. Her feet were warm enough, he decided, and replaced her dainty slippers.

"Tea," Mora announced, carrying a pot on a tray and three cups. The girl placed the tray on a nearby table and began to pour. Gabriel rose from his kneeling position before Amelia. His thigh set up an immediate protest. He limped to a chair across from her and sat.

Mora's hands visibly shook as she handed a cup of tea to first Amelia and then Gabriel. He had to give the girl credit for keeping her wits about her. Even Lady Collingsworth, he admitted, had not fainted or gone into hysterics. He counted himself lucky.

"Mora, Lady Collingsworth remarked that you had been raised on stories of folklore and superstition. Is that true?"

The girl seated herself next to Lady Collingsworth and sipped her tea. "Suppose so," she answered.

"Have you ever heard any stories about men turning into wolves?"

Mora shifted uneasily beside Lady Collingsworth. "Of course, my lord. Everyone has heard those stories, haven't they?"

"True," Gabriel agreed. "But what about men who can take the shape of another person? Have you heard any tales about that?"

Staring into her cup, Mora seemed to be thinking. "The Wargs," she finally answered. "Maybe they could do something like that."

Gabriel leaned forward in his chair. "The Wargs?"

"Forest creatures," the girl provided. "'Tis said they have lived in the woods of Europe for centuries. They make their homes there like other woodland creatures. It's also said a person won't know when one is about because they are so good at blending with their surroundings."

"And these Wargs, they can shift their shapes?"

The girl nodded. "So the tale goes. Like the lady said before, parents use the Wargs to keep their children from wandering off into the woods. I heard once that a Warg could pretend to be your mother or father to lure you to it. Course then it eats you."

Lady Collingsworth's cup rattled against her saucer. Gabriel realized he should have questioned Mora about peasant folklore when the lady wasn't around. She'd had enough to digest in one night.

"You should go to bed," he said to the lady. Including Mora in the sweep of his gaze, he added, "The both of you. I'll stay up and stand guard."

"I could hardly sleep now," Lady Collingsworth said. "And that was before the pleasant bedtime story. Besides, my knees are still shaking to the point I doubt I can climb the stairs."

His leg was aching, but Gabriel rose, walked to where she sat, and scooped Lady Collingsworth up in his arms again. She weighed little more than a sack of flour. She set up a mild protest, but he ignored her. Climbing the stairs made him grit his teeth against the pain in his sore thigh. Once at the top, he moved into her room and settled her upon the bed.

Her arms were still entwined around his neck, and he glanced down at her lovely features. Her eyes were sleepy looking despite her claim downstairs, and Gabriel wondered if the sherry had finally begun its work on her. To his surprise, she leaned toward him, her lips so close he could easily kiss her. And he wanted to, he realized. She sniffed at him; then her plump lips parted and she ran her tantalizingly pink tongue across them.

"You really must take a bath," she whispered. "You must be sweating again."

CHAPTER SEVEN

It had taken Gabriel a great deal of willpower not to lean forward and kiss Lady Amelia Collingsworth upstairs. She might have been drunk. Either because of the sherry or because of the scent he put off around her. Instead, he'd gently untangled her arms from around his neck and left her to find sleep. Gabriel wished he could do the same.

He was bone weary and his wounds ached. Mora had offered to dress them for him again, but he'd told her he'd do it himself. He was too damned tired to do it, so he sat in a chair by the fire in the parlor and rested his head against the cushion. As many things that should have been running through his head, he was surprised by the vision that kept haunting him.

It was the sight of Amelia upstairs when he'd gone back up to make certain the women had settled in. She had been wearing a soft cotton gown while Mora ran a brush through her long hair. Amelia's lids had been heavy, her lips puffy and pink, he thought perhaps from him kissing her that morning. Neither woman had noticed him slinking about upstairs checking that all seemed as it should be. But when he looked at Lady Collingsworth, something had stirred inside of him. Lust? He had to assume so, since that was the only emotion he'd ever allowed himself to feel for women.

Gabriel had spent his life avoiding all emotion except the basest ones. He'd thrown himself into the running of Wulfglen and been content enough there among his horses, an occasional woman to see to his manly needs when they got the better of him. He was not like Armond, who needed social interaction with others, or Jackson, who had a weakness for liquor and women and indulged himself with both far too frequently. Gabriel considered himself the sensible one.

But what was happening at Collingsworth Manor made no sense. What were these creatures that could shift into the likeness of another? Then as easily shift into the shape of a wolf? What did they want with Amelia? And how long could he, Amelia, and Mora hold them off from inside the house? Were their chances better in the woods among the creatures? Could they avoid them and reach Wulfglen safely? His head hurt with all the questions rolling around inside of it and with lack of sleep.

He needed rest so he could think clearly. Gabriel tried to clear his mind, and somehow in the process he drifted off; at least he thought he did. He came awake with a start. He had heard something.

A ghostly figure stood upon the stairs, for Gabriel saw into the landing area from his vantage point inside the parlor. Her long blond hair floated around her as she walked to the end of the stairs and turned toward him. The modest nightgown she wore was not so modest with the glow from the dying fire throwing her in silhouette. The shape of her long legs teased him as she moved steadily toward him. He watched, mesmerized, until she stood before him.

"Lady Collingsworth?" he asked softly. "What are you doing down here?"

She bent and placed a finger against his lips as if to quiet him. A moment later her mouth replaced the soft touch of her finger. He was too surprised to react. Gabriel simply sat, watching the smudges her lashes made against her cheeks, absorbing the soft feel of her mouth pressed against his. Her sweet perfume curled around him, fired his blood, and when she ran her tongue over his lips, he opened to her. He'd berated himself all afternoon for his behavior with her earlier, had told himself nothing like that would happen between them again.

And yet something about her drew him, had drawn him from the moment he saw her in London. He reached up and twisted his fingers into her hair, pulled her down onto his lap. Her round bottom snuggled against him sent a jolt of pleasure through him. He might have been half-asleep a moment ago, but his senses came fully awake now.

He penetrated her mouth with his tongue and she shyly met his challenge. Deeper he delved into her mouth, thinking he wanted to likewise penetrate her elsewhere. The elsewhere pressed harder against his lap, and his hips thrust upward involuntarily. She sucked in a breath, which released him from the spell she had cast over him. Gabriel pulled back from her. Her eyes were only half-open when she glanced at him from beneath her long lashes.

"Go back to bed, Lady," he said. "Go now, while you still can."

She lowered her face as if ashamed, her long hair falling over her cheeks to shield her expression from him.

"It's not that I don't desire you," he said, which felt odd, since he wasn't one to explain himself to anyone, much less worry about hurting their feelings. "It's wrong. You know it's wrong. Go back to bed."

Graceful as a cat, she uncurled herself from his lap and turned away from him. He watched her walk away, the silhouette of her legs still nearly driving him to do something they would both regret. He wanted to stop her, to pull her back into his arms and continue the sin. He wanted it badly. Only when she had walked back up the stairs did he relax. He'd never met a woman like her, at least not a lady.

He'd thought most were silly, chaste creatures only interested in bonnets and gowns and shoes. And of course wealthy husbands. Amelia was a sensuous woman, funny at times, passionate. She intrigued him.

Was that what had happened to his brothers? Had they fallen under a woman's spell? Look where it had led them. To ruin. To marry. To forget the curse that hung over their heads. Gabriel was not in a position to be playing with fire. He had his hands full at the moment. He needed his wits about him, and Amelia Collingsworth greatly compromised his judgment.

Even now his thoughts were centered upon her, when he should be thinking about a plan to escape from Collingsworth Manor.

He rose and walked to the fading fire, using a poker to stoke the flames higher. All of his life he'd only been responsible for himself and the running of Wulfglen. The breeding of horses for sale. Now he was responsible for two strangers. One a girl and one very much a woman. How could he outwit these beasts of the forest? How could he best protect Lady Collingsworth and Mora? And, Lord help him, what if he failed?

She needed a bath and Amelia didn't care what strange happenings were afoot at Collingsworth Manor; she intended to have one. Mora had helped her stoke the stove and put on large kettles of water from the inside pump to heat. They'd had Gabriel carry a copper tub down the stairs and put it before the fire in the parlor. The doors could be closed for privacy's sake. Amelia decided they would all bathe, especially Gabriel, who put off some odd scent that attracted her.

The man had acted strangely toward her all morning. He kept looking at her, as if he expected some type of reaction from her. Did he expect her to be embarrassed about what had happened between them upstairs yesterday? Truth be told, Amelia wasn't as embarrassed about it as she should be. She wasn't positive she was embarrassed at all. Instead, she was rather hoping for a repeat of the incident.

The terrifying incident that had taken place last night she chose not to dwell upon. If she did, she knew she'd go into hysterics. Instead she had focused on this one normal task, something that made her feel as if her world was not crumbling around her.

"Will you accompany me upstairs?" she asked Wulf. "I thought we might go through the rooms and find you something better to wear. Not to mention a razor and a strop."

He ran a hand over the dark whiskers on his cheeks. "You do realize we have more to worry about than how well turned out we all look?"

She frowned at him. "My mother has always said just because your life is a shambles is no reason to let yourself go." When he rolled his gaze heavenward, she added, "Please, I need to do this right now. I don't want to think about last night, or later today, or tomorrow. I only want a hot bath."

His eyes softened upon her—the expression that turned her insides to pudding. "All right," he said. "Mora, keep watch down here," he instructed the girl. "So far, these creatures only seem active at night, but we mustn't let down our guard. Call up if you see or hear anything suspicious."

Mora wiped an arm across her damp brow. "I will for a fact, my lord. I think the lady is right. It feels good to be doing something normal. And I've never seen the creatures stirring about except during the night hours, either. We can take some comfort in that."

"Not too much," Gabriel warned the girl before he turned and followed Amelia from the kitchen and up the stairs. They reached the second landing and she stopped by her room to fetch her soaps and a fresh change of clothes. She had trouble making a decision between a silk striped pink frock and a lilac taffeta.

"Neither."

She turned to see Gabriel leaning against the door frame watching her. "Beg your pardon?"

"Neither gown," he specified. "Something more sensible. Something you can move in."

Amelia frowned and glanced back into her wardrobe. Truth was, she had nothing very sensible. She spotted a bland gray day dress and tugged it out.

"That one will do," Wulf commented.

"It's ugly," she protested. "I'm not even certain it's mine. Looks like something one of my maids would wear."

"Serviceable then," Wulf said. "Sensible."

She wanted to argue. Perhaps she did need something easy to move in. Amelia hadn't thought to bring "running for one's life" clothes along with her. Perhaps it was just as well this gown had obviously been included with her things by mistake.

"Robert's shaving items should be in the room next door," she said. "I'd fetch them for you, but I don't want to go back in there. Not ever."

"Understandable," Wulf said, and shrugged away from the door and disappeared into the hallway. She heard him in the next room a moment later. Amelia fetched a clean shift and a pair of drawers and hid them with her bundle.

"I have what I need."

She turned to see Gabriel in the doorway again, a small bag in hand. Amelia eyed his dirty clothing. "I'm wondering if we might find something for you to wear in one of the other rooms. I know you're too big to wear anything other than Robert's nightshirts."

Wulf shrugged. "His father was a big man. I'm sure Robert kept some of his things up here somewhere."

Amelia moved toward him. "You knew them both, then? Robert's parents?"

Stepping back to allow her to pass, he answered, "When I was younger. Before . . . before things changed."

Lord Gabriel was obviously speaking about the supposed curse that haunted the Wulf brothers. The scandal that had caused their once influential family to be shunned by all of society, with the exception of a few . . . well, only one whom she knew of, the Dowager Duchess of Brayberry.

"I don't believe you are cursed, you know," she said, moving across the hall to the first room. "I believe your parents were unfortunate."

"Given our circumstances, how convenient."

She glanced at him from over her shoulder. "I danced with your eldest brother in public," she declared. "I believe society will soon forgive you."

A slight smile settled over his disturbing mouth. "Forgive us for what? Being insane?"

Amelia moved to a dark oak wardrobe and opened the doors. "Well, for everything, I suppose," she answered.

"My heart leaps with joy over the possibility."

His sarcasm made her lips twitch. "They are a rather boorish lot," she admitted, realizing the garments inside of the wardrobe were mostly old linens and such. She closed the doors and moved past Wulf back into the hallway. "I, for one, find all their rules and silly traditions a bit tiresome. Scandalous people are much more interesting."

"Which is why you married a man you did not love to please them all."

Amelia wheeled around, nearly running into Wulf. "What do you know of love?" she demanded. "Who are you to judge me?"

He wore a hint of a sarcastic smile. It faded. "As you well know, I am no one. And you're right; I know nothing of love. Nor do I care to."

Although Amelia had declared to him that she did not believe in love, it stung somewhat to hear him echo her sentiments. She supposed it was all right for men to be in love with her; she simply would not return so strong or so silly an emotion. "Then we both agree on something." She turned back around and marched into the closest bedchamber. Together, she and Gabriel searched drawers and the wardrobe. They found nothing but were more fortunate two rooms down the hallway.

"And what was last night about?"

They hadn't spoken since they had both declared a disinterest in love. Both were going through a wardrobe where a few items of clothing hung. Items that looked as if they'd come close to fitting Gabriel.

She glanced at him. "Last night?"

He rolled his eyes. "Don't pretend nothing happened."

Her stomach suddenly twisted. "You mean the man . . . or whatever he was? Please, it disturbs me to think of it. I wanted to forget for a while longer."

Gabriel shook his head. "No, I didn't mean that. I meant later, when you came downstairs."

Amelia had trouble recalling much of last night. She strongly suspected Mora had doctored her tea so she would sleep. Suddenly she thought she knew what must have happened. "Oh good lord, don't tell me I was sleepwalking."

He blinked. "Pardon?"

Heat rushed into her cheeks. "A nasty habit I've had since childhood. What did I do? Sing? Dance? Play an instrument? Lord knows I was invited over as a guest more often than other girls when I was growing up for just that reason. I understand I am quite entertaining."

He blinked again. "Quite," he assured her. "And you remember nothing?"

She tried. "No, not a thing. What did I do?"

He glanced away and ran a hand through his hair. "Nothing. You just came downstairs and stood over me for a moment, then went back to bed."

Amelia sighed. "Thank heavens. I've been known to carry on whole conversations while I'm asleep. It's very embarrassing. I warned Mora about it while she was brushing my hair, maybe sensing that events of the past two days might set me into motion. Since we are bed partners for safety's sake, I thought she should know all of my bad habits."

Gabriel was the one who had insisted the two women sleep together in the same room. Amelia had been uncomfortable at first, but she found she felt safer with someone else in the room with her.

"I guess that explains what you were doing," he finally responded, although he still looked a little confused. "I'm glad to know you sleepwalk. I won't have to wonder what you are doing if it happens again."

"And it might," she assured him, holding a white lawn shirt against him and deciding the fit would be acceptable. "I do it more when I'm upset over something. Or so I assume, since reports of my wild antics usually have centered around an event which had disturbed me in some way."

"And you are certain you don't remember anything?"

Glancing up at him, she answered, "I'm positive. Why? Did I do something I should remember?"

He stared down at her for a moment, than answered, "No."

Amelia shrugged and laid the shirt over her arm along with her gowns. "If you find a pair of trousers, bring them downstairs. You don't mind if Mora and I have our baths first, do you?"

Gabriel glanced down at himself. "Probably a wise idea, since I will get the water the dirtiest. It's been a while since I've had the luxury. I'm sure the water is heated now. I'll be down in a moment to carry it to the tub for you."

"Your shoulder," she worried.

He shrugged. "It's nothing. I've had worse scrapes."

They stood staring at each other until the moment grew awkward. Amelia wondered if he was remembering yesterday morning when they were alone together upstairs. She was. Remembering and wishing he would kiss her again, regardless of how inappropriate her thoughts were. Perhaps she simply wanted another diversion. Anything to keep from thinking about last night and what she had seen outside.

"Did you want something else?"

His voice, already low pitched, bordered on seductive. She roused herself. "No," she answered. Since she wasn't certain what to say, she walked from the room and downstairs. After she deposited the clothing and necessities for bathing in the parlor, she returned to the kitchen. Steam whistled from the kettles on the stove. She glanced around, looking for Mora.

The door to the root cellar stood open. The heavy items Gabriel had stacked against the door were moved out of the way. Gooseflesh rose on her arms. Why was the door open? And where was Mora?

"Mora?" Amelia called down the stairs. "Mora, are you down there?"

Silence.

Amelia took a step into the doorway. "Mora, answer me!" she called again.

"It's me, my lady," Mora finally responded. "Just gathering some potatoes for a stew tonight. I thought I'd told Lord Gabriel to fetch me some, but couldn't find any upstairs."

"You should not be down there!" Amelia called. "Come back up this instant!"

"I know, been telling myself over and over it's not right, me being down here by myself, but I didn't want to ask the lord to come down here again. His body will not heal if he keeps exerting himself like he's been doing. And besides, he said we were safe in the daylight hours."

"What's going on?" Gabriel stood at the kitchen entrance, a pair of dark trousers draped over his arm. "What's that door doing open?"

"It's Mora," Amelia told him. "She's gone down to fetch some potatoes."

"Foolish girl," he swore, then draped the trousers over the back of a chair and crossed the room. He was through the doorway, moving down the stairs in a matter of seconds.

Amelia held her breath until the two of them came back up a moment later. Mora had a few potatoes cradled in her apron and Gabriel looked as if steam might come out of his ears. He quickly closed the door and began stacking items against it again.

"Never go down there alone!" he said to Mora once he'd finished. "What were you thinking? Are you daft?"

The girl's eyes filled with tears. "I just wanted to make a nice stew . . . and I didn't want you to hurt your shoulder again. It won't mend if you keep moving things about. Besides, you said yourself whatever is in the woods, they don't come out until dark."

He got in the girl's face. "What if I'm wrong about that? What if one of those creatures had been waiting down there for you? Not only did you put yourself in danger, but the rest of us by leaving the door open into the house."

Tears slid down Mora's cheeks. "I listened for a long while before I went down. I knew no one was there."

He opened his mouth, Amelia felt certain to continue berating the girl, but she intervened. "Please stop," she commanded him. She walked over and placed an arm around Mora's shoulders. "Can't you see how much you've upset her? She didn't mean any harm."

Gabriel took a step back, but the anger remained stamped on his handsome features. "I need Mora to understand how dangerous what she just did was," he persisted. "Do you understand, Mora?"

The girl nodded. "It was foolish. I'm just so used to doing for others instead of having done for me, it seemed natural for me to handle fetching the potatoes."

Amelia squeezed Mora's shoulders. "We're all safe," she said to Gabriel. "The girl understands that she made a mistake. Please carry the kettles into the parlor and fill the tub. We'll let Mora bathe first so she can collect herself."

"All right," he finally agreed, but only after staring at Mora long enough to make the girl burst into fresh sobs. "After we have seen to our cleanliness, we will discuss what we need to do to get ourselves out of this predicament."

Sensing it was best to be agreeable with Gabriel when his temper was up, Amelia nodded. She steered Mora to a table and helped her unload her apron of potatoes as Gabriel set about hefting the heavy kettles into the parlor in order to fill the tub. Amelia had claimed they were all safe, but in the back of her mind, in the far recesses, she knew that was a lie. They were safe for the moment. But for how much longer?

Chapter Eight

Mora had gone sniffling to her bath. Amelia felt rather sorry for the girl and had offered to help her, but Mora had shaken her head and mumbled she wanted to be alone. Amelia admitted she had probably only made the offer because she'd never seen Mora without that dreadful bonnet covering her hair. Amelia was always the first to fall asleep and the last to wake; therefore, she never saw Mora undress for bed or re-dress in the morning. Amelia did suspect Mora had tried her perfume and could hardly blame the girl, so she'd made sure to lay out her soaps and such to be shared.

While the girl saw to her bath, Amelia sat at the kitchen table across from Gabriel. He wore a brooding expression, and she kept silent for the most part. What Mora had done was foolish and dangerous, but as Amelia had already pointed out to him, no harm had come from it.

"You must let it go," she finally said.

He glanced up as if he'd forgotten she sat across from him. "I don't understand what possessed her to do something so foolish," he said.

"She's young," Amelia defended the servant. "And

as she said, used to doing for others rather than having things done for her."

His expression did not soften. "Still, you'd think she'd be too frightened to venture outside of the house alone."

Amelia shrugged. "She said she listened at the door to make certain she heard no one stirring about down there. She also said she didn't want you to strain your injuries. Mora was just being considerate."

He grunted in response but said nothing further. The silence stretched between them. The air grew thick and Amelia had trouble breathing . . . and his scent, it seemed to waft around her head. She glanced across the table and saw him staring at her. She could get lost in his deep green eyes . . . and she did. His pupils seemed to dilate as she stared, to grow long and slitted rather than round. His gaze lowered to her mouth and she swore her lips tingled as if he'd touched them with his own again.

"Pardon me, but I've finished my bath."

Only when Gabriel glanced away could Amelia do the same. Mora looked well scrubbed and she had fetched a clean work dress, but the girl still wore the ugly bonnet upon her head.

"Don't you find that bonnet stifling in the house, Mora?" Amelia asked. "Please don't feel as if you must wear it to keep up an appearance of servitude. Lord Gabriel and I don't care under the circumstances."

The girl bowed her head. Her cheeks bloomed with pink. "It's against my religion to show my hair, my lady. To do so is a sign of pride, and everyone knows pride is a sin."

Amelia glanced across the table at Gabriel. He merely lifted a brow. Although she'd heard of such a religion, Amelia had never really thought pride should be a sin. If one couldn't take pride in their appearance, then what? Realizing it was a rather shallow thought, Amelia rose from the table.

"I'll hurry so the water stays warm for you," she said to Gabriel. "Be nice," she added under her breath.

Be nice? No woman had ever ordered Gabriel to be nice, well, except his mother. He watched Mora as she tied an apron around her slim waist and set about peeling the potatoes she'd risked all of their lives to fetch. He didn't want to be mean to the girl. Her tears had affected him, but she must understand what she'd done had put not only herself in danger but him and Amelia as well.

"I apologize for being so short with you, Mora," he finally said. "I was upset that you would put us all at risk. I only wanted you to understand the seriousness of what you did."

"I do understand," she said softly, never turning to look at him. "What I did was wrong and I won't do anything like that again."

He tried to relax. Ever since he walked into the kitchen and saw the cellar door open, his body had been poised to defend. He liked to fight, Gabriel admitted. In the past, it had been a way to relieve the tension that arose from being a solitary figure—from his infrequent visits with women and his even more infrequent visits to London. He'd been involved in many a tavern brawl over the years, but he'd never faced what he was facing now. He wasn't even certain what he was facing.

"These creatures, Mora. You said they came shortly after you were employed by the head housekeeper here. What did they do to run everyone off?"

She kept her position across the room, wielding her small knife with precision as she peeled potatoes. "I didn't see them do anything," she admitted. "But Constance, the laundress, she said one came to her one night as a man and told her everyone should leave. Then she said the man turned into a wolf before her very eyes."

Gabriel scratched the whiskers upon his chin. He was looking forward to a shave and a bath. "And they all fled, strictly on her word?"

Mora glanced at him. She drew herself up straight. "The woman was respected among the rest of the staff. She'd been with the young lord's parents. No one thought she was lying."

"Odd," he said, mostly to himself. "That it took so little to convince them all to flee."

"Pardon me for saying so, my lord, but it is not a little thing to see a man turn into a wolf, or the other way around. Is it?"

Her stare unnerved him somewhat. As if she looked deeper inside of him than he wanted her to see. As if she knew the truth about him and his family. But she couldn't know. All believed the curse that haunted the Wulf brothers was insanity. No one knew the truth. Or did they? He wondered about his brothers, now married. Had they escaped the curse? Was it over for them? He needed to know, but he wasn't going to find out anything stuck at Collingsworth Manor.

"I suppose it is odd," he finally answered her. "If one believes in such things."

"Seeing is believing," she commented, turning back to her task. "You and the lady have both seen now."

Mora's speaking of the lady turned his thoughts to the parlor. Was Amelia naked now, stretched out relaxing in her bath? As much as he tried to steer his thoughts from such visions, he couldn't seem to help himself. Gabriel still had trouble believing Amelia did not remember coming downstairs last night and practically seducing him. Was she pretending she didn't remember?

"Mora, did Lady Collingsworth say anything to you about sleepwalking?"

The girl took the potatoes she'd peeled and sliced, dumping them in a pot steaming upon the stove. "Yes. She warned me that she sometimes walks in her sleep so as not to frighten me. Now that we're sharing a bed and all. Never seen anyone who did that myself, but have heard of it."

"Did you hear her get out of bed last night?"

Mora turned and looked at him. "No. Slept like the dead, I was so exhausted. Did she do that last night?"

At least he knew Amelia had not lied upstairs. "Yes. She came downstairs, although she doesn't remember it today."

"Poor woman," Mora clucked, turning back to her stew making. "To be widowed on her wedding night, and now all this. She's holding up better than I imagined a dainty social flower like her would do, though, don't you agree, my lord?"

"Yes," he admitted.

"And so kind, she is," Mora added. "Never worked for the upper crust before coming to this house, but I'd heard not to expect kindness from them. I'd heard they were all too caught up in themselves to care for the likes of a servant. Unless she was pretty and the lord wanted . . . well, you know."

Gabriel didn't know, not really. When he was growing up, before the curse visited their father and their lives became hell, they had servants. Gabriel didn't recall anyone in his family being mean to them; he didn't really recall them at all. They were like ghosts in a house who kept everything running smoothly. He'd had to learn to do for himself. Men wanted the coin the Wulfs offered enough to work for them, stable help and the like, but not women.

If the Wulfs wanted their clothes laundered, they took them to a woman in a nearby village called Hempshire. Women were willing enough to take the Wulfs' coin as long as they didn't have to work for them at Wulfglen.

He missed his home, his brothers, and suddenly he knew that he, Amelia, and Mora must leave Collingsworth Manor and make it to Wulfglen afoot. Strength in numbers, and the numbers seemed to be on the wrong side at the moment. He would tell Amelia and Mora as soon as he'd had a chance to clean up. He would tell them over the dinner Mora busied herself preparing.

Amelia entered a surprisingly short time later looking pink and clean and rather embarrassed by the drabness of her gown. "The bath is all yours," she said to him. "But I'm afraid you'll smell like Mora and me because of the soaps we used."

He shrugged. "A definite improvement over the way I smell at the moment." He rose from behind the table, feeling the pull in his thigh where Mora had dug the ball from his flesh and stitched him back together. His shoulder ached, as well, but if Mora thought he wasn't healing properly, no telling what task she might take upon herself next. He did his best to hide his limp as he left the room.

The parlor was pleasantly warm and steamy. He closed his eyes for a moment and simply breathed in the scent of perfumed soap. The scent of Amelia . . . and he supposed now Mora, as well. Gabriel hurriedly stripped from his clothing, glad to part with the stained buckskins. He removed the bandages from his wounds and climbed into the warm water. A long sigh of contentment left his lips when he settled back into the tub to soak. Since there was no one waiting for use of the tub, he took his time.

"Do you think he's all right in there?" Amelia asked Mora. Gabriel had been attending to his bath for a long while.

Stirring the stew she now had simmering over the stove, Mora shrugged. "Imagine he's just enjoying a soak. You can always go see about him if you're worried."

Mora must know her suggestion was improper, but then, being from a lower class, perhaps she did not. If Amelia had voiced such a question to one of her own maids, she would have scurried to check upon the situation. Amelia missed her staff in London, but Robert had assured her one of his staff would be qualified to take over the role of lady's maid.

Of course no staff had been at Collingsworth Manor when they'd arrived. She supposed she should tell Mora it wouldn't be proper for Amelia to go and check on him, that she might accidentally catch him in a state of undress, but why bother under the circumstances?

Now there was an intriguing thought. Seeing Gabriel Wulf naked. Amelia had already seen him bare from the waist up, had seen his leg . . . she couldn't imagine how impressive the entire width and breadth of him unclothed might be. Well, she could imagine, if she tried. But she would not.

"Can I help you?" she asked Mora, needing a distraction from her wicked thoughts.

"You can set bowls out for us," Mora suggested. "The stew will be ready shortly. Wasn't much to put in it. No meat, I'm afraid. I do have half a loaf of bread and a bit of cheese. That will have to satisfy us."

It sounded wonderful to Amelia. All of her life she'd been fed the finest food prepared by the finest cooks, and now, here she was, helping the kitchen help set the table. And looking forward to a meal she might have once turned her spoiled little nose up at. How drastically her life had changed in the space of one day. She would not have believed something like this could happen. And especially to her. For some reason, she'd always thought being wealthy and privileged came with a certain degree of safety.

She'd always been protected, coddled, given the finest of everything. Seldom had she done anything or gone anywhere in her life when someone wasn't along with her. It was, in a way, stifling to her. Perhaps that was why she rebelled so much of the time. Now she'd give anything to be surrounded by servants and her family.

Mora had already set bowls and spoons on the counter beside the pump. Amelia simply had to transfer everything over to the table. It didn't take long. She was in the process of arranging the last bowl when Gabriel returned from his bath. The sight of him nearly took her breath away.

He was dressed in a white lawn shirt, open at the neck, and a pair of black trousers that fit him almost indecently snugly. They outlined the powerful shape of his thighs. His hair was wet and slicked back from his chiseled features, his face now smooth as a baby's behind.

"Oh my," she couldn't help but breathe. He smiled at her, and she swore her knees went weak.

Gabriel walked to the table and sobered. "I have made a plan while I soaked and wish to share it with the both of you."

Mora hefted the pot of stew to the table, ladling a small potion into her and Amelia's bowls and a considerably larger portion into Gabriel's. The girl then fetched bread and cheese. Gabriel seated both women. He settled into his own chair.

"We need to get away from here," he said. "We are too vulnerable trapped as we are in the house."

Mora gasped. "But won't we be in more danger outside, amongst them?" she asked. "At least here we have walls to protect us. To keep them out."

He shook his head. "It would be easy enough for them to force us out. They could wait until we've run out of food and are too weakened to fight them. Foul our water supply. Any number of things."

Amelia shivered. She hadn't thought of any of those scenarios. She wondered if even now the creatures plotted something sinister against them.

"He's right, Mora," she said. "If we left by daylight, if we pack supplies, we might have a chance."

"I'd rather starve to death than be eaten by one of them," Mora muttered.

"We have decided," Gabriel said to the girl. "You must come with us, Mora. I can't in good conscience leave you behind."

Amelia felt a thrill race through her over his chivalry, if it was followed by a shudder of fear over what they had decided. At least they were planning an escape. Planning felt better than doing nothing. Mora, she sensed, was not convinced. Amelia reached across the table and patted her hand.

"We will plan more after we've eaten. I'll need you to help with the supplies. You'll know better what we should take than I would as far as food—"

"Ladies," Gabriel interrupted.

Amelia glanced across the table at him. He sat very still, his nostrils slightly flared. "There is no time to plan," he said. "They've set the house on fire."

She thought he must be joking, but then, no, he wouldn't tease about a thing like that. Amelia couldn't smell smoke. But wait, yes, just a whiff. Then there was no time to think. Gabriel sprang into action.

Gabriel rose from his chair. He glanced around the kitchen and saw the smoke seeping in from behind the cellar door. Damn, they would burn the house from the ground up. Reaching out, he grabbed Mora's arm and pulled her up from her chair, glad that Amelia had the sense to leap to her feet.

"Come on," he said to the women. "We must go now."

"But, but shouldn't we try to put it out?" Mora choked. "What about supplies, clothing? We can't just run out into the night with nothing!"

"We must go!" Gabriel repeated. "They'd expect us to take the time to gather what we can. Our best chance to escape is now, at this very moment."

"The pistol," Amelia breathed. "You do have that?"

Rather than answer, he removed it from the band of his trousers. "Out the front!"

Amelia easily followed into step behind him, but the girl dug in her heels. Gabriel dragged her along. Since he held the pistol in one hand and Mora's arm in the other, Amelia hurried forward and fumbled with the locks. She had the door open a moment later. They were greeted by a man, his eyes glittering, his pointed teeth bared in a snarl.

Gabriel lifted the pistol and shot the man. Mora screamed and Gabriel pulled her behind him, all of them stumbling over the dead man. Gabriel released Mora long enough to shout, "Run for the trees!"

The girl froze. Amelia took hold of her arm, pulling Mora along with her as she ran. Gabriel followed, the pistol cocked and ready, glancing in front of them, behind them, wherever the threat might spring from. He was surprised they weren't suddenly rushed. This was what the creatures had wanted, to get them out of the house into the open.

And like he suspected, they might have believed Gabriel and the women would put up more of a fight from inside of the house or at least that they would take time to gather what they could. At the moment, Gabriel had the advantage. He wouldn't waste it.

The pistol was firmly clutched in his hand as he ran after the women. Even injured, Gabriel easily caught up with Amelia and Mora. The girl tripped over a log and he understood that he had advantages the women did not. He saw clearly in the coming dark. He took Amelia's cold hand in his and instructed her to hold on to Mora; then he led them at as fast a pace as he dared push them, through the woods, into the thickness of the trees, into the thickness of the danger he sensed all around them.

Gabriel knew a shortcut to Wulfglen. As boys, he and his brothers had used it often to visit Robert. On horseback the journey took only a few hours; on foot, being pursued, it might take days. He stopped for a moment to get his bearings, to allow Amelia and Mora to catch their breath; then he pushed them onward. Gabriel now recalled a place where they might spend the night in relative safety. It was an animal den that he and his brothers had discovered while exploring the area around the swimming pond. Gabriel and the women needed water, and the pond would provide that for them. If the water wasn't the cleanest, it would suffice.

"This way," he instructed.

Chapter Nine

Summer had almost ended and now Amelia felt a chill in the night air. Gabriel finally stopped and allowed them to rest. The moonlight glistened on a small pond and it was much easier to see out in the open, but around them there were no night sounds. It was eerie. She rubbed her arms and drew the cool night air into her lungs. Her throat was dry, either from fear or from their harried journey through the woods.

She watched Gabriel. He stood very still as if listening, as if sniffing the air. Surely he wasn't doing that, she told herself. He was just breathing. After a few more moments, he seemed to relax.

"Drink from the pond," he said to them. "The water isn't the cleanest, but I don't suppose it will kill us."

Mora didn't hesitate. She quickly went to the water's edge, bent, and began to drink from the pond. Amelia wet her lips, but there was little moisture in her mouth to aid her effort. Now Gabriel had bent beside Mora and also drank from his cupped hands. Amelia forced herself to move and bend beside Gabriel.

"What does it taste like?" she asked him.

"Fish," he answered.

Amelia deplored fish. She shuddered.

"It's not that bad," Mora offered, wiping her mouth with the sleeve of her dress. "But probably a good thing it's dark and we can't see it. I'll wager it has a green tint to it."

The thought turned Amelia's stomach. "I believe I'll just wait until we come across water that is cleaner."

Gabriel lifted his head and glanced at her. "There is a creek that runs a ways through the woods," he admitted. "But it may be two days before we reach it. Drink now."

His tone was commanding. Amelia wanted to balk; at the same time, she wanted a drink. She drew in a deep breath and cupped her hands into the chilly water. Her first sip gagged her. Gabriel had not been exaggerating. It did taste like fish. She forced herself to drink even though the water tasted horrible.

"What are we going to do now?" Mora asked.

The moonlight shone down upon him, highlighting the silver-blond streaks in his hair. "I know a place where we can sleep," he answered. "It's just over here."

They all rose from the pond's edge. Gabriel led them to what appeared to be a large hole in the ground. "You'll have to climb in," he said to them. "I'll go first. You follow."

"In there?" Amelia wrinkled her nose. "It looks dirty."

Gabriel sighed. "It's in the ground; of course it's dirty. Would you rather stay out here and take your chances with whatever might be tracking us?"

Amelia wouldn't, but she hated small enclosed spaces. "It looks awfully dark down there," she commented.

Mora stepped forward. "I'll go after Lord Gabriel," she said. "I don't like small places, though," she grumbled, and Amelia could have kissed her for complaining.

Gabriel scurried down the hole. Due to his size, it was a tight fit, and just watching him made Amelia short of breath. A moment later he disappeared.

Mora nudged Amelia. "Wonder if anything else is down in that hole," she said. "A body finds a hole in the ground, there is usually an animal that goes with it."

The thought raised the fine hairs on Amelia's arms. "That is not helping," she said. "The only consolation, I suppose, is if there is an animal down there, it will attack Lord Gabriel first."

Mora surprised her by giggling. She had never heard the girl laugh before. It eased some of the tension Amelia felt over having to climb into the hole.

"All right, come on, Mora," Gabriel called, and his voice echoed. "Hurry; we need the cover."

The girl sobered quickly. She took a deep breath and began to climb into the hole. Amelia couldn't watch without feeling a choking sensation close her throat. She glanced around. Here she was in the dark of night in the middle of the woods with two virtual strangers. Her gown was stained and dirty. She had a fishy taste in her mouth, and for all she knew, she was the target of the eyes of some creature that could turn into a man or a wolf.

A scent caught her attention. Wild mint? While Mora made her descent into the hole, Amelia searched for the source of the smell. She found the patch about the time Gabriel called to her. Gathering up a handful, she stuffed the leaves into her pocket and returned to the hole. As frightened of dark, enclosed places as Amelia was, Gabriel was right. She'd rather face what was down there with them than stay up here and face whatever might come along all alone.

Amelia took a deep breath and began to climb. Dirt crumbled around her as she scurried down the hole. The den beneath was larger than she would have thought; at least she could gather that much from what little moonlight spilled down from above. Gabriel reached out and pulled her to him, and the three of them huddled together on the dirt floor. Due to their close proximity, Amelia gladly shared her mint leaves.

After huddling together for warmth, Gabriel instructed the women to get some sleep. Amelia couldn't sleep. She was snuggled up against Gabriel, and his hard, strong body did not make a good pillow. He did radiate body heat, though, and for that reason alone she wasn't tempted to find a more comfortable position. Amelia rested on one side of him and Mora on the other. She could already hear Mora's soft snores and envied the girl for finding sleep so easily under their current conditions.

"We'll have to tease her about her snoring tomorrow."

Amelia jumped. She had thought Gabriel had drifted off to sleep. "A pound says she won't crack a smile," she whispered. "Mora doesn't have much of a sense of humor."

Gabriel shifted so that he was facing her. "I'm surprised by yours," he said. "When I saw you in London, it wasn't something I would have likened with you."

Amelia drew herself up on one elbow. "You remember me, then?" The thought pleased her more than it should. She kept forgetting that she was in mourning. It didn't help that she had never seen Robert's body. It was as if her mind refused to acknowledge his passing, even though Gabriel had told her that she must.

"Yes," he finally admitted. "You stuck in my head for some reason."

Knowing she shouldn't confess as much, she said, "And you in mine."

"Not too awfully long," he said drolly. "You did marry."

Amelia wondered what else she was supposed to have done? Waited for him? Tried to arrange a chance meeting with him through her friend Rosalind? Begged to be invited to Wulfglen so that she might be around him? "I did what was expected of me," she clipped. "You're a man. You have no idea the pressure society and one's parents put upon a girl about making the right match. I wanted a life of my own. It was the only way I could have one."

He reached forward and brushed a stray lock from her forehead. "Now what will you do?" he asked.

She fought down both a flush of pleasure from his touch and rising hysteria. Amelia hadn't had time to think about what she would do. All she had time to think about was what was happening now.

"I don't really know," she answered. "I suppose I'll return to my parents' home, although it will be awkward. I am a widow, but I have never been a wife."

Wulf was silent for a moment; then he said, "Young widows, I imagine, are every bit as in demand on the marriage market as young debutantes."

Amelia supposed he was right, but the realization

brought her little comfort. She'd already been through the husband hunt once; she wasn't that anxious to return to it again.

"Tell me what you know of my brothers and their wives," he said. "Does all seem well with them? When last I left London in search of Jackson, Armond was having trouble with his wife's stepbrother. Was the issue resolved?"

Mention of Rosalind's stepbrother made Amelia shiver. The man had been handsome enough, but he exuded an air of evil that had made Amelia's skin crawl. "The stepbrother is dead," she answered. "A house fire. His mother perished in it along with him."

Wulf's eyes glittered in the darkness, but that might easily be due to the moonlight spilling in from above. "Too bad for the stepmother," he commented. "But then, do they seem happy together? Armond and Rosalind?"

"Oh yes," she assured him. "If I believed in love, I would say they are in it. And Jackson and Lucinda, as well. Rosalind is to have a child," she informed him. "She hasn't said anything, but it's obvious really, even if she chooses gowns that do well at disguising her fuller figure."

"A child? And Jackson has a son already?"

She didn't know whether to voice her opinion and the opinion of many regarding Jackson's son. Why not? Amelia decided. Who knew if either of them would be alive tomorrow? "I don't think the child is Jackson's," she confided. "The babe looks nothing like him, but your brother seems to care for the child as if he were his own, which I suppose is what is most important."

Gabriel snorted. "I cannot see him in the role. If it

were Jackson in this position with two women, he would not be merely sleeping."

Amelia should act shocked by his insinuation, but she was too tired. She merely said what was on her mind. "I think if a woman doesn't wish to have a witch put a curse upon her, she will not give Jackson Wulf a second glance these days."

"Do you believe in such things, Amelia? In witches and curses?"

The use of her given name should upset her, given their short acquaintance, but it did not. Amelia liked him to use the more intimate form of address with her, and she had to admit she liked thinking of him as Gabriel rather than Lord Gabriel. What had he asked her? About witches and curses and if she believed in such things.

"Two days ago, no. Now, I'm not so sure."

He leaned closer. "Do such things frighten you?"

Again, she was too tired to be anything but honest. "Yes."

Closer yet he came, his lips nearly brushing hers. "Do I frighten you?"

Peering at him through her lashes, she examined whether anything she felt at the moment might be related to fear. Yes, her heart beat faster, but the reaction did not stem from being afraid.

"Why would I be frightened of you?" she asked. "You are my protector. My best friend is married to your brother. I might be dead, or worse, if not for you. Why do you ask me if I am frightened of you?"

"Regardless of the other things you mentioned, I am a stranger to you."

How could Amelia tell him that he was not a stranger? That she had memorized his features? That he had visited her in dreams? That she had thought about kissing him long before an opportunity was presented? That she had thought of doing more than kissing him? She couldn't tell him.

"I suppose you are," she admitted. "But at the moment, you're all I have that stands between me and whatever those creatures want."

He pulled back and settled upon his back, staring up at the moonlight. "Do be honest."

She giggled over his dry tone and snuggled beside him for warmth. They didn't speak further, and without the distraction of conversation, Amelia became totally aware of him. Of the slight sound of his breathing, the hard feel of him pressed against her. And his scent. She didn't always notice it. But she noticed it now and tried to identify what it reminded her of.

Spice. Not as strong as clove, not as sweet as cinnamon, but something in between. The scent curled around her and she found herself wondering if it would feel different to kiss him when his cheeks were smooth rather than whiskered? Would it feel different to have him pressed against her while they were lying down, rather than standing?

"You kissed me when you were walking in your sleep."

He startled her again. And, good lord, it was as if he knew she was thinking of kissing. "What?" she asked.

Gabriel turned on his side again. "I wasn't going to tell you, but you came downstairs and you kissed me."

Amelia was glad it was dark. Her cheeks were suddenly burning. "Are you lying to me? I swear I do not remember anything happening between us."

"I'm not lying," he assured her. "But it was different than when you kissed me upstairs."

His shifted position brought them closer, or rather, it aligned them in a disturbing way. Body parts against body parts. "I'm thinking it was you who kissed me upstairs," she pointed out. "And different in what way?"

She supposed his silence meant he was thinking upon the matter. "You lacked . . . passion," he finally answered. "It was as if you were only going through the motions."

It was rude enough to mention the incident if it had indeed taken place, but then to criticize her kissing technique was even worse. "I was asleep," she reminded him. "And obviously not inspired enough to wake."

His teeth flashed briefly in the darkness when he smiled. "I didn't say it wasn't nice. I merely said it was different."

"And it's rude of you to even mention it," she clipped. Amelia was sorely embarrassed that she would seek him out in her sleep and kiss him. Her defenses lowered, such action spoke of an unconscious desire to share intimacy with him, and he was smart enough to realize that.

"Are you warm enough?"

She was warmer than she had been a moment earlier due to her flush of embarrassment. "I'm fine," she answered.

"Then we should get some sleep. We have a long trek ahead of us tomorrow."

The conversation had at least distracted her momentarily from their immediate plight. Amelia wasn't ready to return to the nightmare her life had become. She doubted she would sleep at all once all the worries began to plague her. She really knew nothing about Gabriel Wulf. Nothing but that he was tall, built rather marvelously, and was as handsome as sin. Nothing but that he could seduce a woman with a kiss and just the smell of him.

She supposed he was gallant. Another man might have fled the situation at Collingsworth Manor post-haste and left her and poor Mora to whatever fate befell them. But he had stayed and defended them. Offered his protection. Led them to safety when the house was set afire. They'd seen no smoke or flames in the distance. Gabriel had remarked that it was probably simply a scare tactic to force them out into the open. Which had worked.

Mora's soft snores continued. Amelia wished they would lull her into sleep, but she simply lay there and stared up at the moon directly overhead. The chill found her again and she shivered. Gabriel drew her closer. She didn't pull away. Snuggling closer, Amelia tucked her head beneath his chin. She heard the strong beat of his heart beneath her ear, felt the long length of him pressed against her.

He began to stroke her hair. She hadn't bothered to do more than pull it back after her bath and now she felt certain most of it had come loose. It was soothing, the stroke of his fingers through her hair, and yet it was disturbing, as well. His strange scent enveloped her. She tried to block it out by holding her breath, but that only made catching it harder once she ran out of air.

Slowly, his hand drifted from her hair down her back. Was she supposed to be going to sleep? If his touch was meant to soothe her into relaxing, just the opposite was taking place.

Amelia was aware of his hand on the small of her back. It drifted a little lower and pressed her against him. She swallowed a sudden lump that formed in her throat. They were hip to hip, and she felt the obvious bulge in the front of his trousers.

He groaned a moment later. His hand fell away from her and he rolled onto his back. She glanced at him from beneath her lashes. He stared up at the moon. She lay very still, waiting to see if he would touch her again, but he didn't. It was as if he'd regained control over what had possessed him to touch her in the first place. A pity, Amelia thought.

Deep down in her wicked soul, she was hoping he'd kiss her again. Maybe hoping to prove to him that she did not lack passion in the least. She had to wonder, since she'd been sleepwalking and had no recollection whatsoever of their encounter, how much advantage he had taken of the situation. It would be just her luck that he had despoiled her and she didn't recall it. But no, she was certain that had not happened.

There would have been signs, plus he would have said so had things gone beyond a kiss. And Amelia realized she no longer had reason to hold on to her precious virginity. She was a married woman . . . a widow now. No one would expect her to be chaste. Or would they?

If no consummation had taken place between her and Robert, would she still be able to claim his holdings? A large portion now being the dowry her father had settled upon her. Robert had no living relations; she knew that. He'd once remarked that the men in his family didn't seem to live to a ripe old age. Poor Robert, neither had he.

Guilt came close to consuming her. Here she was, lying next to another man and wishing he'd kiss her when Robert had not even been laid to rest. While she did not love her husband of one day, she should show him respect.

And she would, Amelia decided. She would not harbor wicked thoughts of Gabriel Wulf until her mourning period was over. But that was a year and would she even live to see tomorrow? The thought of dying a virgin greatly upset her. Well, actually, the thought of dying altogether greatly upset Amelia. Perhaps she wouldn't have to mourn Robert for a whole year . . . maybe under certain circumstances a day or two would suffice.

Having fully exhausted her mind, Amelia snuggled up next to Gabriel, wrenching another soft moan from him by doing so, and tried to sleep.

CHAPTER TEN

Gabriel nudged Amelia awake. "We need to get moving."

She groaned, then groaned again when he sat, taking his wonderful body heat. Mora was already awake, staring up at the hole above.

"How do we get up there?" she asked.

"I'll heft you up," Gabriel answered. "See those roots sticking out of the dirt? Grab onto those and pull yourself the rest of the way to the top."

Amelia was thankful that Mora was going first. She'd need to watch her and see how she proceeded. The servant nodded and allowed Gabriel to heft her up. It was a good thing both Amelia and Mora were slight of build, Amelia thought. Less strain on Gabriel. She knew his shoulder must still ache, since that wound hadn't had time to heal.

He lifted Mora with little effort. Beneath the sleeves of his now dirty shirt, Amelia saw his muscles bulge. His arms were wonderfully sculpted, she recalled. Everything about him was wonderfully sculpted. Mora strained to reach the roots sticking out of the dirt.

"Test them first," Gabriel warned. "Be sure they're strong enough to hold your weight."

The girl did as he instructed. When she got hold of a root that seemed sturdy enough to support her, she latched on and pulled herself up. A moment later the girl scrambled out of the hole. Her head appeared, staring down at them.

"I want you to help Amelia once she's close to the top," Gabriel called up to Mora.

Amelia figured that she could get out as well as Mora had done. The fact that Gabriel obviously didn't think the same stung her pride. She wasn't helpless, for God's sake. But she did want out of the hole, and pointing out his error would only prolong her current discomfort.

"Your turn, Amelia," Gabriel said.

She crawled to where he knelt. He placed his hands on her waist and lifted her off the ground. Amelia felt his warm breath against the skin displayed by the neckline of her gown. His face was even with her breasts, and her nipples hardened in response. It was embarrassing. How easily he affected her. Amelia wondered if all women reacted to him the same way. Mora didn't seem affected, but then, Mora was only a girl. Perhaps her woman's emotions hadn't yet developed. Amelia wished hers had not.

"Reach," Gabriel said, and she noticed that his voice sounded huskier than usual.

Amelia tried. She couldn't. Gabriel's hands moved down to her hips and he lifted her higher. Her fingers managed to grasp two thick roots jutting from the ground.

Mora reached her arms through the hole. Amelia realized she must pull herself up a little to reach the girl's hands. She also wondered if Mora would be strong enough to help her out.

An attempt to push herself up using her feet against the damp den wall made dirt suddenly crumble in all around her. The hole above began to disappear. Mora yelped and pulled her arms away. Then Amelia fell. Gabriel caught her and in a jumble of arms and legs he rolled them deeper into the den. He was on top of her and Amelia could hardly breathe, but then, she could hardly breathe anyway, the dirt was so thick in the den. And it was dark. Darker than midnight.

Gabriel might be squishing her, but Amelia realized he was also protecting her. Dirt continued to fall from the top of the den, chunks of it pelting Gabriel rather than Amelia. She was terrified of being buried alive. Amelia pressed her face against his neck and squeezed her eyes closed. How long she clung to him she had no idea. It seemed like an eternity before she no longer heard the pelting noise of dirt clots hitting Gabriel's back.

"Are you all right?" he said close to her ear.

"I think so," she whispered. "Are you?"

"Yes, I'm all right. We need to lie very still until I know nothing else is coming down on top of us."

Above, they heard Mora call to them. "Don't answer," Gabriel warned softly. "You could bring more dirt cascading down on us."

Amelia hated not answering the girl's calls, but what else could she do? And what exactly *were* they going to do? She suspected there wasn't much air trapped in the small den with them. Just the thought sent panic coursing through her.

"You must relax, Amelia," Gabriel said against her ear. "Breathe slowly."

Surely he felt her quickly rising chest—her heart pounding. She did need to calm down, but under the circumstances, she didn't see how. "I'll try," she said. "But I have a problem with small, dark places. My brother once locked me in a dark closet for hours."

He was silent for a moment; then curiosity obviously got the best of him. "Why did he do that?"

Amelia wasn't careful with her words. "Because he was a mean little bastard who loved playing the worst pranks on everyone. We were playing hide-and-seek at the time."

Gabriel surprised her by laughing in her ear.

She tensed beneath him. "I don't think anything regarding our current situation is humorous," she said crossly.

Once he stopped laughing, he said, "No. But I've never met a lady who drank and cursed and did both so well."

A blush would be appropriate, but Amelia didn't bother to summon one. Wulf couldn't see it anyway. "My brother isn't so mean now," she admitted. "And I wasn't above pulling a good prank or two."

"You?" he said drily. "And you look like such an angel."

Amelia was not an angel. She had a very wicked side. They both might die at any moment and she was still harboring indecent thoughts about Gabriel Wulf. Still wondering things she should not be wondering. Like what it would feel like if they were both naked right now.

"How are we going to get out?" she asked. That was what she should be thinking about.

Slowly, he rolled off of her. He sat, although the den roof was hardly tall enough for him to do so. "I'm going to dig us out," he answered.

Gabriel knew there wasn't much air trapped with them in the den; he also knew Amelia was on the verge of panic. He had to proceed quickly but carefully, since he wasn't sure how long the roof over them would hold before it came crashing down on them. He slid slowly along the damp, packed dirt of the hollowed-out den to where the dirt had crumbled in on them from the opening. Above, he still saw a portion of light, although the opening was now much smaller than it had been when they had climbed inside last night.

There were no tools he could use to shovel, so he had to use his hands. He set to work. Amelia's growing panic was a palpable force inside the small den. Without anything to distract her, she was reacting to her childhood fear of being locked inside somewhere she couldn't get out. Gabriel thought conversation would keep her distracted, although he wasn't usually a talkative man.

"Tell me more about your family," he said to Amelia.

He thought she wouldn't answer, that fear had taken over her and robbed her of the ability; then she said, "They are typical. Father and Mother married because they were a good match. They seem content enough with one another. My brother is three years younger than me. I miss them."

Gabriel glanced over his shoulder. Amelia looked very small and frightened, like a little girl, although he knew for certain that she was not a little girl. He was much too aware of her physically.

"I miss my brothers, as well," he admitted. "We are closer than most, maybe because for some time now, we're all each other has had."

Damn, he had never admitted anything so personal to a woman. It was the circumstance, Gabriel assured himself. He had to continue a conversation in order to keep her from panicking and possibly putting them in more danger.

"Well, I never thought it was fair," she said. "The way society judged your family for something your parents did. The way they always quickly jump to the worst conclusions. Like when that girl was found dead in the stable of your family townhome. Everyone naturally assumed Lord Wulf was responsible."

Focusing on his slow digging, he said, "We are many things, but we are not murderers." Then he recalled that he and Armond both had worried that Jackson might be in some way connected to the woman's death. Only because of the timing of the murder and the fact that Jackson had been in London and then later, when another murder occurred, he'd been in London again. Gabriel realized he was wrong to think for one moment Jackson would be tied to hurting a woman. Jackson loved women and they loved him.

"Are you bitter?"

Her question surprised him. And confused him a little. "Bitter about what?"

"Being denied your right to rub elbows with those of

your station? Being forced to live in the shadows of society? I think I would be."

Gabriel kept digging. Was he bitter? "I've never cared to be part of society. Most of them are silly and shallow. Lazy and conceited. No, I am not bitter."

She made a huffing noise. "But you are judgmental. You can't judge everyone by the actions and opinions of a few."

He glanced back over his shoulder at her. "Of course I can," he told her. "Especially when the society you defend are like sheep being herded by dogs. They cannot think for themselves; they have to be told what to believe and what opinion they should have upon every matter and every person."

"That is not true," she argued. "I like to think I am my own person, that I am free to form my own opinions. And to express them," she added. "If you judge all by what you believe about a few, you are just as guilty of being a snob."

She was opinionated, obviously, and Gabriel found the trait attractive about her. And he supposed she was right and he was judgmental. Perhaps a little jaded. He had thought to put her in a category along with how he assumed most ladies of her station were, but she was in a category by herself. Truth be known, he could not be a proper judge of ladies of her "station" anyway. He'd never spent much time around them. He supposed he was a hypocrite. None of the things he admitted to being was worse than what he truly was. Cursed.

He'd dug his way to the smaller hole, the dirt that had caved in, actually making reaching it less difficult than it normally would have been. Carefully, he began to widen the hole. It didn't take him long to widen the space enough so that he could climb out. He poked his head out and glanced around. He didn't see Mora anywhere, and luckily, he didn't see any unwanted company.

"Amelia, I am going to crawl out. You come out behind me in case I need to help you."

Allowing her to go first would be better, but Gabriel knew that climbing back down might start the cave-in all over again.

"I'm frightened," she whispered. "What if the dirt starts caving in again? I could be trapped here alone."

"That isn't going to happen," he assured her, and hoped he was right. "Just be careful when you're climbing out. Try not to rush yourself."

"Anything to get out of here," she said, and he was relieved she showed both courage and determination in the face of her fear.

Gabriel shimmied out of the hole. The ground around the opening was unstable at best. It felt heavenly to breathe in air that wasn't coated by dirt. He lay on his stomach, looking down into the hole.

"All right, come on, Amelia," he instructed. "Nice and slow."

Below, he saw her appear. She looked up at him, her face a pale oval in the darkness.

"Crawl up on your belly," he instructed her. "Just move slowly and carefully."

She started out that way; then, as if her fear had taken hold of her, she crawled so quickly toward the top that the dirt began to crumble around her again. Gabriel lunged forward and grabbed her arm; then he was pulling her out, rolling away from where the ground began to cave in around them. In a matter of seconds, the den caved in entirely.

Amelia gasped for breath beside him. They both sat and stared at the place that might have become their grave. They were coated with dirt, but they were alive.

"You saved my life," she whispered. "Again."

He reached out and wiped a smudge of dirt from her cheek. "Let's find Mora." He rose and extended a hand to help her up.

It was odd, but any time they touched, a strange tingling coursed through him. A current. He helped her to her feet, and together they walked toward the pond. They spotted Mora a moment later, sitting by the water's edge.

She glanced up as they approached. Her eyes widened and she placed a hand against her heart. "I thought the both of you were dead," she said. "I didn't know what to do. I couldn't go back to Collingsworth Manor."

"We're all right," Amelia assured the girl, brushing dirt from the skirts of her serviceable dress. "We couldn't call out for fear it would cause more dirt to cave in upon us."

Mora looked shamefaced. "I was afraid to stay there because I thought I might fall in with you. I guess I'm a coward."

Gabriel bent beside the girl and washed his dirty hands in the pond. "You could have easily caused a worse cave-in," he assured her. "You did right to get away."

The girl nodded toward the pond. "While I sat here wondering what I should do, I noticed that small hole there where a few fish have gotten in and can't get out. I was thinking of trying to catch one and eat it."

He found that odd, that Mora would be thinking of eating if she was too worried about their fate. As if she realized that same thing, she blushed.

"I had to think of myself," she said. "How I would survive out here without you and the lady."

Amelia bent beside Gabriel. She wrinkled her nose at the green-tinted water, then stuck her hands into the water to wash. "I suppose you were being practical," she said to the girl. "And you are more levelheaded than most young girls, Mora. It wasn't as if you could go for help."

Mora shook her head. "No, I couldn't, my lady. Was afraid to venture back into the woods alone."

"All's well that ends well," Amelia assured the girl. "How would you have eaten a fish had you caught one?" she asked.

Mora grinned and pulled her potato-peeling knife from her pocket. "Could gut it with this. Have to eat it raw, though."

Gabriel saw Amelia blanch. "I hate cooked fish," she said. "I couldn't imagine eating one raw."

He smiled slightly. "Try," he said to her before he went in after one.

Chapter Eleven

Gabriel held up a hand to signal Amelia and Mora to stop. He listened, his gaze scanning the trees surrounding them as he tried to identify the sound. There it was again. A creak. A wheel? There was obviously some sort of conveyance coming down the road a few yards to their left. He had decided they would not use the road. If they were being hunted, and he was certain they were, the road would be the logical place to look for them.

"Why are we stopping?" Amelia whispered behind him.

"Someone is coming," he answered. "We'll move closer to the road and watch."

"I don't hear anything," she said after a moment's pause.

He gave her a look that usually silenced whoever thought to annoy him by babbling at the mouth. As he suspected, it didn't work on her.

"Well, I don't," she huffed.

Gabriel motioned them forward. The vegetation grew thicker as they approached the road. The brambles and branches caught at their clothing and hair. At least at his and Amelia's hair. Mora was wise to have worn her bonnet. He expected Amelia to complain, but she did not, if her expression told him easily enough that she was displeased.

Her stomach grumbled and he knew he should have forced her to eat raw fish that morning. She had actually gagged and carried on so that he had relented in the end and allowed her to go without eating. She had to be starving. Hell, he was starving and he had managed to make himself eat raw fish.

Once the road came into view, Gabriel found a place for them to crouch and hide. He didn't suppose he was lucky enough for whoever it was coming down the road to be one of his brothers, he hoped recently returned from London.

"Where are they?" Amelia whispered beside him. "I can clearly see down the road and I see no one."

His hearing was superior to hers. But he couldn't explain that to her, not without making her as fearful of him as she was of the creatures that hunted them.

"Patience is a virtue," he remarked.

"I care little about being virtuous," she countered. "I'd rather have a ride to Wulfglen, a nice hot bath, a fresh change of clothes, and a full stomach."

She had him there. Her sauciness made him smile, and Gabriel wasn't used to being so easily entertained. Amelia's very nearness stirred him to lust. He had kissed her twice, and he wanted very badly to do it again. His thoughts should not be on what he'd like to do to Lady Collingsworth but focused upon their situation and how to best keep both women alive and from harm's way.

They sat in silence. Mora's stomach grumbled and Gabriel wondered what they would do for food. He could easily catch something, but they would be foolish to build a fire. It would lead those looking for them right to them. He'd gotten the women safely from the house, but without food and shelter, how much longer could he keep them safe?

Finally a cart being pulled by a man, another walking by his side, came into view. Both men looked like peasants. One walked with a cane; a stick really was all it was. Neither man was particularly big. Gabriel saw no visible signs of weapons, which he knew meant nothing. They looked harmless enough . . . but looks were often deceiving.

"There they are," Amelia whispered, her eyesight only now able to make out the cart and the two men. "Do you think they might help us?"

"They have no horses," he said, disappointed. "I doubt they have anything to spare. I can't see where they could help us. Best to just let them move on past."

"Not help us?" she echoed, her big blue eyes widening. "Why wouldn't they help us? Three men are better than only one when it comes to protection. We could offer to pay them if they accompany us to Wulfglen."

She had a twig in her hair and he loosened it for her. "We would have to tell them what we are running from," he pointed out. "I imagine they would think we are all mad, don't you?"

"'Spect if they are from around these parts, they might not be so surprised," Mora offered. "And they are peasant folk, which is plain to see. They've probably grown up on the same stories I grew up on. They believe in strange tales easier than most."

"Maybe they at least have some food they could spare," Amelia piped up. "Anything. I promise I won't complain."

The hope in her eyes was his undoing. She was hungry, Mora was hungry, and Gabriel felt incompetent to take care of them properly. He'd never had to take care of anyone but his younger brother before. Certainly not two females. Gabriel had a few coins in the purse stuffed inside his pocket. When he'd set out to search for Jackson, he'd never imagined it would take him as long as it had or be as expensive.

"All right," he agreed. "But I go alone. You two stay here in the brush, hidden. Understood?"

The women nodded and he rose from his crouching position, his thigh aching from all the pushing he'd done last night and earlier today. He'd pulled Mora's stitches open, but he wouldn't tell her. They had worse things to worry about.

Gabriel walked out on the road and started toward the men. They drew up when they saw him, looking wary as he approached. He let his hands hang down by his sides so they could see he wasn't armed, if the pistol still rested in the waistband of his trousers beneath his shirt.

"Good afternoon," he called.

Neither man spoke, but neither did they suddenly draw weapons, so Gabriel continued toward them.

"I've had a mishap," he called. "My horse threw me and I've been walking for two days. I wondered if you could spare any food?"

Both men looked at each other. "Can you pay?" one called.

"I have a little, not much," he answered. He probably had more than these two would see in a year's wages, but only a fool would let that fact be known. It wasn't that Gabriel couldn't take both men if they tried anything, but he didn't want to fight in front of the women if it could be avoided.

"How much you got?" one of the men asked when he drew closer.

"That would depend on what you have to spare," Gabriel answered.

Both men walked to the back of the cart. "Taking supplies to our families," one said. "Otherwise we wouldn't have much. But if you've got coin to pay for what you take, I suppose we can replace it easy enough."

Gabriel might have been relieved, but he didn't plan to let his guard down until an exchange was made and the men were out of eyesight. They threw a tattered canvas back and displayed their supplies. There was more in the cart than he would have suspected.

"Got big families," one of the men grumbled. "Break our backs to feed them all."

Most of the supplies Gabriel couldn't use. Flour, sugar, things for baking that would do them little good. "I need something to tide me over until I reach my home," he specified. "Do you have dried beef? Bread? Cider?"

"Where might your home be?" one of the men asked.

Gabriel wasn't about to tell them. Most had heard of the Wulf brothers. If the scandal attached to their names didn't make the men shy away, the wealth attached to the name would make them greedy.

"Three or four days out maybe," was all he provided. "Never walked it before, so I'm not certain how much longer."

"All alone, are you?" one man asked, his gaze scanning the area.

Gabriel's senses went on the alert. "Yes," he answered.

"Not a good thing," the other said, smiling at him. "These roads are dangerous for a lone man."

"Especially one turned out as fine as you are," the other added. "Plain to see you're not of the working class. A London dandy would fare worse than most on the road alone."

Both men chuckled. Gabriel smiled pleasantly at them. Let them think him a dandy. He glanced down at the supplies again. While he busied himself looking over the fare, he fully expected one, if not both men to try something. He made an easy target in their eyes despite his size. They wouldn't expect he'd know how to defend himself. They were in for a surprise.

"Gabriel! Watch out!"

He glanced up to see Amelia standing in the road. Because of the distraction, he wasn't ready for the blow when it came. The man with the stick hit Gabriel across the shoulders, aiming for his head, he suspected, but not tall enough to reach. The blow staggered him. The man might be short, but he had strength.

"Didn't tell us you had company," the other man taunted Gabriel. "Now she's a sight for sore eyes, that one."

"Pretty," the man with the stick said, then swung.

Gabriel ducked the blow, which was again aimed at his head. He'd once told his brother Armond that the rules of society no longer applied to a family shunned by the ton. Manners were something Gabriel had forsaken some time back, and still, it bothered him to fight in front of Amelia. Gentlemen did not subject genteel-bred ladies to such vulgarity, or so he'd once been taught.

"Hey, there's another one. One for you and one for me," the man with the stick chirped.

Mora must have joined Amelia on the road. Gabriel used the distraction of the women to his advantage, stepping forward to grab the man's stick. He brought it up and smacked the man hard in the face. The force broke his nose, and blood spurted down his face.

"Hey!" the other man bellowed.

Gabriel stepped forward and delivered him a sound punch that sent him reeling backward. The man with the bloody face charged Gabriel. They landed in the dusty road. Gabriel hardly fought by Oxford rules. He rolled, gained his feet, and kicked the man in the ribs. The man grunted and drew his knees up to his chest. Gabriel paused long enough to push his hair out of his face and wipe his sleeve across his bloody lip. He was attacked from the back.

The other man had retrieved his friend's stick and clearly intended to beat Gabriel senseless with it. He took one blow to the back. The stick landed hard on his injured shoulder and he stifled a groan.

Wheeling to face the man, Gabriel was shocked when he saw Amelia jump on the man from behind.

The man bellowed and easily threw her lighter weight off of him. Then he shoved her and she landed hard in the dirt. Gabriel saw red.

He charged the man and easily wrestled the stick from him. His temper simmering, Gabriel broke the stick in half. The man's eyes nearly bulged from his head.

"We don't hit girls," Gabriel said, very low, nearly a growl. "Didn't your parents teach you that?"

Rather than answer, the man scrambled away, turned tail, and ran in the opposite direction.

"Wait," the other one yelled, staggering to his feet. He ran after his partner.

Rushing to Amelia's side, Gabriel helped her to rise. "Are you hurt?" he asked.

She shook her head. "He just knocked the breath from me for a moment."

Gabriel sighed with relief. Then he got angry. "What were you thinking? I told you to stay put."

Her hair had come loose from the braid Mora had fixed for her before they set out that morning. Wispy blond curls framed her dirt-streaked face, and still she managed to look like a princess. Amelia placed her hands upon her hips. "I thought you needed help," she answered. Her gaze suddenly landed upon the broken stick lying on the ground. "I guess I was wrong." Her big blue eyes lifted to him. "How did you break that in half? I've never seen a man do anything like that before!"

Gabriel had let his temper get the best of him. It wasn't something he should do in front of normal folk, like Amelia. Rather than answer her, he glanced down the road toward Mora. "Come, Mora," he called. "Pick out supplies for us. You'll know best what we need."

The girl started toward them.

"You didn't answer me," Amelia reminded him. "How could you possibly break a stick that thick in half as if it were no more than a twig?"

He couldn't explain his unusual strength any better than his unusual eyesight or his superior hearing. But Gabriel knew he must offer her some type of explanation. "Have you seen men brawl before, Amelia?"

She frowned up at him. "Well, no, never, but still . . ."

Gabriel moved to the back of the wagon with Mora. "Rage gives a man strength he might not otherwise have. The fool was lucky I didn't snap his neck as easily as I snapped the stick. He shouldn't have touched you."

"Sent those two running," Mora remarked as she sorted through supplies. "Thought fancy men fought with fancy manners." She eyed him oddly beneath her lashes and Gabriel thought it best to turn both women's attention toward something other than his fighting skills.

"What do we need here?" he asked the girl.

Mora had separated a few items from the rest. "Jerky doesn't have to be cooked," she said. "Two loaves of bread. Some cheese. Apples. A jug of cider for when we can't find water easily."

Pulling the tattered canvas from the wagon, Gabriel laid it on the ground to make a pack for their supplies. Amelia still stared at him suspiciously. He tossed her an apple to distract her. Hungry as she was, it worked. Once they had what they needed, he tied the canvas and toted it over his shoulder. He dug in his pocket, removed some coins, and tossed them on the back of the wagon.

"You're paying them?" Mora exclaimed. "After what they tried to do to you?"

Gabriel had been taught well at one time in his life. He maintained those values, he supposed, regardless of what had later happened to his family. "If I don't pay them for what I take, it makes me a thief, which is no better than what they are. Come, we need to get off the road."

Shoulder stinging, leg throbbing, he led the women off the road and back into the brush. At least they now had food, so they wouldn't starve. But how long until whatever was tracking them caught up? Gabriel saw no signs of trouble. He didn't smell either man or beast on their trail. It was eerie. It made him more nervous than if they'd had to fight every step of the way they'd come so far. Like everything else that had happened to him since he'd arrived at Collingsworth Manor, this did not make sense.

CHAPTER TWELVE

Night was close to falling by the time they stopped to rest. Amelia was nearly too tired to chew the stringy jerky they'd taken from the wagon earlier, but she tried and she did not complain. She watched Mora bandage Gabriel's shoulder using torn strips from her petticoat. The stick had broken the wound open again, but Mora said it wasn't too bad.

Amelia's gaze drifted over Gabriel's powerful chest, the bulging muscles in his arms. He was strong as an ox, anyone could see that, but was any man strong enough to snap a thick stick in half, as if it were merely a sapling twig? She didn't need to have seen a brawl before to know Gabriel's strength was not normal.

And how did he seem to know when to stop and wait, when to move, when to rest, when to push on? She'd watched him and it was almost as if he heard things no one else heard, saw things no one else saw. Amelia supposed she was being silly. Perhaps what he said was true and during a battle a man did possess more strength than seemed humanly possible. Gabriel had played in these woods as a boy. Perhaps that was why he seemed so at home in them. She feared she'd become paranoid with all that had happened to her since she'd arrived at Collingsworth Manor.

"Now the leg," Mora said, bringing Amelia back from her thoughts. "I should take a look at that, too."

"The leg is fine." Gabriel shrugged into his shirt. He reached for a loaf of bread and broke off a small chunk. "If you two want to clean up in the creek, better do so now. We'll settle in shortly and sleep."

"I'm too tired to care about cleaning up," Amelia said. And she was. She felt as if when she closed her eyes she would be instantly asleep. Besides, she imagined the water would be chilly and she was already anxious to settle in beside Gabriel and let his body heat warm her. She wished they could have a cozy fire to sit before, but Gabriel said it wouldn't be safe.

"I'll go," Mora said. "Need to wash my hands."

"Don't be long," Gabriel instructed. "If you hear or see anything suspicious, call out to me. I'll hear you."

Amelia's gaze roamed their secluded spot for the night. The creek was only a short distance, lined with trees for good cover. She supposed if Mora screamed, the sound would carry to them easily enough. She should go with the girl, but her legs refused to obey the wishes of her mind. Instead she finished chewing the stringy jerky and swallowed it down.

"For future reference, any time I am confronted from this night forward, you are to remain hidden as I told you to do," Gabriel said.

Her gaze snapped to him. The moonlight danced upon his hair, almost illuminating the pale streaks interwoven with the darker color. "You're welcome," she said. "If I hadn't distracted the men, you might not have gotten the upper hand."

He stared back at her intently. "If I had not gotten the upper hand, do you have any idea what they planned to do to you?"

The possibility had not occurred to her. Amelia assumed a man wouldn't hit a woman; of course she'd been proven wrong quickly enough. She'd also assumed no peasant would dare assault a lady of her obvious station. Wrong again, she supposed. "I didn't think about that at the time," she admitted.

"I have come to realize there is a clever brain inside your pretty head. You should use it more often. And from this night forward, you must listen to my instructions and obey me in all things, Amelia."

What a backhanded compliment. Amelia had decided being a widow might not be too bad. She would have no one to answer to, and now he was suggesting she answer to him.

"You are not my husband, my father, or any relation to me," she said. "Not that I planned to ever obey anyone who was or is anyway, but that is beside the point. As a gentleman, it is your duty to protect Mora and me. As a lady, I have no obligation to you except to be grateful."

He took a bite of bread and slowly chewed, staring at her all the while. It unnerved her more than if he'd raised his voice to her. She squirmed on the stump she sat upon.

After he swallowed, he said, "This is not some social tea we are involved in. This is life-or-death. And I am no gentleman. It would make the task of protecting you and Mora easier were you to listen to my instructions and obey them. If you have no wish to reach Wulfglen alive, then I suppose the choice is yours to make."

She blinked at him. She'd expected he'd insist. "You don't care if I live or die?"

He wiped his mouth with the back of his hand; then he looked at her again with his unsettling eyes. "If I didn't care, I wouldn't ask."

His admission immediately defused her temper. Amelia felt silly for arguing with him in the first place. Of course he cared what happened to her and Mora. He would not still be with them if he didn't. He'd risked himself today to see that they ate tonight. She should be more beholden to him.

"You are more gallant than you will admit," she said. "It was a good lesson you taught Mora today about thieves. You say that you are no gentleman, but I haven't seen you act in any way that would lead me to believe your claim. It is obvious to me you had good training by your parents, regardless of what they did later."

Glancing away, he scanned the tree line of the creek as if in search of Mora. Amelia had hit a sore spot with him. She was curious, and she'd never been one to stanch that curiosity.

"Do you think of them often?" she asked. "Your parents?"

Gabriel didn't look at her when he answered, "No."

She found his answer odd. "Why not? You must have fond memories of your life before. I mean before they—"

"I do not think about them," he interrupted, turning to look at her. "Or my life before. Leave the matter alone."

Amelia tried. She failed. "But why—"

"Because it hurts," he interrupted again. As if he'd revealed too much of himself, he glanced away again. He stared out into the darkness as if he saw things that she could not.

Gabriel Wulf might be a man, big, strong, beautiful, but now Amelia saw something else in him. She saw his vulnerability. She saw the young man he must have been at one time, hurt by the uncaring decisions of his parents. She rose and went to kneel beside him.

"I'm sorry," she said. "I didn't mean to stir painful memories."

He glanced down at her, now masking the vulnerability she'd seen a moment earlier. "Yes, you did. Because you are a woman and that is what women do. You are not satisfied unless you are wrenching some emotion from a man. Anger, lust, pain, it's all the same to you."

Amelia blinked up at him. What a horrible notion to have about women. "Have you never had a woman be your friend?" she asked. "A woman you could trust with all your secrets? With all your hopes and dreams? Do you even like women?"

His eyes, cast now with a faint blue glow, moved over her. "Women serve their purpose. No, I do not hate them."

Blood rushed to her cheeks. She understood his insinuation and it angered her that he would view women in this unfavorable light . . . that he might view her the same way. "If you feel that way, you don't really like women then."

He leaned closer to her. "Is that what you want, Amelia?" His voice was very low. It raised gooseflesh on her arms. "Do you want me to like you? To share my hopes and dreams with you?"

Staring into his eyes, she was tempted to say the first thing that came to mind. Yes. She did want him to like her. She did want him to share his deepest thoughts with her. But she could not confess as much to him. She was barely a widow and he was a man who had once been her dead husband's friend. Judging by what he'd just said, he was also a man who wouldn't know what to do with a woman's love if she gave it. And besides, Amelia did not believe in love.

"I suppose you could start by telling me why you have developed such a nasty attitude toward women, or is it just me you're angry at?"

Her question made the sensual smile hovering around his mouth disappear. He pulled back from her. "I'm not angry with you. A little annoyed about your actions today, putting yourself at risk when I am capable of handling any situation on my own. More than a little annoyed that you seem to have difficulty following simple instructions."

He wanted to be in charge, Amelia understood. He was the man and therefore the smarter, stronger one among them. It was an attitude most men shared. One that drove her crazy at times. Amelia had trouble dealing with men who thought just because she was pretty she was also useless except for decoration. She knew her attitude was not readily accepted in her social circles. At least Robert had patronized her by pretending to be interested in her views and outspoken opinions on just about everything.

"Women, along with children, are meant to be seen, not heard, is that what you're saying?"

Gabriel ran a hand through his hair and made a snorting noise. "Seems to me you're the one doing all the talking, and putting words in my mouth while you're at it. It's simple really. All I want from you is to follow my instructions while we are in the woods. Once I get you to safety, I don't really care what you do."

Amelia supposed she loved a stimulating argument as well as the next person, but his words hurt her. He only cared about his duty, or what he felt was his duty. That of getting her to safety. He didn't really care about her, as a person. And that meant when he'd kissed her, he'd only kissed her because she inspired something in him other than gentle emotions. It bothered her that she cared when he obviously didn't. And she was afraid her expression might give her away.

She rose. "I should check on Mora," she said. "And probably clean up while I'm there, although as I said, I'm so tired I'd rather just go to sleep. Of course I only go with your permission," she added sarcastically.

His lip quirked. A half attempt at a smile. "Permission granted," he shot back just as sarcastically.

Back straight, Amelia set off for the creek. She felt his eyes following her. He wasn't at all the man she'd molded him into with the aid of her silly daydreams. In her imagination, he had shared all his secrets and his dreams with her and she had shared hers with him. She had no idea that he was closed off and secretive, a private person, although it had also been silly of her to assume that he wasn't exactly what he was. The Wulf brothers had always been shrouded in mystery. She certainly should have taken that into account.

Amelia realized in that moment that the reason she hadn't thought rationally about Gabriel Wulf in the past was simply because she hadn't thought rationally about anything. She'd convinced herself she was different from her boring debutante friends; then she'd lined up for the marriage mart like a lamb to the slaughter just like the rest of them. She'd married a man she did not love because he seemed like a sensible choice to her parents.

She'd done what was expected of her. She wasn't brave or shocking at all. The realization deflated her somewhat. If Amelia had been brave enough to have refused Robert's proposal of marriage, she wouldn't be in her current predicament. She'd still be safe and blessedly ignorant that the world wasn't what she once perceived it to be upon first glance.

Lost in her reflections, she was surprised when she stumbled across Mora in a state of half dress and without the worn work bonnet that Amelia had never once seen her without.

In the moonlight, Mora's pale blond hair shimmered in waves down to her hips. Her back was turned, her work dress and chemise pushed down around her waist while she washed. There were binding strips lying on the ground next to her.

"Mora?" Amelia called, so as not to startle her, but of course she did. The girl jumped up and wheeled around. As an afterthought, Mora splayed her hands over her breasts, but not before Amelia got a look at them. And they were not the breasts of a girl.

"I'm sorry," Amelia blurted, and she knew she should turn her back and afford Mora privacy, but she couldn't help but stare. Then she glanced at the bindings lying on the ground and she knew what they were for. "Why do you bind your breasts, Mora? Why do you hide your hair?"

Mora stared at her defiantly for a moment; then as if she remembered herself, she bowed her head. Her glorious hair swung over her shoulders to hide her face. "It was my brother's idea," she answered. "He was afraid for me to work in a fine house where the lord of the manor might take too much notice of me. He said I was to bind my breasts and hide my hair, and pretend to be younger than I am so that I would not bring shame upon myself."

Amelia moved closer. "How old are you?"

Turning her back, Mora picked the bindings off the ground and began wrapping her breasts. "Eighteen last fall."

The servant was barely younger than Amelia, and Amelia did not consider herself a child. "Do you feel you must follow your brother's wishes, even though you are no longer at Collingsworth Manor? You are with me and Gabriel."

It took Mora a moment longer to finish her bindings and pull her chemise and dress back up. "Lord Gabriel is a man. A young, virile man. I don't think my brother would like me showing myself to him."

When Mora turned to face Amelia again, she saw for the first time how truly lovely the girl was. She had done everything to make certain she appeared plain and uninteresting. Like an insect that changed its color to blend with a branch or a leaf so that no one would notice it.

"Do you really think Gabriel would take advantage of you in that manner?" Amelia knew that despite his claims of not being a gentleman, deep down he still was, whether he wanted to be or not. "How could you mistrust him so when he has risked his life for us?"

The girl, only Amelia must stop thinking of her as a girl, lowered her eyes and chewed upon her fuller lower lip. "I want to trust him," she admitted. "But I know he lusts for you. What if he turns his lust on me simply because you are a lady and he cannot behave as he wishes with you?"

Amelia was shocked by Mora's forthrightness. "Lord Gabriel was once my husband's good friend," she said. "I am barely a widow. You mustn't say such things."

Twisting her hair into a knot at the back of her neck, Mora asked, "Why? They are true. I've seen the way he looks at you, and the way you look at him."

Heat scorched Amelia's cheeks. God, was she so obvious in her attraction toward Gabriel Wulf? Mora placed the ugly bonnet upon her head and transformed back into the plain girl both Amelia and Gabriel had thought she was.

"You won't tell him, will you?" Mora asked. "I would feel uncomfortable if he were to regard me as a woman. I feel safer with him while all his manly attentions are focused upon you, my lady."

Amelia wasn't certain she wouldn't be uncomfortable with Gabriel looking at Mora as a woman, as well. It was a jealous response she had no business feeling. Still, she felt uncharacteristically torn about deceiving him. Amelia moved to the water's edge to clean up.

"I won't tell him for now," she finally said. "But at some point, you must. It isn't polite to deceive a man doing his best to protect your life, Mora."

Mora settled beside her. "I know, my lady. I will tell him. It really isn't that important that he know anyway, is it?"

Amelia supposed it wasn't that important. The only thing Mora was hiding from Gabriel was that she wasn't a young girl and that she was a lot prettier than he probably realized. "I don't guess so," she admitted. "But still, remember you promised me to tell him at some point."

Mora nodded. Shyly she asked, "Will you tell me about your life in London? Were you like a princess there?"

London and her life seemed like a dream. Amelia shrugged. "No, I was not a princess. But my father is a duke and I do hold a certain standing among my peers. I actually complained often that I thought London life was boring. I would give anything to be that bored again."

The girl reached out and patted Amelia's shoulder. "I think your life must have been grand indeed," Mora said. "All the balls you must have attended. The lovely gowns made for you to wear. And you are so beautiful. I'm certain you had many suitors chasing after you."

Thinking back, Amelia supposed she did have all of those things, but she had never paid much attention to them. She had taken them for granted. She had taken too much for granted. But she didn't want to think about that. Instead of answering Mora, she said, "Tell me about your life, Mora. You said you are an orphan, but you do have a brother, correct?"

Mora dipped her hand into the chilly water. "Yes. He's taken care of me most of my life. Then he said it was time for me to go out in the world and earn my own way. I was glad to get a position at Collingsworth Manor, but then, well, as you know, things did not work out well."

The chilly water wasn't so much invigorating as it was uncomfortably cold. But the conversation was nice. It had never occurred to Amelia to befriend a person of the working classes. Well, why not? Everything else about her life had changed. "I hope we can be friends," she said to Mora. "I think under the circumstances, we both could use one."

"I never thought I'd be a friend to a grand lady," Mora responded. "I expected to be scrubbing your floors and have you never even notice me."

And probably that would have been the case, Amelia admitted, had her life not been irreversibly changed at Collingsworth Manor. "I suppose it is odd how things sometimes work out," she said, thinking it was also odd that she was in the company of Gabriel Wulf when once she only dared to dream about him. And thinking of Gabriel made her realize they had tarried too long. He'd come looking for them if they didn't return soon.

Amelia washed out her mouth and reached in her pocket for a mint leaf to freshen her breath. She offered Mora one; then together they rose and walked back toward where they would sleep for the night.

They had found a couple of worn blankets in the men's cart and had taken them. Gabriel had spread them on the ground. He still sat where Amelia had last seen him, although he would have had to move around to position the blankets.

"We'll lay on the one and cover ourselves with the other," he said. "It should at least be warmer."

Given the size of the darker shapes the blankets made on the ground, Amelia realized they would have to sleep very close together.

Gabriel rose. "I'll clean up before I join you," he said.

Mora bent to the task of straightening the blankets, but Amelia watched him walk away. She loved the way the moonlight danced upon the lighter streaks in his hair. His tall shape made a formidable shadow, moving toward the stream. Then she noticed what she thought he was trying very hard to make unnoticeable. He was limping again.

He'd told Mora the wound to his thigh was mending. He'd said it was fine. Amelia wondered if that was the truth.

"The bed is ready," Mora said. "It isn't proper, the both of us sleeping with a man," she added in a hushed whisper.

"It isn't proper for either of us to be sleeping with a man," Amelia pointed out. "But it is safer, and he is warm. Or haven't you noticed?"

Mora smiled up at her. "He is that," she admitted. "Puts off a nice heat. Doesn't make a good pillow, though," she added.

Amelia frowned. So Mora had noticed, as well? Amelia climbed beneath the covers. The ground was hard, the blankets probably lice ridden. But she wouldn't think about that. There were many things she wouldn't think about, for if she did, she feared she'd start screaming and never stop. Instead, she tried to remember what her life had been like only three days ago. She tried to remember Robert's face. He'd been rather handsome with his pale complexion and his dark eyes. But every time she brought his features to memory, he would turn into a beast, with claws and fangs and fur.

She shivered. Mora's soft snores sounded a moment later. Amelia had never met anyone who could fall asleep as fast as the servant. But then, maybe Mora was used to crawling to her bed exhausted from her work duties, finding sleep easily. Amelia lay awake until Gabriel returned. She scooted over next to Mora to make room for him.

In the silence, she heard the slight intake of his breath when he bent to crawl beneath the blanket next to her.

"It's your leg again, isn't it?" she whispered. "It hurts more than you are leading us to believe."

He didn't answer.

"Maybe we should rest tomorrow. Allow it—"

"Go to sleep, Amelia," he interrupted. "You know we cannot stop. We cannot rest until we reach Wulfglen."

She did know that. And she imagined he knew what was best for him. Or she hoped he did. She started to shiver a few moments later. Gabriel reached out and pulled her closer. Amelia snuggled up next to his warmth. He seemed warmer than usual, she noted. Good lord. They were all pretenders. Mora was pretending to be young and plain. Gabriel was pretending his leg was not hurting him. And Amelia was pretending she wasn't affected by his closeness. His heat. His scent. Everything about him.

"I didn't mean that earlier," he said quietly. "About not caring. I do care what happens to you. I care what happens to Mora. Sometimes not caring is simpler."

Amelia agreed with him. Instead of following her feelings for Gabriel Wulf all those months ago, refusing to marry Robert and pursuing what her heart had told her in that moment she saw Gabriel in London, she had done what was simpler. What was expected of her.

"I'm not who I thought I was," she said. "Maybe that frightens me more than anything that has happened to me since I arrived at Collingsworth Manor."

Amelia was surprised when he ran a hand over her hair. "Seldom do any of us get to be what we really want to be in life. You're not who I thought you were, either. You have shown amazing strength in light of all that has happened to you. I admire you, Amelia."

He admired her? Well, it wasn't a declaration of love, but then, she kept forgetting, neither of them believed in love. Whatever it was, it was enough to flood her chilled body with sudden heat. It was enough to get her through the night, and in their circumstances getting through the night was all they had.

"Good night, Gabriel," she whispered, then snuggled closer to him, allowing his heat to warm her body and his words to warm her heart.

Chapter Thirteen

Gabriel knew he couldn't continue to hide his worsening condition from Amelia and the girl. He woke covered in sweat. Amelia had turned away from him during sleep, as if she had needed to escape his heat. He'd taken a look at the wound last night by the creek. It was swollen and festering. The wound needed to be lanced and cauterized. He had neither tool nor fire to do either. Their plans had to be changed.

The women had packed up the camp, what little they had. Amelia had helped without complaint. For the time being, her spoiled life in London had faded to the furthest recesses of her mind. He admired her for that. That she adapted as she had. She was stronger than he thought. She was stronger than she knew.

"There is a village called Hempshire we might make by nightfall if we move quickly today," he said to the women. "I thought our original plan of reaching Wulfglen was more important than the delay going out of our way to reach the village would cost us. But now it is important that we reach the village first."

Amelia came to stand before him. Her long hair was

twisted into a knot at the back of her head. She didn't look the part of a grand lady now, but he couldn't say she wasn't still every bit as appealing as when decked out in her finery. In fact, she was more appealing, at least to a man like Gabriel.

"It's your leg again, isn't it?" she repeated the question she'd asked last night. "It's infected."

"What?" Mora now hurried to join them. "You said it was fine. You said—"

"I know what I said," he interrupted the girl. "I thought I could hold out until we reached Wulfglen. The wound needs to be lanced, cauterized. There's a blacksmith there who often shoes my horses. He can do it. And we can get food, horses, or perhaps even a hack of some sort. We'll be safe there. At least until we set out again."

"And you believe we can reach this village before nightfall?" Amelia asked.

"If we move quickly," he repeated. "And encounter no trouble along our way."

Glancing around, Amelia rubbed her arms in the early-morning chill. "Why haven't they caught up with us? Why haven't we seen them? Or at least heard them?"

Gabriel had been wondering the same thing. It was as if the trouble they had encountered at Collingsworth Manor had stayed there. Why hadn't the men, creatures, whatever they were, given chase? He wasn't complaining. He found it odd, is all.

"I don't know," he answered her. "But we'll count ourselves fortunate and hope our luck holds. Let's move."

Rising from his position on a rotting tree stump, he did his best not to wince with the pain in his leg. That the wound had become infected angered him. Gabriel was supposed to be the strong one. The sensible one. The one in control of his emotions and his situation at all times. At the moment, he felt weak, and he abhorred weakness in anyone, mostly in himself.

Gabriel's father had been weak. He'd taken an easy path to end his troubles. Gabriel's mother, even weaker. They had needed her to be strong for them, to help them, guide them, love them despite what foul blood ran through their veins. Cursed blood. She had abandoned them to make their way alone. Sterling had been weak. Fleeing when he was no more than a boy, running from what none of them could escape. Jackson, with his love for whores and liquor, had been weak. Armond had surprised Gabriel the most. He had thought the two of them were the strongest, at least in will. But Armond had found his weakness. A woman.

He must resist Amelia's temptation. He'd admitted things to her he had not admitted to anyone else. He'd felt things for her he'd not felt for anyone else. He couldn't afford to lose his head given their current predicament. He damn sure could not afford to lose his heart. Not to her, not to any woman. Not ever.

Nor had he wanted to talk to her last night about his parents. He resented them, Gabriel admitted. He counted them as weak. And if he shared his father's cursed blood, he had vowed to be nothing like the man. He had in the past not formed much of an opinion about women because he'd never really had to, with the exception of his mother. She had taught him that women lied. Women were not to be trusted with his heart. And as far as hopes and dreams went, he had allowed himself to have none. They seemed silly and unproductive for a man who had no future.

But Amelia had tempted him to be open with her. He had feelings for her he'd do better to suppress.

"Are we going?" Amelia asked.

Gabriel realized he was staring at her. Mora giggled and he shook his head to clear it and headed off toward Hempshire. Amelia carried the blankets, Mora the canvas with their supplies. Gabriel would be doing good to put one foot in front of the other.

The day passed in agony. It was bad enough to have the leg throbbing as it was, but having to hide his pain was worse. He knew Amelia and Mora would insist they stop if they knew walking had become pure torture for him. By the time the sun began to set, he could no longer hide his limp. Ahead, through the trees, he saw rooftops, smoke rising from chimney stacks. He knew his companions couldn't see them yet, so he said nothing, but the sight of their destination close at hand kept him going.

"Shouldn't we stop and rest?" Amelia asked a while later. "My feet hurt."

"Mine, too," Mora quickly added.

He kept his teeth clenched and kept walking. He heard Amelia sigh behind him, but she said nothing further. He imagined her feet did hurt, but he knew she'd only raised the complaint for him. He found it somewhat endearing, although he tried not to.

"Wait."

He halted at Amelia's whispered instruction. He turned to look at her. She closed her eyes and inhaled. "I smell smoke."

"Cooking fires and the like," he assured her. "We're almost there."

She opened her eyes and her face lit up. Damn, she was beautiful. "How long can we stay? Long enough to pay for a bath and a bed?"

He'd need to send Amelia and Mora off somewhere while the blacksmith tended to his leg. "A bath for sure," he answered. "There's a tavern in the village. I'm sure a bath can be bought in one of the rooms upstairs."

"Sounds like heaven," Amelia breathed behind him.

"A hot meal sounds good," Mora piped up. "Something I don't have to chew for two days to swallow."

Amelia laughed and even Gabriel found it easier to smile. He was certain they made an odd sight when they entered the village a short time later. Night was quickly falling. He walked with Amelia and Mora to the tavern first. The downstairs was still empty. Patrons would make their way for a pint once they'd had their suppers at home. The man polishing his scarred bar frowned upon seeing Gabriel.

"No fighting," he said before Gabriel could call a greeting. "Just now got the place fixed from last time you were here, Wulf."

Gabriel grinned at him. "It wasn't that bad, Nate. Besides, I paid you more than enough to replace the broken chairs and tables."

"That's true," the man grumbled. "I suppose you can bust the place up all you want as long as you keep paying more than the cost to fix it back up. Turn a nice profit from you."

Feeling Amelia's and Mora's curious regard, Gabriel

turned to business. "I have a couple of ladies with me who'd like a hot bath and a hot meal."

"I've got both," Nate said. "Be best to get the women taken care of and out of here before the men start wandering in for a pint."

Digging a couple of coins from his pocket, Gabriel slapped them down on the scarred bar. "I trust the ladies will be safe here with you. I need to see Bruin."

"They'll be fine. Bruin is no longer here, though," Nate told him. "Took his family and disappeared a few days ago. Got a new man. Seems all right. A lot of new faces around here since last you visited."

Gabriel turned to the women. "You'll be all right here until I get back. Take your baths and have a hot meal. Just in case." He withdrew the pistol from the back of his trousers and slid it into Amelia's pocket.

She placed a hand on his arm. "Are you sure we shouldn't come with you? Is there not a physician here who could look at your leg?"

He shook his head. "No, the blacksmith is the best I'll be able to do. You and Mora stay here until I return for you. Understand?"

"But—"

"You said you would follow my instructions," he reminded her.

She lifted a brow, perfectly arched and just a shade darker than her blond hair. "Out there, I said I would obey you. And that was a lie even when I said it."

He tried not to smile. "Stay here," he said to both women. Gabriel limped from the tavern.

The blacksmith's barn was at the end of the road. There were horses in a corral out back, Gabriel noted.

Good. He didn't have much coin, but perhaps even a small deposit on a horse and cart would be enough. If Bruin still lived in the village, Gabriel knew it would be. He'd done business with the man often, had even visited his cottage on occasion when he'd had to go and fetch the man.

Gabriel had also found many an excuse to visit the village . . . and the tavern. Not so much to drink. He did not share his younger brother's fondness for spirits, but it usually only took Gabriel showing his face in the tavern to start a good brawl. Men were stupid while in their cups, and one usually managed to say the wrong thing to him before the night's end.

Fighting worked to relieve a man's tensions. Of course something else worked better, but he'd tried to get by with as little feminine companionship as possible over the years.

Ironic that he was now stuck with one, at least until he could get her safely to Wulfglen. If he could manage to even get himself there. He heard the hammer of the smithy before he entered the barn. Heat from the man's fire made it almost unbearable inside the stifling barn. Gabriel waited until the man paused in his hammering before calling out.

"What happened to Bruin? I was here only four months past and he said nothing about leaving."

The fellow was big, with big arms. His shirt was soaked with sweat and clung to his barrel chest. He wiped a beefy arm across his brow. "Don't know what happened to the man who had the place before I came. He and his family just took off one night, the way I heard it. Was just passing through myself, but have done this work before, so I agreed to take over." Moving forward, the man extended a sweaty palm. "Mullins is my name."

Gabriel took the man's hand and shook. "Lord Gabriel Wulf. I often bring my horses to Hempshire to be shod."

Mullins glanced outside the open door. "Got them with you?"

"No," he answered. "I have a problem. A festering wound to my thigh. I planned to ask Bruin to lance and cauterize it."

The man winced. "Nasty business that will be. Have you the stomach for it?"

Gabriel lifted a challenging brow. "Have you?"

Mullins threw back his head and laughed. "That I do. Come and sit and I'll stick a knife on the fire."

Gabriel limped toward a metal bench where he'd often sat and watched Bruin forge the shoes for his horses. Mullins drew a long, nasty-looking knife from his boot and stuck it on the raging fire.

"Wouldn't think you'd need something like that here," Gabriel said, nodding toward the knife.

The man shrugged. "Haven't been here long enough to know if I do or I don't. The folks hereabout seem mostly decent. Was traveling with my two cousins when we stopped at the tavern. My cousins stayed on, as well. Help me with the horses."

Gabriel glanced around. The place was full of shadows and iron.

"Not here," Mullins said, as if he knew Gabriel had been looking for the men. "Can fetch them, though, if you think we'll need them to hold you down."

He smiled. "No need," he assured the man.

Mullins laughed again, then picked up the knife. The blade glowed red. "Shuck your trousers, man, and let's get to it."

Rising, Gabriel unfastened his trousers and slid them down his legs. He was grateful the shirt he'd taken from Collingsworth Manor was long enough to cover his privates. Not that he was particularly modest, but he felt vulnerable enough with a stranger wielding a glowing knife.

Mullins whistled through his teeth at the sight of the wound. "Needs cut, all right," he said. "Surprised you're not out of your head with a fever."

It was hard to respond. Gabriel was busy steeling himself for the pain to come. He nodded toward his leg and the man brought his stench and his knife closer.

"Ready?"

Again Gabriel nodded.

Gabriel didn't watch, choosing to stare at the red flame of the fire burning in the large grate. The man did the job quickly. He'd sliced Gabriel before the pain reached his brain. When it did, he ground his teeth together to keep from shouting out with the pain. He glanced down at the cut. Pus and blood bubbled up and ran down the sides of his thigh.

Mullins removed a dirty rag from his pocket and extended it toward Gabriel. He hated to be rude, but he wasn't about to place that vermin-ridden rag against the wound to stanch the blood. Instead he tore the sleeve of his shirt from the shoulder. It wasn't much cleaner, but at least it was his own dirt and sweat. Mullins walked back to the fire and placed the knife in the flame again.

"Bet you yell this time," he said with a grin.

The man seemed to be enjoying himself too much at Gabriel's expense. His thigh stung like the dickens, but he knew he had to press the wound, get as much of the infection from it as he could before Mullins cauterized it closed again. He was drenched in sweat by the time he'd managed to press the wound several times. His sleeve was soaked in blood and worse.

"Ready?" Mullins called again.

Sucking in a deep breath, Gabriel nodded.

"You're strong," Mullins said, respect flavoring his gruff voice as he returned to Gabriel. Mullins pressed the knife to Gabriel's thigh.

The red-hot burn of the knife made Gabriel jerk. He nearly gagged on the smell of his own singed flesh. His mind screamed with the pain, but he clamped his lips together and bit back a response. Mullins had bent down beside him. The man removed the knife and glanced up at Gabriel.

"I heard you were."

Pain clouding his mind, Gabriel didn't understand what the blacksmith meant. As Gabriel grappled with the sharp sting, the burning sensation in his thigh, the man slowly lifted his knife, pointing the blade toward Gabriel's throat.

"Strong," the man explained. "Was told to be on the lookout for you if you happened this way. Was told to take care of you."

Dawning registered when the man's eyes began to glitter in the shadowed darkness of the barn. He was one of them. Damn, Gabriel had left his pistol with Amelia.

"What do you want?" he managed to ask through the pain. "What are you?"

Mullins grinned, and his teeth looked pointed and sharp. "We want the woman," he answered. "And you dead. Any dead who bear witness to our plans. We've waited a long time."

Gabriel had placed himself in a vulnerable situation. Something he would have never done had his mind not been fogged by the pain in his leg. If he could keep the man, creature, whatever Mullins was, talking long enough to recover, he might have a chance.

"What are you?" he repeated.

Mullins brought the knife closer to Gabriel's throat. "A man, the same as you are. A man with gifts."

Curse? Gifts? Gabriel imagined it was a matter of opinion. "How does your kind shift into another person?"

"Not all can," the man answered. "Those gifted practice at it for years. But enough talk."

Talk was exactly what Gabriel needed to recover enough to defend himself. "Why lance my wound, then cauterize it if you were planning to kill me anyway?"

Mullins grinned his toothy grin again. "To make you suffer more."

Gabriel slumped, as if resigned to his fate. He wanted information from the man and also needed a little more time to recover from having his wound lanced. "If you're going to kill me, I'd like to know your plans."

Mullins shook his shaggy head. "No point in that. Time to die. Sorry, it's only orders."

The man made the mistake of pulling back his hand

to stab with more force. Gabriel used his good leg to kick Mullins in the face. He tumbled backward and Gabriel quickly jumped to his feet. Pain shot through his leg, but he tried to ignore it and concentrate on defending himself. His wounded leg nearly folded beneath him when he kicked at the man again, aiming for the knife in his hand. Mullins howled in pain, then rolled and gained his feet.

"Got no chance against me," he hissed. "Best to just lie down and die."

"You first," Gabriel said, then lunged forward and delivered a solid blow to the man's face. Mullin's stumbled back again, but when he glanced up at Gabriel, his features were contorted. He was changing himself. Were Gabriel's chances better against a man or a beast?

Mullins lunged forward, swiping at Gabriel with the long claws now jutting from his fingertips. Maneuvering with his injured leg was difficult. Gabriel took a scratch to the arm before he managed to get out of the way.

He needed an advantage, and at the moment Mullins had them all. To strengthen himself, Gabriel thought of Amelia and Mora, left to the mercy of Mullins and his kind. Rage managed to make it past Gabriel's pain. It bubbled up inside of him and Gabriel welcomed it, did not fight for control of his emotions as he usually did. When Mullins growled low in his throat, Gabriel growled back at him.

The response caused Mullins to draw up, or Gabriel had to assume that was the reason the man simply stood staring at him. The contortion of Mullin's features unnerved Gabriel. It reminded him of a time years before, when his father had transformed before them all one night at the dinner table. That nightmare had haunted Gabriel for years.

"You are one of us-s-s," Mullins hissed, his voice distorted, but not so much that Gabriel couldn't understand him.

"No." Gabriel shook his head. He lifted his hand, tried to ball it into a fist, but the claws jutting from his fingertips would not allow it. Gabriel stared at his hand for a moment, his brain refusing to acknowledge what his eyes told him.

Mullin's deep laughter, garbled, which made it more hideous, drew Gabriel's attention back to the threat the man posed, not only to him but also to Amelia and Mora. He ran his tongue over his teeth. They were sharper, his eyeteeth longer . . . like fangs.

"I am not like you," he spat at Mullins, then found strength he would have never had . . . not as only a man. He leaped forward and slashed his claws across Mullins's throat. The man gasped, his deformed hands clutching at his throat. Blood spilled down his neck, and his legs went out from beneath him. Gabriel stood over Mullins, watching the life drain from him. Only in death did Mullins reclaim his shape as a man.

Gabriel drew in deep breaths between the fangs that had lengthened in his mouth. He held up his hand again, willing the claws to retract. Never had he come so close to transforming. Why now? But he thought he knew. Amelia . . . and the girl. He had to protect them, and protect them with everything he had, even his curse.

In a matter of minutes, Gabriel felt the pain of his claws retracting into his fingertips. He groaned and stumbled to sit again. His breathing ragged, he reached up and tore the other sleeve from his shirt. Gabriel wrapped the material around his throbbing thigh, yanked on his trousers, and set off at as fast a pace as the injury would allow. He had to get to Amelia and Mora now. He had to get the women out of the village!

Chapter Fourteen

Amelia relaxed in the short tub, allowing the warm water to soothe her. There was no perfumed soap. The rough lye would probably take the top layer of her skin off, but Amelia didn't care. Not at the moment. She was clean. She was safe. There was hope they would reach Wulfglen alive.

Mora had been starving and wished to eat first rather than bathe. Amelia left her in a kitchen at the back of the tavern, licking her lips over a thick bowl of stew, fresh bread, and thick slabs of cheese. Amelia's stomach growled at the thought of the feast she'd have waiting for her when she found the energy to rouse herself from the soothing water. The thought of dressing in her dirty clothes held little appeal. But she supposed she must.

Sighing, she rose from the tub, grateful that a fire burned in the grate and the room was warm. A thin towel had been set out for her to dry herself with. Amelia snatched it up and set to work on her dripping hair. She'd only begun to dry her body when the door suddenly burst open. Amelia squeaked, clutching the towel to her breasts. Gabriel stood framed in the doorway. He looked somewhat wild. His eyes seemed to glow back at her, and the sleeves of his shirt were missing.

"We have to leave," he barked. "Now!"

"What?" The thin towel barely covered Amelia from the tops of her breasts to the tops of her thighs. "What's going on?"

"Dress quickly." He came into the room and began gathering her clothes. Her undergarments he tossed aside. He dug the pistol from the pocket of her gown and shoved it beneath his shirt into the waistband of his trousers. Then he held the tattered gown toward her.

"Put this on."

"But my underthings," Amelia protested. "I can't go around without—"

"There isn't time!" he nearly shouted. "They're here."

Chill bumps rose on Amelia's arms, but they had nothing to do with her still-damp body. She understood what he meant. He shoved the gown at her and turned back toward the door.

"I'll get Mora. Meet us downstairs. Hurry, Amelia!"

Amelia dropped the towel and scrambled into the dirty gown. She ran to the heap of her discarded underwear and found her slippers; sorry as they were, she slipped them on and ran downstairs. She heard Gabriel arguing with the tavern owner.

"What do you mean, she's gone? Gone where?"

"I don't know," the man answered. "I left her in the back, but when I went to fetch her like you asked, she wasn't there. The back door was standing open."

Amelia joined Gabriel downstairs. "Where is Mora?" she whispered.

"Gone," he growled. "Maybe taken."

Her heart lurched. "We have to find her."

Gabriel pulled her toward the tavern door. "There's no time. We must escape now."

He was strong and Amelia had trouble struggling against his hold, but she did. "We can't leave Mora! No telling what those beasts will do to her!"

"Stop fighting me," Gabriel ordered. "I'll come back for her. I swear to you, but for now, I must get you safely out of the village."

Amelia hated the thought of leaving Mora behind. All of Amelia's life, she'd only thought of herself. What she wanted most and how best to get it. Mora wasn't just a servant; she'd become a friend. But Gabriel was right. They must get away before—

Low growls from the shadows cut into her thoughts. Glittering eyes watched them. Amelia fought down a scream. Gabriel pulled her to a horse tied in front of the tavern. The animal reared, or tried to; tied as it was, it couldn't do much but prance nervously in place.

"What's going on?" Nate called from the tavern door.

"Get inside! Bolt your doors!" Gabriel yelled to him. "There are wolves roaming the village."

Amelia was yanked up upon the horse's back. The animal reared again, and she nearly slid off the back.

"Hold on!" Gabriel shouted.

She wrapped her arms around his middle, closed her eyes, and pressed her face against his broad back. The horse shot forward and they were thundering down the road that wound through the village. She didn't want to look behind them. She wanted to keep her eyes closed and pray they made it safely away, and without her falling from the horse and breaking her neck, but she did look.

Several dark shadows chased them. Two were nearly upon the horse's heels. Amelia fumbled with Gabriel's shirt, slid her hand beneath and down the flat ridges of his stomach to remove the pistol from his trousers. She cocked the pistol with one hand, turned, and fired, bringing down the first wolf.

Gabriel veered off of the road, turning the horse so sharply Amelia nearly fell. In her struggle to hold on, she dropped the pistol. They crashed through the underbrush lining the road and into the trees. Branches tore at her clothing. She bent her head and pressed her face against Gabriel's back again.

Forever it seemed they rode. Amelia wondered when the beasts would catch them, when she would fall off the horse and surely be killed, given the pace to which Gabriel pushed the animal. Amelia had never seen a man handle a horse the way Gabriel did. Twisting and turning, taking the animal deep into the forest, seemingly able to see where they were going when darkness had fallen and Amelia saw nothing but blackness all around them.

Suddenly Gabriel brought the gasping horse to a halt. He slid down, reached up, and plucked Amelia from the animal's back. He slapped the horse's rump and sent it running.

Amelia gasped. "Why did you do that? Now we're afoot again."

"We need shelter. I know a place, but the horse must race ahead in hopes they will follow. The pistol," he said. "I need it."

Amelia wanted to whimper. "I dropped it," she said. "It was when the horse veered and it was that or fall off."

He was silent for a moment. She knew he was upset over the loss of the weapon. "All right, come on, then. We must fight with our wits tonight."

He took her hand and then they were running through the brush. Several times Gabriel had to stop for a moment and Amelia knew his leg must be killing him. The night closed around them, made eerier by the knowledge that they might be set upon at any moment.

Shadows and shapes passed in a blur. They stumbled upon a small cabin before Amelia managed to make it out in the darkness. There were no lamps burning inside. No smell of a fire from the chimney. The door creaked when Gabriel eased it open. He pulled her inside and eased it shut. Then he stood very still, listening.

Amelia listened, too. The cottage was as silent as a tomb. The night chill rose gooseflesh on her skin. She shivered, but she didn't know if it was from being cold or frightened.

"This is where Bruin and his family lived. It's deserted," Gabriel finally said, his voice quiet. "Stay here. I'll be back in a moment."

As quietly as he usually moved, the leg must have hampered him, because she heard him creeping through the cottage. He returned a moment later and she felt the scratchy wool of a blanket being shoved toward her.

"You must strip from your clothing, Amelia," he said. "Animals hunt by scent. I need to take our clothes into the woods and get rid of them."

Had any other man asked her to strip naked in front of him, Amelia would have thought it was a ploy to seduce her. She knew Gabriel would not ask if their lives were not at stake. Although she wasn't modest, it felt strange to undress in the same room with a man, one who was doing the same, by the sounds of it. Once she'd stripped from the worn gown, Amelia wrapped a blanket around her and held her discarded clothing toward Gabriel.

"I'll be back in a moment. Stay inside; be very quiet."

He was gone before she could argue. Amelia didn't want to be left alone. Her heart pounded so loudly she felt certain anyone within a mile could hear it. On shaky legs, she slumped down a wall to the floor and waited. The blanket was scratchy against her skin. It was the least of her worries. She had begun to think Gabriel would not return when the door eased open. She nearly screamed, but he called out quietly to her.

"Here," she said. "On the floor."

With a slight groan he settled beside her. He was winded. When she reached out to touch him she also realized he was quite naked. She snatched her hand back.

"Where's your blanket?"

"Could only find one," he huffed. "Truth is, I knew I'd move better without having to hold on to something draped around me." With another grunt, he rose. She heard him go into the next room. Not long after, she heard him come out and pad off somewhere to her right. When he squatted beside her again he shoved a stale chunk of bread into her hands.

Starving, Amelia tore a chunk of the bread off and stuffed it into her mouth. It tasted like heaven.

"There's some cider. A few apples. They left in a hurry. Didn't take anything with them."

"Why?" she asked.

"Frightened away, I'm guessing," Gabriel answered. "Mullins, the new blacksmith, came to Hempshire to watch for us if we passed this way. He needed a reason to be here so he wouldn't look suspicious. I imagine he and his men frightened Bruin and his family away in the night."

A thought raised the hackles on the back of Amelia's neck. "Then, is this where they are staying?"

"No," Gabriel assured her. "I don't smell them here. They would have eaten the food Bruin and his family left behind. I imagine they took up residence at the blacksmith barn in the village. They wouldn't want to take the chance of missing us if we passed through."

"Will they come here?"

He didn't answer for a moment. "I don't think so. They will assume we'd want to get as far away from Hempshire as we can. They'll look for us in the woods."

Amelia felt far from comforted, but for the moment they had shelter, at least some food, and maybe a measure of safety. "What about Mora?" she whispered. "We can't leave her behind. Not with those beasts. They might kill her."

Gabriel sighed. "My first duty is to get you safely to Wulfglen, Amelia. I am sorry for the girl. I do not wish to leave her behind. I will in fact return and try to find her after I have you safely away."

Once, the situation would have suited Amelia fine. It no longer did. She couldn't bear the thought of poor Mora at the mercy of the beasts that frightened her so. "I will not go until we at least make an effort on Mora's behalf. We are all in this together, aren't we? What does it say about me if I let you leave her behind?"

Gabriel didn't respond for a moment. "She wouldn't expect us to stay," he finally said. "You know that."

"One day," Amelia bargained. "Tomorrow, we can go to the village and have a look around. If we don't see her, we will move on."

"It's insane to go back to the village," he argued. "Mora wouldn't expect you to put yourself in danger for her. She has the sense not to put herself in danger for you."

Amelia recalled that Mora had left them to fend for themselves when the den had caved in on her and Gabriel. Perhaps the girl would not expect them to rescue her if she'd been captured. Amelia couldn't help believing what had happened at Collingsworth Manor was somehow her fault. It was Amelia whom the beasts had wanted, and Gabriel and Mora were both innocent bystanders.

"One day," Amelia begged. "If we don't see her, we will go, I promise."

He was silent for so long Amelia wondered if he'd drifted off to sleep; then he sighed. "One day," he agreed. "And I'll go alone to look for her. You'll stay here."

Amelia knew she'd be pushing her luck if she argued further with him. Although she wanted nothing more than to get away from the threat that must surely surround them, she felt better knowing they wouldn't leave Mora behind without making an effort to rescue her.

"I keep thinking this must be a dream," she said softly. "That I will wake up in my parents' fine home in London and laugh that my imagination provided me with such a tale."

She handed a piece of bread to Gabriel in the darkness. "And if you are dreaming and you wake tomorrow, would you still marry Robert Collingsworth?"

Amelia could say with certainty that she would not. She realized now that she should have married Robert for more reason than to please her parents. She was curious as to why Gabriel had asked. "Would you want me to?"

The question was brave, but then, circumstances called for bravery. He said nothing for a moment and she thought he wouldn't answer her. "No," he finally answered softly.

Her heart sped a measure, not with fear this time but with hope. "Why not?" she ventured a step further.

*Why not? Indeed. Gabriel didn't know why he had an*swered "no" to her question. He'd known from the moment he saw her she was not for him, no matter that he couldn't get her from his mind. What had just happened to him in Hempshire left little doubt about what he was, what he might easily become. He was not a fit husband for any woman. He'd known that long ago. That was why he'd pledged his vow along with his brothers.

"Because he could have never made you happy," he

said. "There is a difference between being happy and being content. Why settle for the one when you can have the other?"

He knew that better than anyone. A woman such as Amelia should have never settled. Settling was for people who had no choice. Like him.

"Are you warm enough?" he quickly changed the subject. Gabriel had found a pair of coarse Cossacks in the small bedroom Bruin shared with his wife. Putting them on had been painful. He'd hurriedly rifled through a few women's items, but the blacksmith's wife was a sturdy woman and anything she'd left behind would swallow Amelia. They'd had a strapping son around the age of ten. If worse came to worst, Amelia could probably wear something of the lad's.

"The blanket is better than nothing, but I would prefer to be dressed."

The fact that she wasn't dressed beneath the wool blanket wasn't something Gabriel could easily forget. Thoughts of her pale creamy skin tortured him. What had happened in Hempshire tortured him. Why had he nearly transformed? He'd never done so before. Was the confrontation with Mullins what had triggered the curse? Or was it Amelia? Gabriel had seen the look of repulsion and horror on her face when she was threatened by men who could shift their shapes. If she knew about him, she would be just as terrified and repulsed. How much longer did he have to be only a man? How much longer until her trust in him vanished?

"There are clothes you can probably fit into in the cottage," he managed to find the decency to say.

She didn't answer. He glanced at her and saw that

her eyes were closed. She was exhausted. She had to be to fall asleep given their circumstances. But she also must trust him to let down her guard for even a moment when they might still be in danger.

He reached for her and pulled her against him. She snuggled next to him, her warm breath dancing across the skin of his neck. Her soft curves beneath the scratchy blanket tantalized him. He ran his fingers through her tangled hair. She moaned softly and snuggled closer, her lips now nearly pressed against his neck. His senses stirred, the baser ones coming quickly to the surface. Was it the beast in him responding to her or simply the man?

His hand tightened in her hair. He pulled her head back to look down at her. Her lashes fluttered and she opened her eyes. She did not pull away as he expected she might do. Better for her if she had. Her lips parted. He couldn't take his eyes off of them. So sweet and plump. Then he was leaning toward them, as if he had no will to stop himself.

Chapter Fifteen

Amelia knew he was going to kiss her. Maybe it was wrong, but she wanted to feel something besides worry, fear, hunger, and cold. The day she married Robert Collingsworth seemed like a lifetime ago. The life she lived in London seemed unreal—like a dream floating in a bubble. Now there was only Gabriel and her, and the darkness that surrounded them.

"Are you awake?" he asked softly.

She assumed he couldn't see that her eyes were open. The only reason she saw his was because they glowed in the dark.

"Yes," she whispered.

"If I kiss you will you remember it in the morning?"

She smiled over the reminder of her sleepwalking at Collingsworth Manor. "I will remember," she promised him.

His lips brushed hers, like a whisper at first before he took full possession of her mouth. Amelia opened readily to him, her blood heating when his tongue slid into her open mouth to caress hers. His scent curled around her. Warmth spread through her chilled bones. Her arms crept up around his neck, uncaring that the blanket wrapped around her fell away to her waist. The contact of flesh against flesh was like the shock of touching metal when static laced the air.

Gabriel gently pulled her on top of him so that she straddled him. Her nipples hardened against the feel of his smooth, warm skin. The heat radiating from him felt unnaturally warm, and she worried about his leg. Then his hand slid slowly up her stomach to cup her breast and she couldn't think beyond sensation. His thumb brushed across her hardened peak, forcing a moan from her lips.

"I want to taste you here," he said, slowly tracing the circle of her nipple.

The suggestion alone made her ache. Amelia knew she should try to gain control of her emotions. As shocking as she was at times, she'd never gone so far with a man before. But Gabriel was not just any man, and as much as she pretended that she did not believe in love, she feared love had found her anyway. Maybe love wasn't something a person could escape from when it was right—when it was destined.

"I want you to," she said bravely.

He leaned forward and kissed her neck before bending his head to her breasts. The first touch of his warm mouth against her nipple sent a jolt through her. He teased her nipple with his tongue before taking the sensitive bud into his mouth. He suckled her and the gentle tug of his mouth made her stomach muscles tighten; then, lower, she began to throb.

She twisted her fingers in his hair. He sampled one breast and then the other, teasing and tasting until she grew breathless—until she writhed against him. Beneath her, she felt his hardened member press against her. What she felt was impressive and more than a little intimidating, but then his scent curled around her and she was lost in a fog of her own desire.

"Gabriel," she whispered, "make me feel something other than fear. Make me forget this night might be our last."

He pulled back to look at her. In the darkness, his eyes were twin balls of blue fire. "You don't know me, Amelia. Not really. You only see what I want you to see."

She wanted to know him. His hopes and dreams—his secrets. But tonight she wanted to know him as she had never known a man before. "Will you deny me this one night together?" she asked. "Neither of us knows what tomorrow will bring."

For a moment, she thought he would refuse her. He seemed to struggle with himself, which Amelia found rather humiliating. She knew she wasn't unattractive, and she knew Gabriel found her physically appealing. Most men, she imagined, would not refuse her offer under any circumstances, but then, Gabriel was not most men.

She started to pull away, but he stopped her. He trembled when he touched her. It was a heady elixir, to know how strongly she affected him. She leaned forward and kissed him. His mouth was warm and responsive. Below, he pressed against her and her pulses leaped. She pressed back, stealing a slight groan from him. Amelia was careful not to shift her weight against his injured leg, but she wondered how long she could maintain the presence of mind to remember that he was in no physical shape to be doing what they were.

His scent, his kiss, his touch, all worked against her to steal reason. There was nothing but hands and mouths and sensation. No wolf at the door. No danger lurking in the shadows. Just her, him, and the night gathered around them.

The blanket still draped her lower half, but beneath it she was naked. The coarse trousers he wore both irritated and stimulated her sensitive skin. When he bent to sample her breasts again, Amelia threw her head back. He rubbed his erection against her and she arched against him, pressing until the friction nearly drove her mad.

Gabriel's hand slid down from her breast and he touched her there, in the sensitive place between her legs. She gasped and pressed harder against his fingers. Her nails dug into his shoulders. He stroked her, his skilled fingers playing her like a fine instrument until she hummed, until she moved with him, against him, whatever it took to keep the wonderful pressure building inside of her.

*Gabriel knew he should have refused her. He had de*ceived Amelia. She didn't know what he truly was. She didn't know about his curse or the beast that prowled even now beneath his skin. The beast that urged him on, that gave him strength when he should have none, that even dulled the pain in his leg so that all he felt was his desire for her—his instinct to mate. She saw him as her protector, but there was no one to protect her from him. Not even himself.

The offer she made was too sweet—to forget for one night who she was and who he was and simply be together. She was the strongest form of temptation. The feel of her soft, smooth skin, the wetness between her legs, her scent, all combined to rob him of the ability to resist her. He couldn't stop himself; he didn't want to.

Deep down, he knew it was more than the beast urging him to take her. It was the man who wanted to be only a man in her eyes. If only for one night. For the first time since he learned about his curse, he welcomed his weaknesses—his lack of control. He forsook them for the simple joy of feeling—the temptation of being only a man making love to the woman he desired above all other women. But the man in him still ruled . . . at least for now.

"You should stop me before I can no longer think with a rational mind," he found the will to warn her.

Her hips moved and she pressed against him. "I don't want you to stop," she responded breathlessly. "Gabriel, please don't stop."

He stroked her velvet softness, the small nub that controlled her passion. His member throbbed painfully, hungry for the feel of her wrapped around him. He paused long enough to unfasten his trousers and free himself. Her moan of disappointment had him quickly returning to the source of her frustration . . . and his.

Amelia thought she would die when he paused in his steady stroking. Then she felt the hard, long length of him released from his trousers, felt him pulse against her, and she swallowed loudly. She didn't want to stop him, but then again, she was hesitant. Her mother had gleefully told her about blood and pain during a woman's first time with a man, making it sound worse than it must be, Amelia had suspected, in order to dissuade her from engaging in such activities before marriage. Perhaps her mother hadn't exaggerated . . .

Then he touched Amelia again and all doubts fled. The pressure that had built was suddenly back. She moved not only with and against his fingers but also along the hard length of his shaft, making him slick with her dew. Higher and higher she rode the crest of a wave, but she wanted more. She wanted him inside of her. She shifted on top of him so that the large tip of his member was suddenly poised at her entrance.

His hands twisted in her hair and he pulled her face back so that she was staring into his eyes. "You push me beyond my control," he said, and the sound of his deep voice alone nearly sent her beyond hers. "Are you certain you want this, Amelia? If you don't, you had better say so now, while I still have the control to ask."

There was no going back for her. There was possibly no tomorrow for her. She would have Gabriel Wulf as her lover tonight, and the rest of the world be damned. She'd waited all this time to become a woman, and now she realized in the secret places in her mind, she had been waiting for him. Robert had only represented duty, another way to please someone other than herself. Gabriel had pulled her heart from its protective barrier and made it his own. She wanted to belong to him. Heart, body, and soul.

"I want you," she whispered.

He groaned softly in answer; then he thrust into her

and the pain came sharp and quick, forcing a loud gasp from her lips. He twisted his hands tighter in her hair and pressed his forehead against hers.

"I'm sorry I hurt you," he said. "I thought it best to get that part over so we can move on."

He didn't allow her time to respond before he was moving on. Deeper into her, stretching her, forcing the air from her in little gasps. He was large and Amelia reconsidered her decision, at least until he released his hold on her hair and his fingers were back to work their magic. The combined sensation was what had been missing before, and as he stroked her, penetrating her deeper and deeper, the pressure built inside of her.

She was aware of everything about him. His scent, the feel of his smooth muscled chest against her breasts—the heat radiating from him, the glow in his eyes as he watched her. The way he filled her, kept filling her, as he moved deep inside of her. His hands gripped her waist and he lifted and lowered her until Amelia understood the rhythm, also understood that if she positioned herself a certain way, the stimulation he'd provided with his fingers was unnecessary.

She used her knees on either side of him to give her leverage, lifting and lowering herself upon his thick shaft until his breathing was as labored as her own and his eyes flared a brighter blue.

"God," he rasped. Then he kissed her.

It was that added element, his mouth claiming hers, his tongue penetrating her as he penetrated her below, that sent her spiraling out of control. Amelia's nails dug into his shoulders and she rode him harder, faster, until she exploded into a million pieces. As she convulsed around him, she broke from his lips to bite his neck, gently and, she supposed, not so gently. Warmth flowed through her, around her, and she felt as if her soul had left her body, spiraling up to hover above her. He still moved inside of her, prolonging the pleasure that seemed to go on and on. Suddenly he tensed beneath her, his hands tightened on her waist, and he pulled her off of him.

She felt the warm spill of his seed against the inside of her thighs. His body jerked and convulsed as hers had done and she knew he had found his pleasure. He pulled her closer and she rested her head against his shoulder, breathing hard against his neck, listening as he struggled to bring his own breathing back to normal. It was the most glorious thing Amelia had ever experienced.

"God," he said again.

Amelia snuggled closer against him and sighed. "I am a woman now."

He gently stroked her hair. "You were always a woman. An extraordinary woman."

Her lack of experience had her wondering if what had just happened between them could have been as wonderful for him as it had been for her. "Did I please you?"

He laughed. "If you had pleased me any more, I don't think I could have survived it."

His praise warmed her nearly as much as the heat radiating from him. As her body began to register the shock of what Gabriel Wulf had just done to her, she remembered his injury. She pulled back to look at him.

"Your leg," she whispered.

Gabriel pulled her closer. "To hell with that," he said. "You are good medicine. I forgot all about my injury."

Amelia wasn't convinced. Carefully, she slid from on top of him. Her thighs were sticky with his seed and, she imagined, her virgin's blood. "What I wouldn't give for a bath," she said, settling beside him before pulling the blanket around them.

"I can't give you that, but I imagine there is a pump and bucket outside. I'll get you some water to wash with."

She wondered if he could even manage to rise. Amelia thought of offering to fetch the water herself, but she knew Gabriel wouldn't let her go outside, not while he wasn't certain they were safe. Besides, she wasn't positive her trembling legs would support her. She hadn't had time to absorb what had just happened between them, what she had in fact instigated. Would he think less of her now? Did he love her? He'd certainly never said that he did.

As she watched him, he fumbled beneath the blanket draped around them, obviously pulling himself back together; then he rose. He grunted with the pain but said nothing. He bent and offered her his hand.

"There is a soft feather mattress in the next room. If I had been thinking clearly, I would have suggested we go in there. The floor is hard and probably none too clean."

Amelia was thankful the darkness hid her blush. She had copulated with Gabriel Wulf in a blacksmith's cottage on the floor. She had managed to shock even herself. If he'd been thinking clearly? Did that mean that he hadn't known his own mind when he had made love to her? Did he regret his actions already? Should she regret hers? Amelia didn't believe she could if she wanted to. Were these sudden insecurities and doubts what her mother had hoped to spare her from? The gnawing fear in her gut that he did not feel about her as she felt about him.

Since he still stood with his hand out to her, she placed her smaller one in his. He pulled her to her feet and she clutched the blanket to her breasts. He kissed the top of her head and turned her toward the next room.

"Go. I'll join you in a moment."

She went, and Amelia knew she was being foolish, but for one moment when he opened the door and disappeared, she wondered if he would ever come back.

Gabriel wasn't so blinded by emotion that he forgot to be careful. He moved as silently as his injured leg allowed and found the pump, a bucket next to it as was custom. A thousand emotions assaulted him. Guilt, disappointment for his weaknesses, lust to have her again, worry that he should leave her. But he couldn't leave her. She wasn't safe without him . . . she wasn't safe with him.

He glanced up at the nearly full moon overhead. The wolf was closer now; Gabriel felt it. Had he fallen in love with Amelia? The widow of a onetime friend, a woman as different from him as night was from day? He wanted to say that he hadn't fallen in love with her. That she was no different from the other women he'd taken his pleasure of in the past, but he knew that was a lie. She was different.

Maybe he had known that on some deep level the first moment he saw her standing on the streets of London. Maybe that was the reason he had dreamed about her.

Now that the fading embers of lust had banked, his

leg hurt like hell. All the rationalizing in the world couldn't erase the fact that he'd just taken Lady Amelia Sinclair Collingsworth's virginity. A right that should have been reserved for her husband. At least reserved for a man who could offer her a future. At least for a man who was only a man and nothing more.

And now Gabriel understood that being with a woman he had an emotional tie with was different. He was different when he was with her. He liked pleasing her, watching the expressions cross her face. He liked it too much. He suddenly very much wanted to experience that again with her.

Gabriel worked the pump. Although it nearly killed him, he bent and stuck his head beneath the chilly water in order to clear his mind. He would not go back inside and make love to her again, this time on the soft mattress in the small room another man once shared with his wife. Gabriel swore he wouldn't, but the wolf beneath his skin urged him to forsake his pledge. To ignore every pledge he'd ever made to himself.

Could he stop what he felt happening to him? Gabriel glanced up at the moon, nearly full in the night sky. For a moment, he merely stared, mesmerized. The moon called to him, seduced him as easily as Amelia had seduced him. The wolf beneath his skin crept closer to the surface. The beast gave him strength, whispered dark thoughts in his head. He still smelled Amelia's scent on him.

He closed his eyes and breathed it in, let it heat his blood and fire his lust for her again. Glancing toward the darkened cottage, he picked up the bucket and moved toward the house and his prey.

Chapter Sixteen

Gabriel was having the dream again. The one where he watched his father turn into a wolf at the dinner table. Only it wasn't just his father who was transformed. Gabriel looked down and saw his hands, misshapen, covered by fur, long claws jutting from his fingertips. Then Mullins was there, laughing at him. "You are one of us," he hissed, then laughed again until his neck split open and blood gushed from the wound. Gabriel came awake with a start.

At first, he had no idea where he was or why. Then he saw Amelia and the night before came rushing back to him. He'd returned to the cottage with every intention of ravishing her again, but when he'd stood over her in the small bedchamber, looking down at her sleeping countenance, her features those of an angel, the man had gained control of the beast. He'd slid off the coarse trousers, washed up as best as he could, and slipped into bed with her. And finally, he'd found sleep himself.

Amelia was now perched on the side of the bed staring at him. She wore a pair of snug trousers and a white shirt that laced at the neck, although her breasts did not allow her to lace it closed and offered him a tantalizing peek at her cleavage. He saw the dusky color of her nipples through the shirt. When he could take his eyes from them, he noted her hair had been brushed and tied back with a black ribbon. She looked fresh and ripe for the picking.

"You must have found some of the lad's clothes," he said. "I knew from my search last night you wouldn't be able to wear Bruin's wife's things."

"Yes," she answered. "I always wanted to wear men's breeches."

"You don't look like a man in them," he responded, allowing his gaze to run the tantalizing length of her.

He thought she might have blushed. She rose from the edge of the bed. "I found food. Not much, but a few dried apples and the other half of the loaf you brought me last night. Are you hungry?"

She'd returned to the bed with her scavenged items and stood looking down at him.

"Hungry for you," he answered honestly.

She blushed again, but with pleasure, he thought. "You are in no condition to . . . well, I shouldn't have seduced you last night," she admitted.

"Regrets already?" Gabriel tried to rise and winced. He quickly settled back against the pillows, the scratchy blanket draped over his lower half.

"I have no regrets," she announced before placing the food items on the bed and leaning forward to press her cool palm against his forehead. "You feel unnaturally warm. I think you have a fever."

Gabriel snatched her hand and brought it to his lips. "A fever for you," he assured her.

Amelia rescued her hand and placed both on her hips. "Stop trying to seduce me. You are in no condition; in fact, I worry that you are in no condition to look for Mora, either. Perhaps I should go."

Her words sobered him. "That is not an option," he assured her. "I will go. The sooner the better, so that I can get you safely away from here."

She tilted her dimpled chin up. "I can help," she insisted. "I know you think I'm relatively useless, but—"

"I do not think that," he interrupted her. "I might have at first. I misjudged you."

And he had. Amelia was an extraordinary woman. An extraordinary lover. She was brave and thoughtful and none of the things he might have at first glance assumed about her. She was too damn good for him, that was certain.

She smiled softly at him, then quickly frowned. "You find me useful in what way? I remember what you told me when we were in the woods. About women serving a purpose."

Damn. As if things were not complicated enough between them. Now Gabriel must appease her female sensibilities, something he had never cared to do before. "The village is dangerous, Amelia," he explained. "I don't know who is friend or foe. I'll be better able to concentrate on finding Mora if I know you are here safe."

Gradually, her frown faded. "I suppose you're right." Her beautiful blue eyes suddenly filled with tears. "I hope Mora is alive. I feel this is my fault. If we hadn't forced her to come with us—"

"She would already be dead," Gabriel assured her.

"The man posing as the blacksmith said they didn't want any witnesses left behind. That would include all of us."

Gabriel steeled himself and bent forward to reach for a pair of trousers Amelia had obviously draped across the end of the bed for him. Pain shot through his leg, but he managed to grab the clothes. He'd never had a woman take care of him before. Not since he was a young boy. He rather liked it. Throwing the scratchy blanket aside, he managed to gain his feet. Dressing nearly killed him, not to mention ignoring Amelia, since she stared boldly at him.

She wasn't shy, his Amelia. Gabriel immediately corrected the thought. She wasn't his. She would never be his except for in the way she was his last night. If they did manage to reach Wulfglen safely, they had no future together. Especially not now.

"The leg looks horrible," she commented. "But the rest of you is quite something."

He lifted a brow while fastening his trousers. "How do you know? You don't have much in the way of comparison."

She smiled and he wondered if she realized how seductive it was, her smile. "I may be many things, but I'm not an idiot. You are a beautiful man, Gabriel Wulf. If you hadn't chosen to hide yourself away in the country these many years, I imagine you would by now have become an expert at beating women off with a stick."

The reason he'd hidden himself away robbed him of the ability to enjoy her flirty banter. The sooner he found out about Mora, the sooner they could move on and, he hoped, reach the safety of Wulfglen. Gabriel had no idea how long he could keep the wolf inside him at bay, but it wasn't something he ever wanted Amelia to know about him. Let her think him beautiful; let her think anything but that he was a monster.

Gabriel pulled on his boots. He tugged on a shirt Amelia had found for him. Then he began his search for a suitable hiding place for Amelia while he was gone. While he went from room to room studying the floor, Amelia followed.

"Did the man . . . creature say anything else to you in the blacksmith's barn?" she asked. "About what they have planned and what I had to do with it all?"

He shook his head. "No, not really. Only that they'd been making some sort of plans for a long time."

"What are we looking for?" she asked a few minutes later.

"An indentation of any sort. I'll wager Bruin has a small area under the floor where he kept his valuables, maybe his spirits and food supplies."

Rather than comment, Amelia began searching, as well. A few moments later she called to him from the kitchen area. "Here, Gabriel. I've found it."

He joined her in the small area where a cookstove and a crude table and chairs sat. She was down on the floor beneath the table, having pulled a worn rug back to display exactly what he'd described to her.

He and Amelia pulled the table aside. Bending to grab the small latch of the hidden entry to the floor pained him, but he got it open. The smell of dirt and stored vegetables wafted up.

"Good," he said to her. "We'll leave it open. If you

hear anyone come around while I'm gone, get inside and close the door."

She nodded. "Are you sure you should go?" she asked. "I can see the leg is paining you. Maybe you should rest today and go out tonight, under cover of darkness."

The suggestion was plausible, but Gabriel felt he might have already waited too long to help poor Mora. "Time is important," he said. "You know that."

She bit her full lower lip. "Yes, I know. Please be careful, Gabriel."

Reaching out, he brushed her cheek. It seemed only natural to lean forward and kiss her. His lips lingered against hers for only a moment before he pulled away, readied his strength, and rose from his kneeling position on the floor. After instructing Amelia to bolt the door behind him, Gabriel left the relative safety of the cottage in search of Mora. He had no idea what he would find in the village.

He wound his way through the woods and back to the village. Gabriel moved more slowly than he would have liked, but the leg held him up. He now paused in the cover of foliage to study the village ahead. Hempshire looked deserted. He wondered if the blacksmith's barn should be the first place he looked for Mora.

It seemed natural. Mullins had said he had two cousins who helped him. Gabriel was betting the cousins had the same "gifts" as Mullins. Setting off again, Gabriel tried to keep to the foliage as much as possible. It thinned as he drew closer to the village. Luckily, the blacksmith's barn sat on the edge of the village closest to him.

A few horses milled around in a corral out back. It had been dark last night when he'd stolen one of them and he and Amelia had made a mad dash from the village. Now, in the daylight, he saw one horse he recognized. His own lame mount he had ridden to Collingsworth Manor upon. He would bet that most of the horses in the corral had once been in Robert's stable.

Gabriel leaned up against the barn when he reached it, resting his throbbing leg. Sweat coated his brow and he wondered if a fever had taken hold of him. In the stillness, he heard the mumble of voices coming from inside the barn.

Gathering his strength, he moved around the side of the barn toward the back. He would be spotted easily from the front entrance by anyone moving through the village. He had to walk through the horses and they snorted and stomped. Horses usually took well to him, at least his own horses. The one he'd ridden to Collingsworth Manor simply regarded him curiously, as if it wondered where he had been and what he was currently doing. Perhaps the other horses were responding to his scent, Gabriel realized. Maybe it had been the reason the one he'd stolen last night had been so wild to handle. It might have smelled the wolf in him.

Two rear doors opened up into the stable. Gabriel paused at them, listening. The voices were clearer, but not clear enough for him to hear their conversation. He slipped through the doors. A few stalls stood at the back of the barn. Gabriel glanced cautiously in each as he passed. They were empty.

"How could they have escaped you?" one man

asked. "There are only two of them, for God's sake, and neither with our talents."

"The man handles a horse like no man I've seen before," another man defended. "And the woman, she shot at us."

"We must stop them before they reach safety. We've waited too long to execute our plans. We can't have them ruining everything."

Gabriel heard a soft snort in the silence that followed. "Who do you think would believe them if they did manage to reach safety?" someone asked. "The two will most likely be charged with the husband's murder and assumed to be lovers."

"Wulf won't be taken seriously, perhaps. His family has no influence among society. The woman, though, you know we have plans for her."

"It wasn't supposed to work this way," one man argued. "You know the rules set down long ago. She is not weak or suffering. What we plan for her is nothing short of murder."

The hair on the back of Gabriel's neck bristled. No one was going to hurt Amelia. He'd kill any man or beast that tried.

"She could have lived at one time. She could have been useful, but now all of that has changed. The plan has changed, as you all well know."

"Miss High-and-mighty in the tavern thinks they will come back for her," a voice proclaimed. "I told her she was naught but a servant and she placed too much hope in two of the higher class. But she insists they will return for her. She claims they are not like others of their station."

"She is being guarded well, correct?"

"Aye, five men in there on watch just in case she's right. We'll give it a couple of days to see if we can catch a bigger fish with a small one; then we'll have to make her disappear."

Gabriel's heart pounded loudly. Mora was still alive, thank God. He wasn't too late, but she was under heavy guard, her captors obviously hoping he'd do just what he had and come to rescue her. How to get her out without getting himself killed or captured in the process? He needed a plan, but his leg throbbed and he felt foggy headed. At least he knew Mora was safe for a couple of days while they waited to see if he might return for her.

"Wulf. He's dangerous. He killed Mullins, and how he did that, I'd like to know."

"Cut his throat as we all saw," another man provided.

"But how did he get the drop on him to cut his throat?" the same man asked. "Mullins was a hard man to take by surprise."

"Don't know, but he will pay for killing one of our own. An eye for an eye. We don't have to feel any guilt over killing that one. He's already brought down too many of us."

Just how many were there of these creatures? Gabriel wondered. Creatures with some sort of plan. He had still to understand what that might be, but now he knew they had no intention of letting either him or Amelia live. Slipping away, Gabriel moved as silently as his throbbing leg would allow through the back of the barn. He suddenly needed to see Amelia, to touch her, to know she was safe.

• • •

Amelia felt useless. There were a few supplies in the dark hole beneath the table. There was a stove, probably wood outside to stoke it with, but she had no idea how to start a fire, much less how to cook a decent meal. Gabriel needed better nourishment than what he'd been getting. He needed to get stronger to fight off the infection that was no doubt running through his body. She was certain what had happened last night between them hadn't helped his condition.

She supposed she should feel guilt of some sort, shame perhaps that she had given her virginity to a man who was not her husband, but she couldn't dredge up those emotions. There were too many others rolling around inside of her.

Every second Gabriel was gone was pure torture. She worried about him. She worried about Mora and her fate. What if Gabriel didn't come back? What if she never saw him alive again? Such thoughts made her chest hurt, made catching a breath difficult. Such thoughts broke her heart. He was unlike any man she knew. He was honorable and strong and compassionate, even if he wished he were not. He might not be the fairy prince she once dreamed he was, but he was better. He was real.

A soft rap on the door made her jump. Amelia hurried to the bolted door and listened. A moment later Gabriel called softly to her. Relieved, she threw back the bolt and opened the door. He limped inside, spotted a chair, and immediately headed toward it to sit down. His eyes didn't look quite right to her.

"You need a doctor, Gabriel," she worried.

"That will have to wait," he said, then smiled at her. "Mora needs to be rescued."

Amelia's heart leaped with joy. "She's alive?"

He nodded. "She's being kept under guard in the tavern. They think we may come back to rescue her. They are using her as bait."

Amelia pulled out a chair and sat beside him. Her knees were weak with relief. "How are we going to get her out?"

He lifted a dark brow. "How am I, you mean? You aren't going anywhere near the village."

The arrangement would have suited her fine at one time. Amelia knew Gabriel wasn't in any condition to charge to Mora's rescue, but the two of them together might free their friend.

"I am capable of helping you," she said sternly.

He sighed. "I know you are brave, Amelia. I know so much more now than I did in the beginning. You're stronger than I thought you were. Had none of this happened, had you married Lord Robert Collingsworth and gone on with your life, I don't think it is something he would have even known about you. And I'm sorry for him because of that. For not having the chance to know how truly extraordinary you are."

Her heart melted. Gabriel hadn't said he loved her, but he'd just come very close. Perhaps he did not even realize it. She prayed they would have the time for him to do so. But time for poor Mora was running out.

"When will you go?" Amelia asked.

He swiped a sleeve across his brow. "Tonight, under cover of darkness like you suggested this morning. You need to be ready to run when we return. Find what you can pack in the way of food. Maybe some clothes like you are wearing for Mora. She can move faster in men's trousers."

Amelia put a plate of dried apples, bread, and a small chunk of cheese in his lap. "You need to eat, Gabriel. Then you need to rest. I still think I should go with you and help."

She watched as he picked at the food. The fact he seemed to have no appetite wasn't a good sign. "You're going to have to trust me, Amelia," he said. "Can you do that?"

If not him, who else in the world could she trust? He'd kept her alive and safe this long; she had faith he would continue to do so. At least if he was physically able. "I do trust you," she said, and because he wasn't eating much anyway, she took the plate from his lap and placed it on the table. "Get into bed."

A lazy half smile shaped his sensual lips. "Is that an invitation?"

Despite the fact that he was glassy-eyed, obviously exhausted, and in pain, Amelia found him nearly irresistible. She tamped down her woman's feelings for him and tried to fix a stern expression on her face. "None of that," she said. "At least until you are better."

"I can be better if that is your wish, Amelia."

Her heart thudded against her chest. How could he be better than he was last night? The thought intrigued her, would have intrigued her more under different circumstances.

"And I thought you were not a rake." She returned his half smile and helped him rise from his chair, steering him toward the small bedchamber and the soft feather mattress.

Once he sat upon the edge of the bed, she helped him get his boots off. She'd cleaned up that morning with water from the bucket Gabriel had brought in last night. The blood on her thighs had been a rather shocking sight. Proof positive that she was no longer a maiden. Amelia returned to the bucket, poured a little water into a sturdy crock, and fetched a rag she'd found in a pile of rags she had to assume were used for such things.

After wringing out the rag, she returned to the bed. Gabriel now lay back against the pillows. "Remove your shirt," she said. "The cool water will help bring down your fever."

Tugging the garment over his head, he asked, "And when did you learn so much about tending to the sick?"

"From Mora," she informed him. "She knows a lot about such things. While you were leading us through the forest, focused in on everything else around us, we talked with one another. I was worried about your leg and she told me a little about healing herbs and ways to bring fever down, and I told her a little about my life in London."

"Mora has a lot of life experiences to be so young."

Amelia ran the wet rag over his brow. "I should tell you something about Mora," she said. "I promised her I would let her tell you, but I feel you should know."

His eyes had closed; now they opened. "What about Mora?"

Trailing the rag down his neck to his chest, she answered, "She isn't that young. Maybe a year younger than me. She chose to hide it from us by binding her breasts and wearing that bonnet to make her look plain. She thought she must disguise herself to stay safe while working for the upper crust. Her brother had once assured her she'd be taken advantage of otherwise."

Gabriel's green eyes narrowed. "When did she tell you?"

Amelia shrugged. "She didn't tell me. I discovered her one night cleaning up by the stream without her bonnet and her bindings. She promised me she would tell you, but she still wasn't sure you could be trusted. She thought you lusted for me and might turn your attention her way, knowing you couldn't very well seduce a lady of my station."

His copper-colored nipple hardened when Amelia swiped the wet cloth over his chest. She stared at it, fascinated that his nipples could harden the same as hers.

"She was right, I did lust for you," he admitted. When she glanced up at him, he added, "I do lust for you."

Amelia hoped it was not a simple case of lust for him, although she had once believed lust was the same as love. She knew that wasn't the truth now. She might have been attracted to Gabriel Wulf from the moment she saw him, might have flirted with wicked thoughts of him, but it was only after coming to know him that she had really fallen under his spell.

"Then maybe she was wise to keep her secrets," Amelia responded, trailing the cloth down his corded stomach muscles.

He placed his hand over hers. "She had no need to fear me," he said. "I was taught better than to take advantage of serving girls. I have recently discovered when I want one woman, only the one woman will do."

Amelia swallowed loudly. Gabriel was obviously trying to seduce her. And it was working. Which was ridiculous given his condition. Still, his intoxicating scent suddenly seemed stronger. She had trouble thinking clearly and shook her head in an effort to regain control. "I need to look at your leg. Maybe pressing a cold rag to the wound will help bring down your fever."

"Go ahead," he suggested, that half smile hovering over his lips and his eyes focused intently upon her.

If he meant to rattle her, he succeeded. Amelia tried to keep her mind on tending to him, telling herself she could take care of him without being seduced in the process. She set the rag aside and reached for the fastenings of his trousers. If she hadn't had to figure the workings of men's trousers that morning when she dressed, she wouldn't have known how to proceed. Once she loosened the trousers, she took hold of either side and tugged them down his lean hips.

His manhood immediately sprang forth, long, hard, and intimidating enough to send her running were she still a maid. Instead, the sight of him fully aroused sent heat coursing through her, all of which settled between her legs. She had a nearly uncontrollable urge to touch him there, to wrap her fingers around his width and see what he felt like.

"Go ahead," he repeated softly, as if he'd read her mind.

She startled, wrenching her gaze from the impressive sight of him. Amelia assumed he had not read her mind and was merely bringing her back to the task at hand. She regained her grip on his trousers and pulled them down his legs, careful not to be rough with his injured one. Grabbing up the rag, she returned to the bucket and crock and rinsed the rag.

The man had no shame. He hadn't even reached for the scratchy blanket to cover himself with while her back was turned. Amelia would pretend not to notice he was sprawled out naked before her. Tawny-colored flesh, muscles, and of course the nasty wound to his thigh. The place where he'd had the wound lanced and cauterized looked red and swollen. She sat on the edge of the bed and pressed the cool cloth gently against his thigh.

"I hope this helps with your fever," she commented.

"You have me in bed, naked, and at your mercy. There's only one thing that will stop the fever that rages inside of me now."

She glanced up, immediately ensnared by his strange eyes. Her lips felt dry and she unconsciously moistened them. Surely he wasn't well enough to do what his eyes suggested he wanted to do. And she shouldn't encourage him. Amelia tried to keep her mind focused on bathing him. She ran the cloth over his smooth skin, her fingertips at times coming into contact with his heated flesh. She wanted to run her hands over him, not the cool cloth. She wanted to feel all that muscled flesh pressed against her naked.

Last night had been wonderful, but she suspected most men and women did not couple on the floor while the man sat propped against a door, the woman straddling him. She couldn't avoid his private area. Nor could she ignore the constant reminder that he was aroused and obviously wishing to engage in activities he hadn't the strength to perform.

He sucked in his breath softly when she touched him there with the cool rag. She tended to him, but all the while she couldn't get the desire to replace the rag with her fingers from her mind. Gabriel pulled the cloth from her hand a moment later. She glanced up into his eyes, not surprised by the heat she saw there, but surprised that it probably had nothing to do with his fever. He took her hand and guided it to his hard member. Her fingers wrapped around him as if she could not command them. He felt like steel wrapped in velvet.

When she tightened her hold on him, he closed his eyes and groaned. Afraid she had hurt him, she snatched her hand away.

"Don't stop," he said softly. "I love the feel of your hands on me."

"We shouldn't," she whispered. "You are in no condition to—"

He suddenly reached out and grabbed her, pulling her down on top of him. "I think I'm a better judge of what I can or cannot do than you. I want to make love to you again. I want to feel you beneath me, your skin against mine. I want to please you in ways you have never dreamed of being pleased."

She should resist him, not because she wanted to, but because it wasn't right. Not when he was hurt. Not when he was flirting with a fever. She wasn't so selfish she would compromise his health for a few stolen hours of pleasure. But his scent curled around her, weakened her will. He was irresistible. When he reached behind her and cupped her head, pulling her lips down to his, she did not stop him.

*Gabriel knew that lust drove him. Not any sort of nor*mal lust he had felt before, but an animalistic lust to mate with Amelia. It had dulled all feeling except the throbbing of his cock—the need to be inside of her. And still, the man wanted more than a quick coupling, his own satisfaction of finding release from the torture of his desire for her. The man wanted to make slow love to her. The man wanted her to feel the same pleasure he felt. The man wanted to see the beauty of her face when release found her.

He kissed her, seduced her with his tongue, for he knew she was thinking more rationally than he. Gabriel wanted her to care about nothing but the pleasure he could bring her. For a while, he wanted everything to fade into the background. He wanted there to be just the two of them, giving and taking.

His hand slid down and he gathered her coarse shirt and pulled it up, breaking from her lips only long enough to pull it over her head. Her soft breasts pressed against his chest. Her skin felt cool and smooth as glass against the hotter, rougher texture of his. She was perfection. His hand slid along the slim slope of her back, around and in between them to unfasten the trousers she wore. She'd had her worn slippers on when he'd arrived back at the cottage. He heard her kick them off, and each one landed with a soft thud against the floor.

Together, she and Gabriel rid Amelia of what little clothing she still wore. He flipped her on her back.

While she touched him, he did the same, cupping her breasts, bending to tease her nipples, then sliding one hand down her flat stomach to the soft hair between her legs. She parted them for him, already past being a shy maiden her first time with a man.

Not that she was ever shy, he recalled. He liked that about her. That she came to him with very few inhibitions. Most men preferred a reserved wife in bed and a lusty mistress on the side. With Amelia, a man would have no need for a mistress. She wrapped her hand around his sex again and he nearly exploded. He wasn't used to controlling his needs in bed. The women he'd lain with in the past were simply vessels to ease his lust. He'd never wanted to actually make love to one.

It had been shallow of him, he realized. As he was afraid to feel more than he should for any woman, it had also been a defense. It was too late now, so he lowered his defenses and allowed himself the true pleasure of being with a woman, this one woman. Gabriel gently took her hand from him and slid down her silken skin, trailing a path with his tongue to her navel. Lower yet he went until he was lodged between her legs, until he could pleasure her with his tongue as he had done with his fingers.

She gasped softly. Her body tensed. He supposed he'd managed to shock even a woman who was by most standards shocking herself. Then he made love to her with his mouth and he felt her surrender to him. Her hands crept into his hair, twisting, pressing him against her. He loved the taste and the scent of her. It fired his own burning blood.

His cock throbbed. His animal instincts to claim her rose. He took her to the edge; then he slid up her body, captured her lips, and entered her warm, tight passage. It was heaven and hell. Being inside of her. He wanted to explode, to spill his seed, but he held back, moving inside of her, angling himself so that he stimulated her as he'd done with his tongue. Her breathing grew ragged and she matched his movements. Her nails dug into his back and still he pushed her. Faster, harder, until they were both sweating and gasping for breath.

He felt the first tremors of her climax, felt her tighten around him, and he lost control. He pumped harder and she shattered, her nails digging into his back, her legs wrapping around him. She moaned his name, and poised upon the crest of his own release, he knew he should pull from her. But he could not. The beast inside of him would plant its seed, for that was the reason an animal copulated. Continuance of their race.

The climax took him before he could reason like a man. He thrust deep into her, spilling his seed. He had never done so before inside of a woman. He'd always been responsible with the women he'd lain with. Not only for their sake, but for whatever child he might spawn's sake. Gabriel held himself up on his elbows so he wouldn't crush Amelia, and she stared up at him, her features so beautiful it was even painful for him to look at her.

A sated half smile rested upon her kiss-swollen lips, and even though he shook from the force of his climax, he bent to kiss her gently. Gabriel rolled to his side and pulled her along with him so that they were still joined.

She snuggled against him, and together they tried to return to earth from the heavens.

Gradually their breathing calmed. He eased from her, but he did not release her. He liked the feel of her in his arms. He liked too damn much about her. And he was fooling himself if he wanted to place such an unthreatening term as "like" to his feelings where she was concerned. He knew it went much deeper than that. What was happening to him was proof even if he tried to deny his feelings. Denying them obviously did no good where the curse was concerned.

He played with her hair and she drifted into sleep. Gabriel should rest, as well. Now that he'd made love to her, the pain in his leg returned. It was bad enough to raise bile in his throat. A moment later the first stomach pain shot through him. It was so sharp it took his breath away and made his body jerk.

"What is wrong?" Amelia mumbled sleepily.

"Nothing," he managed. "I need to go outside for a moment."

She didn't protest when he slipped from her arms. Gabriel managed to pull on his trousers despite the pain in his leg and the sick feeling rising up from his stomach. He grabbed his boots and limped through the cottage. He thought the cooler air outside might clear his head, but he barely made it outside before another sharp pain in his stomach doubled him over. He dropped his boots by the door and stumbled farther from the cottage, thinking he was going to be sick.

On hands and knees now, he waited for the bile to come up in his throat. Then he noticed his hands. Fur covered them and claws jutted from his fingertips. Sweat coated his brow and he shook his head, blinked, hoping when he looked again he wouldn't see what he thought he saw. But he did see it. Another pain sent him to the ground. Gabriel pulled his legs up against his chest. His very bones hurt. He glanced up at the sky, where a full moon bathed the countryside in bright light. It was happening. As much as he wanted to deny it, he knew it was too late for him.

God help him. God help Amelia. She had just lain with a monster. Now was not the time, dammit! Never would there be a good time for this. As his body began to convulse, to change its shape, Gabriel howled out in pain and frustration. Good God, what would he do to her? He tried frantically to hold on to human thought. Had he closed the door behind him? Yes, he was sure he had. Would he get in anyway? What was getting ready to happen to him? Or worse, to her?

Chapter Seventeen

Amelia chanced a glance outside the cottage window. It was one of many chances she'd taken since dawn first streaked the morning sky. She'd awakened in the middle of the night to find Gabriel gone. Although she knew he meant to free Mora under cover of darkness, Amelia couldn't figure out why he hadn't woken her before he left. She was supposed to gather clothes for Mora to change into, gather what food she could find, and make a small pack, and she had done both, but what if Gabriel and Mora had returned, frantic to make their escape, and she'd still been sleeping?

It didn't make sense. Certainly she had been exhausted, not only from making love with a man who had no business making love, but also from being on the run since she'd left Collingsworth Manor. Still, she had trouble believing Gabriel hadn't woken her to do as he'd instructed and be ready lest he and Mora return a short time later. Amelia wondered if she'd talked in her sleep to him, made him think she was awake when she hadn't been. Either way, the fact that neither Gabriel nor Mora had returned made Amelia sick to her stomach.

Had he been captured? Killed? No, she couldn't believe that, but yet the possibility kept torturing her. She'd nearly worn a path in the floor from pacing these long hours past. Once, she'd heard a wolf howl in the distance and she was certain the creatures were coming for her. She'd hidden for over an hour in the place beneath the floor, but no wolf had come. No men breaking down the door. Where was Gabriel? And how long should she wait for him before she took action and discovered on her own why he hadn't returned?

Amelia couldn't wait any longer. Better to do something constructive than continue to make herself ill with thoughts of what might or might not have happened to Gabriel. If he'd been taken prisoner, she must help him escape. How, she did not know. There were no weapons in the house. Both she and Gabriel had checked and double-checked. The blacksmith and his family had even taken the kitchen knives, if they seemed to have left most everything else behind.

Perhaps she could formulate a plan on the way to the village, she decided, and rushed to the door, unbolting it and stepping outside. The first thing she spotted was Gabriel's boots. They were sitting outside and in a place she hadn't been able to see from looking out the window. The hairs on her arms prickled.

She saw no signs of struggle; otherwise, she might believe he'd been pounced upon and taken as soon as he walked outside. And if that were the case, the creatures would have come inside and probably killed her in her sleep. A hundred scenarios ran through her mind as she moved carefully from the safety of the cottage.

She didn't get far before she spotted him, lying on the ground naked, shivering uncontrollably.

A cry of alarm left her lips and she ran to where he lay. Amelia bent beside him and touched his forehead. He was burning up. Tears filled her eyes and streamed down her cheeks. "Gabriel," she croaked.

Amelia wasn't certain what to do. Get him inside, she knew, but how? He was twice her size. She cradled his head in her lap.

"Gabriel, can you hear me?"

He moaned softly but didn't respond.

She tried again. "Gabriel, open your eyes. Look at me."

His long lashes fluttered. He opened his eyes, but they were bloodshot and glassy. "Amelia?"

A sob of relief left her lips to hear him respond. "We have to get you inside."

"What happened?"

Amelia shook her head. "I don't know. You were gone this morning. Can't you remember leaving the cottage last night?"

His damp brow wrinkled. "No . . . yes." When he glanced up at her again, she saw something in his eyes besides confusion. She saw fear.

"You must leave," he whispered. "You aren't safe with me. You aren't safe here."

She ignored his worries. How could she leave him? He was sick, might even be dying. "I'll go," she lied. "But only after we get you into the cottage and into bed."

"You must go now," he said, and his voice was stronger. "Now, Amelia!"

"No," she argued. "When I know you are safely in the cottage. Then I'll go. I promise, Gabriel."

His body still shook, but he at least stirred, as if he wanted to gain his feet and go back to the cottage. Amelia grabbed him from beneath his arms, and together they managed to get him to his feet. She then draped his arm around her shoulder.

"Lean on me," she instructed. "I'll help you walk."

He did, but not fully, she knew. Amelia couldn't support his weight, but her promise to leave obviously gave him strength he should not possess. It was slow, but luckily he hadn't ventured far from the cottage before he'd collapsed last night.

They made it to the cottage, then through the door and into the bedchamber. Amelia helped him into bed and pulled the scratchy wool blanket over him.

"Now go," he rasped.

She'd gotten him where she wanted him; there was no need to carry on the pretense that she would leave him to fare as he might. "I'm not leaving you," she said. "Not like this. Not ever," she added softly. "I love you."

For a moment she thought his eyes filled with tears, but she couldn't be certain because he blinked and looked away from her. "You don't," he said. "You can't. I'm not who or what you think I am. Please go, Amelia. I want you to be safe. I want you to have the future you deserve. Go east. Stay to the woods. You should reach Wulfglen at the most in two days' time. You'll be safe there."

She didn't know if she had a future, but she did know that if she did, she wanted Gabriel Wulf to be a part of it. "Close your eyes; rest," she coaxed. "You'll feel better after you've had some sleep." Amelia rose and fetched some water and a clean cloth. She tried to bathe his face, but he grabbed her wrist, surprisingly strong for a man knocking at death's door.

"I won't feel better!" he growled. "Not until I know you have gone! You can't stay here with me. It's suicide."

He was clearly out of his head. She couldn't help him. He needed someone who could. "All right," she said. "I'll go. I'll go now."

Gabriel released her wrist, and it was if all the strength had drained from him. She had to go to the village. She had to rescue Mora, and together they had to find someone to help Gabriel. She started to rise, then leaned over him. "Do you love me, Gabriel?"

He opened his eyes, but she saw that it took effort. She thought he wouldn't answer, maybe did not have the strength; then he said, "It seems as if I must."

Then he closed his eyes and she knew he'd fallen into unconsciousness. She didn't think beyond saving him, beyond saving Mora. Amelia rose and quickly rif-fled through the clothes left in the wardrobe. She found a baggy coat and a man's cap. The lad's boots were a bit too large, but she found a pair of thick wool socks that would help. With a glance over her shoulder, she ran through the cottage and out the door.

She knew which direction to take to Hempshire. Amelia stayed to the trees until the option was no longer available. She bent and rubbed her hands with dirt, then her face. Pulling the cap from her pocket, she twisted her hair up and shoved the cap on her head. It was too large, which was good, since it covered most of her face.

Her heart pounded so loud she heard it in her ears, but she would not go back. She'd spent most of her life thinking only of herself. Now Gabriel needed her. Mora needed her, and she would not let them down. Only a woman as strong as Gabriel Wulf would ever make him happy. And she intended to be that woman.

The village was nearly deserted, but she noted that a few stood around, and she also had to assume the few who did were probably not normal country folk. They were watching, they were waiting, but they were waiting for a tall blond man and a woman. Amelia kept her head ducked and she walked along the road into Hempshire. She hoped she resembled a ragged orphan, which wasn't an unfamiliar sight in England. Her heart pounded louder as she moved toward the tavern. There were two men out front. Amelia kept her head ducked and moved past them.

"Hey, you, lad," one of the men called. "What's your business in Hempshire?"

Her pounding heart now rose in her throat. Amelia kept her head ducked and tried to recall the many cockney accents she'd heard all of her life among the lower staff who worked for her parents.

"Got no business, sir," she said, making her voice gruff. "Just passing through. Is there some scraps I could have from the tavern?"

She peeked from beneath her lashes at the men. They were rough-looking sorts. One shrugged. "Go around the back and into the kitchen. Some scraps left from our breakfast."

Nodding, she hurried to do as he instructed. What luck to be given access to the tavern. She was sure there were guards inside, and how she would get past them to find Mora, she hadn't a clue. One step at a time, although time was important. She dared not leave Gabriel alone for long in his condition.

The back door to the tavern stood open, she imagined to let out the heat from the stove. Amelia stepped inside. Kettles of water boiled on the stove. On a crude table were the leavings from breakfast. She grabbed a hard scone and stuffed it into her mouth. A burly man walked in and she nearly choked.

"What are you doing in here, lad?" he demanded.

Swallowing the scone with a loud gulp, Amelia ducked her head. "The men out front said I could have leavings from breakfast," she rasped. "I've got no money and I'm starving. On my way to London to find work."

Although she didn't dare glance up at the man, she felt him studying her. "Want to make a coin or two before you go?"

It would be odd if she didn't, so Amelia nodded, the cap bobbing on her head.

"Take these kettles to the first room at the top of the stairs. Fill the tub."

Her luck was holding. She assumed they kept Mora a prisoner upstairs, and now she had an excuse to go up and look for her. Amelia wondered if she could even lift the heavy kettles. She had to; that was all there was to it. Another opportunity like this one wouldn't come along again.

"Get to it," the man snapped. "You can eat when you're done."

Already plotting how she might get Mora out of the

tavern, and worried that guards would be posted upstairs, Amelia walked to the stove. She grabbed a thick towel and wrapped it around the kettle handle, having learned her lesson at Collingsworth Manor. The man grunted and walked into the outer room. The kettle was big and heavy and it took both hands for Amelia to carry it. As she lumbered through the tavern room, she saw the man who'd instructed her talking to two other men who each had a tankard and sat sprawled at a scarred table.

"Found someone to do your work, I see," one man remarked to the burly man, and all three laughed.

Amelia kept her head down and shuffled along. When she reached the stairs, she wondered how she'd ever make it up them with the heavy kettle. She had to. For Gabriel. For Mora. Setting her mind to the task, Amelia gathered her strength and started up the stairway. The men in the common room talked quietly among themselves and paid her little heed. Were they men at all? She had to assume they were not. It chilled her to the bone to know she was in the company of such creatures. It frightened her more to think about how she might free Mora without being taken prisoner herself.

She wouldn't be able to help Gabriel. She certainly wouldn't be able to tell her captors about his condition or his whereabouts, not unless she wanted to seal his fate. The stairs were not so tall to climb, but they seemed like it.

Finally, she reached the top. There were five rooms; she knew that from her short stay there. All the doors were closed except that of the room closest to her, the one where she was to fill the tub. Amelia approached it cautiously, struggling with the steaming kettle.

At first glance, she didn't see anyone in the room. She stepped inside. There, next to the window that looked out on the street below, stood Mora. Amelia was so happy to see her she nearly cried out. She bit her lip to keep from doing so and set the kettle on the floor.

Chapter Eighteen

"Fill the tub, lad," Mora said. "I assume that is what you were sent to do."

Her tone was a bit confusing, as if she were allowed to give orders, but Amelia couldn't see past her own happiness at discovering Mora alive and obviously well. The young woman wore her glorious hair loose around her and a silky robe that, upon further inspection, Amelia realized had once been part of her trousseau. Where did Mora get it? Most likely from the creatures that had ransacked Collingsworth Manor once they had forced them all to flee for their lives.

"Mora," Amelia called softly. "I have come to rescue you."

Mora's head snapped in her direction, sending her long hair floating around her. She looked a bit like an angel there by the window, the sun streaming in to illuminate her pretty features. "Amelia," she breathed.

Placing a finger to her lips, Amelia cautioned her to be quiet. Amelia glanced meaningfully over her shoulder. "There are three of them in the common's room and two posted out front. I don't know how we will make it past them."

"Where is Gabriel?" Mora asked, keeping her voice to a whisper.

Amelia's eyes filled with tears, but she quickly blinked them back. She must keep her wits about her. "He's sick. Very sick. He needs a doctor, Mora. I came to help you escape, and I thought together we might find someone to help him. I fear he might die if we don't. The leg is still infected and now he has a fever."

"Where did you leave him?" Mora asked, moving toward her. "I hope not somewhere he can be easily discovered."

"Of course not," Amelia assured her. "We've been hiding in a cottage just a ways outside the village. The blacksmith and his family once lived there."

"You stayed because he could not go on?" Mora asked.

The fact that Mora wanted to question her regarding Gabriel when the two should be discussing how they might escape tried Amelia's patience. Her nerves were already stretched to the limit. She shook her head.

"No. We could have pushed on, but I didn't want to leave you behind. I talked Gabriel into staying long enough to see if he could find you."

Mora stared at the floor for a moment. "I told them you would stay for me," she said. "They said you wouldn't. I almost wish I had been wrong."

Mora's admission confused Amelia. "We have no time for this," she whispered. "We need to figure out how we can escape. We have to find help for Gabriel."

Suddenly Mora moved past her to the door. She stood blocking Amelia's way. "I can leave any time I wish," she said. "It is you who must stay."

A horrible suspicion began to dawn upon Amelia. She took a step back. "What are you saying?"

Mora did not answer, but her eyes began to glitter. Amelia gasped and retreated farther into the room. "Oh my God," she whispered. "You are one of them."

The woman flinched as if Amelia's fear wounded her. "Don't look at me like that," she snapped. "As if I am not human. As if you find me repulsive."

Amelia could only shake her head in denial of the truth. She hadn't seen this coming. "Why?" she managed to croak. "Why have you deceived us?"

Mora's glittering eyes now hardened. "Because it was my duty," she answered bitterly. "The duty that I've known would someday be mine since I was a little girl. I am part of the plan, a plan for the betterment of all my people. My life has never been about what I might want, but what is expected of me."

Amelia was still reeling from the shock of Mora's deception. She felt no sympathy for the woman. "You accept a duty to deceive and murder those who befriend you?"

Mora flinched again. "Murder is not part of our plan," she defended. "At least it wasn't until Gabriel Wulf intruded. And I suppose, to be fair, until Vincent could not play his part as was taught him. For some, the beast is stronger than the person. Vincent did not have control of it. It had control of him."

Now that her shock had begun to fade, Amelia battled her anger. "What about Robert? You murdered him!"

The deceiver straightened her spine and walked to the bed. "Lord Collingsworth was not long for this world. To further our plan, we have one of our own working as a physician in London. Your departed husband visited him shortly before your marriage. His heart was weak, Amelia. It was a family fault. We doubted he could even survive his own wedding night. So we took our places. We secured positions in Lord Collingsworth's employment and we waited for him to return for his wedding night. We were supposed to wait until he expired of natural causes, but Vincent could not wait. He wanted to claim you. He took matters into his own hands."

To know that Robert had died from being frightened to death sickened Amelia. "How can you affiliate yourself with these creatures, Mora? These murderers?"

The glitter returned to Mora's eyes. "You have lived a spoiled and silly life, Amelia. You have no idea what it is like to be hunted for sport. To starve because the forest can no longer feed your people. Once the Wargs were content to hide away and live their lives among other forest creatures, but we can no longer survive hidden away. Now we use our skills to infiltrate your highest ranks. To gain power for our kind. One day, we will rule the world."

Amelia shivered. Could these creatures possibly do what they planned? Vincent had shifted his shape to look like Robert. If the creatures could do that, she supposed they could take over anyone's life. Mora, Amelia realized, had been a chameleon. The young woman even spoke differently now. She was educated. So many things were obvious now that hadn't been before.

"You're the reason they never attacked us in the woods," Amelia now understood. "They had no call to attack us with one of their own planted among us. You would make certain we never reached safety."

Mora perched on the end of the bed like a queen. She dug through a valise, one that Amelia realized belonged to her. "I told them I needed time with you," she explained. "Time to learn your habits, your expressions, your speech patterns. It was never our plan for me to take your place. Not if Vincent had done his duty. But since he didn't, it was decided upon quickly. That day in the root cellar was when I was told."

"How can you deceive us even now?" Amelia whispered. "I called you friend."

Mora shrugged. "I have my duty, just as you once had yours within your society. You call me friend, but had we reached safety, you would have quickly forgotten the bond we forged with one another. I would become a servant again in your eyes and nothing more."

Was that true? Perhaps at one time, but Amelia had changed. "You don't know me at all," she said to Mora. "I didn't know myself, not until I made this journey. You are wounded when I call you an animal, yet you act like one. Did no one teach you about love? Compassion? Without them, you can never be human."

Color suffused Mora's face. "I have been taught all I need to be taught to survive," she bit out. "I know my duty. The cause of all before the needs of one. Victory at any cost."

"And now your duty is to kill me. To take my place among society," Amelia said. "Those who know me, those who love me, will never be fooled by you."

Mora lifted a brow. "Does Gabriel Wulf know you? Does he love you? I fooled him once, you know. At Collingsworth Manor."

It only took Amelia a moment to understand how

and when Mora had fooled Gabriel. "I didn't sleepwalk at all," she said. "But he hardly knew me then. And even so, he said the kiss he shared with me while I was sleepwalking was different than one we had shared earlier the same day." To add insult, she added, "He said you lacked passion. You couldn't fool him now."

The smug smile on Mora's lips faded. "Can't I? If he's still alive, maybe I will see, just to test myself."

"What are you going to do to him?" Amelia demanded.

Rising from the bed, Mora joined her. "I hope nothing. I hope he will simply die of his infection. It will be easier for everyone."

"One less murder you must cover up," Amelia spat.

With a shrug, Mora opened the door. "The coachman and the footman at Collingsworth Manor will never be found. The young lord is now resting peacefully in the fields, where it is obvious he expired due to his weak heart. Frightened when he did not return to me, I took a horse and tried to make my way to Wulfglen, where I knew my friend Rosalind and her husband would be in residence. As for Gabriel Wulf, I will be upset to learn he died of a fever in this small village so close to his home, but I never met the man, so I won't have to pretend to grieve overly for him."

It seemed too quaint, too easy, for Mora to simply step in and steal Amelia's life. "You'll never get away with it," she assured the woman.

Again, Mora lifted a brow. "Won't I?"

Before Amelia's eyes, Mora began to shift. Her features changed and Amelia was suddenly staring at her mirror image. The color of Mora's hair, her blue eyes, had given her an advantage when it came to shifting into Amelia's form.

"Do you still believe I can't fool anyone?"

Mora had perfected Amelia's voice. Was she still having the nightmare? It seemed more plausible than the truth staring her in the eye.

The deceiver smiled. "I'm rather good at mimicking. At the same time, I still don't know enough about you to feel comfortable taking your place. They will let you live for a while longer because of that," she said. "After I see if Gabriel is alive, or if he is coherent enough to believe I am you, I will return to question you further."

"You'll be wasting your breath," Amelia assured her.

Mora ignored her. "Any last words you want me to pass on to him, to make his own passing easier?"

Amelia's temper had gone from simmering to a raging boil. She couldn't stand the thought of Mora deceiving Gabriel again. Saying words to him that Amelia wanted to say. Touching him. Perhaps kissing him one last time. Her hands had fisted into balls. She flew at Mora, using her nails like claws, and managed to mark her face before the woman recovered. Mora grabbed Amelia's wrists, her strength beyond that of what a normal woman should possess. She flung Amelia across the room, where she landed on the bed.

Mora shifted back into herself and marched to the door. "Men!" she shouted. "The lad is the woman we've been waiting for, you idiots. Come up and guard her."

Amelia felt sick. Not only had she managed to get herself taken captive; she had also given Mora Gabriel's location. They would let him die or possibly kill him . . . and it was Amelia's fault. What was she going to do? How could she save Gabriel?

He must do something, but Gabriel couldn't remember what. He struggled up from the dark folds of unconsciousness. It was more peaceful, the darkness, to surrender to it, but something kept niggling at him, urging him to wake, warning him that he had something important that he must do. He felt a cool hand against his forehead. He was burning up. Amelia was with him . . . but wait, he'd told her to go, hadn't he?

With effort, he pried his eyes open. His vision was blurred for a moment, and then slowly a face swam into focus above him. Amelia's face. He had told her to go, he remembered that, but he didn't remember why. And it was important. He recalled making love to her. He recalled her snuggled against him in sleep. Then he remembered the pain. It had sent him outside. His hands had been misshapen like in his nightmares. Fur had sprouted out on them and long claws had jutted from his fingertips.

Then he remembered nothing, not until morning, when Amelia had roused him. He'd been outside, naked and shivering, burning up from a fever. She'd helped him inside and he'd ordered her to leave him. Although he couldn't remember, he suspected the wolf had finally risen up in him. His curse was upon him and Amelia was not safe.

"I told you to go," he said, and his own voice sounded foreign to him. Low and raspy.

"I couldn't leave you as you are," Amelia said. "You know me better than that, don't you, Gabriel?"

He had come to know her, as he once believed he would never know a woman, never want to know a woman. "You're not safe here."

She smoothed the hair away from his forehead. "The creatures don't know where we are. They'll stick close to the village in case we return for Mora. I'll be safe here for a while."

Amelia didn't understand that he might be as much of a threat to her as those hunting them. Gabriel wasn't sure. What would he do while in wolf form? How would he behave? Like a snarling beast that would tear her from limb to limb? Or would he simply have the mentality of an animal? Dangerous when threatened but otherwise content to be left alone? If she stayed and his infection didn't kill him, she would see. She would know. She would be terrified and disgusted.

"You must go now," he managed to say. "You can reach Wulfglen in two days if you move quickly, if you don't stop to sleep. You can go and bring back help."

Again, the feel of her cool hand against his forehead. "You'll be dead by the time I return," she said. "I won't go, and you don't have the strength to force me." Her hand moved around the back of his neck and she lifted his head, placing a cup to his lips. "Drink some water."

He was dying of thirst. His throat was dry and scratchy and he drank so he might better talk her into leaving. The cool water tasted like heaven. He would have emptied the cup, but she suddenly took it away.

"Not too much," she said. "It will just come back up otherwise."

How did Lady Amelia Sinclair Collingsworth know

that? She said she'd talked to Mora regarding tending the sick, but surely they had focused on what they might have to do for his leg and didn't get much further. Mora. He suddenly remembered what else he had to do that was important.

"Mora," he rasped.

For a moment, Amelia looked startled. "What?"

"Mora," he repeated. "I must rescue her. They said they would only wait two days before they made her disappear."

Amelia's tense features relaxed. "You are in no condition to help Mora. Best think about yourself now. The girl will have to deal with her own situation."

Why was Amelia acting this way? He'd expected just such an attitude from her when he first met her at Collingsworth Manor. But she wasn't like this. He'd come to know that about her. She hadn't wanted to leave Mora behind the night they escaped the tavern, and she wouldn't want to leave her to her own fate now.

"What's wrong with you?" he asked. A chill wracked him and he shivered uncontrollably for a moment. Her image became hazy to him. Once he could speak again, he continued, "You would never leave Mora to her own fate. You care too much about her."

Something crossed her lovely features. Guilt? "I care more about you. I love you."

Gabriel remembered that she had told him she loved him. He remembered the soar of his heart before it plummeted. He also remembered what he'd said to her when she asked if he loved her in turn. It had not been what she deserved to hear, but then, she didn't deserve to be deceived by him, as he had deceived her from the beginning. He did love her, as he had vowed to love no woman. He was weak when he should have been strong against her. He was weak now as fever raged through him, and he was weak against a curse that had been put upon his bloodline centuries ago.

"You shouldn't love me," he said. "I am not worthy of your love."

Amelia regarded him curiously. "Why?" she asked. "Because of your family? The rumors that insanity will someday strike you down? Because you were a friend of Lord Collingsworth's and I was for one day his bride? Why are you unworthy?"

Her image blurred and focused again above him. She had a scratch on her cheek Gabriel didn't remember seeing before. He tried to lift his hand to touch her, but he didn't have the strength. Gabriel thought of the claws jutting from his fingertips last night, wondered if they were still there when she'd found him unconscious.

"What happened to your face?" he asked. "How did you get that scratch?"

Her cheeks bloomed with color. "I don't know," she answered. "But a little scratch is hardly need for concern when you are dying."

Gabriel might very well be dying, but Amelia would never admit to that. It was the same as admitting to defeat. She would try to convince him he wasn't dying. She would try to give him hope—strength to fight. Now she acted as if she expected him to give up. What would happen tonight when the moon came out? Would he turn regardless of his fever and his weakened state? As a wolf, would he be sick or strong?

"What time is it?"

"It is late," she answered. "Nearly dark."

She touched his cheek. That's when he noticed that her hands were rougher than he recalled. True, they had gotten rougher since their journey through the woods, but still, he'd thought they were soft against his skin when he'd made love to her.

"Close your eyes," she coaxed. "Go to a place where there is no pain. No worry. Go to a place where your suffering will end."

Gabriel snatched her wrist. She jumped. He yanked her close, surprised that he had the strength to do so. "Who are you?" he demanded.

For a second her face paled. She moistened her lips. Very calmly, she answered, "You know who I am. The fever has made you delirious."

Was that true? Was Gabriel hallucinating? No, he'd know Amelia anywhere, her scent, her touch. This was not Amelia. "I don't know who you are, but I know that you are not Amelia." His nostrils flared. "You are wearing her perfume, but she has no perfume with her. Your scent beneath it is not the same as hers. But I know who that scent belongs to now. You deceived us in more ways than one, Mora."

Her soft smile faded. The blue eyes staring down at him hardened. "Let go of me," she bit out. With surprising strength, she wrested her arm from him. She rose from the bed and stood rubbing her wrist. "What normal man has the ability to tell a person by their scent? I found it odd at Collingsworth Manor, and I find it odd still. Anyone else would not be able to tell that I am not Lady Amelia Sinclair Collingsworth. And the only one who can will soon be dead."

Gabriel's sudden fear for Amelia overpowered the fever that raged in him. "What have you done to her? If you hurt her, I'll—"

"You'll what?" Mora goaded. "You are not in any condition to threaten me. If it will ease your way into death, she is still alive. For now. I need her. I need to know about her life, her past, so that I can take her place among society."

Struggling to rise, Gabriel asked, "For God's sake, why?" His head spun and he fell back against the pillows, fighting dizziness, fighting nausea. "What is this great plan of yours?"

Mora had wisely positioned herself out of his reach. She shrugged. "It isn't my plan," she said. "It's the Wargs' plan. I am simply a tool they use, as are all of us among them who can shift into the likeness of another. We are pretenders. And our duty in life is to serve. Through a few, many will benefit."

Gabriel couldn't stand to look at Mora standing there with Amelia's face. "Show yourself to me," he said. "I will go to my grave at least knowing the face of my killer. If I am still uncertain as to what you actually are."

For the briefest moment, she looked sad. "I am not your killer. The injury to your leg, the fever, those things will kill you. I have no need to dirty my hands. As for what I am, I am human for the most part. It is said the Wargs were favored by the ancient gods. They gave us the powers we have in order to guard mankind . . . but mankind turned on us. We became hunted, cast out, and soon we learned to live in the shadows."

"Why don't you just stay there?" Gabriel suggested. "And you say you will not kill me, but you will kill Amelia once you've wrested all the information you need from her. She wouldn't leave and save herself because of you. How can you live with your deception?"

Mora turned her back on him. "I am regretful that she must sacrifice for me, even though I should not be, because our survival is more important. You ask why we do not remain hidden. We cannot survive any longer in the woods. There is not enough game to feed us. We have grown weary of being hunted, of being whispered about around night fires. We are stronger than mankind. We are favored. It is only right that we should rule."

Gabriel had trouble comprehending all she said, due to his weakened state. Some of it didn't make sense. "At Collingsworth Manor, why didn't you simply let them in? Why the pretense?"

When Mora turned to face him, she no longer looked like Amelia. She didn't look like the Mora he knew, either. How she had managed to make herself look plain must have been a trick in itself. Her hair was long and thick and fell to her slim waist, nearly the same shade of pale blond as Amelia's. She wore the clothes Amelia had worn when last he saw her, too. She was nearly the same height, the same build. Her eyes were blue, although a darker shade.

"I could have," she admitted. "I needed to have Amelia's trust even if she was captured. I still needed time to study her, to get to know her. I convinced them all that to let us flee would work more to our favor. It would give me the time I needed, although there is still much I do not know about her."

"And now I understand that you must at least in some ways resemble the person whose place you take," he said.

"Yes," she admitted. Mora sighed. "Enough talk. Shouldn't you be dying?"

Now that Mora had brought the matter to his attention, Gabriel realized he didn't feel as weak as he had earlier. He was still hot, but not burning up. Did the coming of the wolf bring him strength? It must, because he'd been able to make love to Amelia when he should have been too ill. What else could the wolf do for him?

"There is one thing your kind cannot plan for," he told Mora.

She lifted a brow again, an unconsciously haughty gesture that would suit her well among society.

"Some of us will not simply lie down and die." The pain hovered just beneath the surface, and Gabriel allowed it to come. As a man, he could not save Amelia. But as something other than a man, he might still give her a chance.

CHAPTER NINETEEN

Amelia was trapped. The men who had mistaken her for a boy earlier had been called to account by Mora, and now two were stationed outside the door, one downstairs, and two outside. They weren't about to allow Amelia to escape. Mora had forced Amelia to hand over her clothes and, oddly enough, had offered her the luxury of the bath she had ordered for herself. She'd also had food brought up to Amelia. She felt rather like a goose being fattened for Christmas dinner.

She had used the bath, mostly because she hadn't had a proper one since she made love to Gabriel, partly because she needed the time to think about her situation and how she would get herself out of it. In her valise, Amelia had found clothing. Her own clothing. Her perfume. Whatever Mora would need to convince those at Wulfglen that she was the distraught Lady Collingsworth.

Would Rosalind see through Mora's disguise? Had they become good enough friends for Armond's wife to know the woman presenting herself as Amelia was in fact an impostor?

And why was Amelia even allowing herself to believe it would come to that? If Gabriel weren't sick, possibly dying, she would never give up hope of being rescued. But he was, and the thought of him at Mora's mercy nearly drove Amelia insane with worry and with anger. After all he'd done to protect her, to protect even a woman who had no need of it, Amelia felt useless when he now needed her to be strong. Nothing in her life had prepared her for what had happened at Collingsworth Manor on her wedding night, for what had happened every day since.

Still, Amelia had survived. She had done what was necessary, what Gabriel told her to do for the most part. And in the process, she had discovered things about herself she had never known before. She was frightened of the men guarding her, for she knew they were more than men. But she was more frightened for Gabriel. Mora had said his infection would kill him, but what if Mora wasn't patient enough to wait for a death from natural causes for him? Amelia had to do something; she just wasn't certain what.

Glancing around the room, she looked for something she might use as a weapon. The room was sparsely furnished. The tub still sat in the middle of the room, the water now cold. There was a crock for pouring fresh water into the basin. A candlestick. Amelia walked over and picked it up. It wasn't heavy enough to render a man unconscious.

She glanced at her valise again. She'd dug a sensible gown from the valise to put on after her bath. Truth be told, she preferred the lad's clothes. They had been much easier to maneuver in. For the first time since her escape from this very tavern, she wore undergarments again. She'd kept the sturdy boots, knowing if she did manage to escape, they would serve her better than one of two pairs of slippers that had been stuffed inside the valise.

Amelia lifted her perfume, uncorked the dainty bottle, and sniffed. It seemed stronger than she remembered, and her eyes watered. She had grown accustomed to going without it. She'd replaced the bottle when a thought occurred to her. She glanced back at the sturdy crock and the basin. Snatching the bottle back up, she moved toward the items. The crock was full of fresh water. Amelia poured a little into the basin; then she unstopped the perfume and poured the whole bottle in the water. The scent was so strong her eyes watered again.

She took the crock to the tub and emptied what water remained. Now what to do? She needed the men posted outside the door to come into the room. Snatching up the empty perfume bottle, she hurled it against the door with all her strength. It shattered. Quickly she rushed to the door, bent, and picked up a large shard of glass. She'd barely made it back to her position in front of the washbasin when the door swung open.

One of the men walked inside, glass crunching under his boots. "What are you up to?"

Poising the sharp shard against her wrist, Amelia said, "I will not take part in your plans. I will kill myself first."

The man's eyes widened. He yelled for the other man before he lunged toward her. Amelia dropped the glass, grabbed the basin, and threw the contents in his face. The other man was already reaching for her and she swung the basin and hit him square in the face. He stumbled back and fell to the floor. The man whom she had doused had his hands over his eyes, rubbing frantically.

"God, it stings!" he shouted, and Amelia knew she had only a moment before both men recovered. She leaped over the fallen man, and then she was running, out the door, into the hallway, and down the stairs. She couldn't be quiet, not in the clunky boots she wore. The man posted in the common's room glanced up from a table where he sat, surprise etched on his features.

"Hey!" he shouted, struggling to his feet.

Amelia had the advantage. She was already in motion and she made her decision to try the back door. It had stood open and unguarded earlier. She prayed that was still the case. The kitchen area was overheated. A pot sat simmering on top of the stove, no doubt for whatever dinner the men had planned. She snatched it up, uncaring this time if she burned her hands. As soon as the man who'd been guarding the downstairs came through the entry, she hurled the contents of the pot in his face. He howled with the pain and she threw the pot at him for good measure. Then she was at the back door, which indeed still stood open. She was out a second later, running for her life and for Gabriel's.

The pain caught Gabriel by surprise. It came so quickly he didn't have time to prepare. He clutched his middle and bent over. He glanced up, gasping with the pain. Mora still stood watching him. He saw no victory in her eyes but rather a sad resignation. She thought he was dying.

"Surrender to it," she said softly. "Let death take you quickly."

Would the change come faster if he did what she suggested? If he surrendered rather than fought? Gabriel closed his eyes and willed the wolf to him. The curse that had hovered over him and shaped his life, had once stolen his dreams and his future. How he hated the beast that prowled beneath his skin, but this once he must surrender. He must bow down. His pride fought the notion, for it whispered of the weaknesses he detested in others. The weaknesses within himself.

Fangs lengthened in his mouth. He felt them with his tongue. As he stared at Mora through the haze of pain consuming him, he saw the moment she realized he was not dying . . . he was changing. Her eyes widened. She took a step back, although he imagined it was an unconscious gesture.

His eyes burned inside his skull. Claws burst through the skin of his fingertips and he nearly shouted out with the pain. Instead, he held them up for her to see.

"You didn't plan on this, did you?" he asked, his voice raw and garbled.

"You are one of us," she whispered, clearly shocked.

"Never," he growled. "I am cursed! I do not choose to become this monster inside of me. But for Amelia, for her life, I gladly embrace it."

The pain was excruciating, but he kept his focus on Mora and what she would do now that she knew she wasn't dealing with a dying man, but a creature, not unlike herself. She didn't do what he expected. She didn't shift her shape and become a beast. She ran from him. The pain in his leg was nothing compared to the pain of transformation, but Gabriel forced himself to rise from the bed. He must rescue Amelia, if it was the last thing he ever did in this life.

Amelia ran. She had to reach Gabriel. She had to protect him from Mora, if it wasn't already too late. The thought of him weak and sick, at Mora's mercy, propelled Amelia toward the cottage at a speed she would have once never suspected she possessed.

Shouts sounded behind her. An alarm had been raised. Amelia picked up her skirts and picked up her speed. The boots were harder to run in than her dainty slippers. They were heavier and too big. Still, she managed as best she could, pushing herself onward toward the cottage. She knew the creatures were now aware that the cottage was where she and Gabriel had been hiding, but she had to save Gabriel. How she would accomplish that without a weapon of any kind, against a woman who was no ordinary woman, she didn't know. Only that she must try.

Crashing through the woods, Amelia nearly collided with a dark shape. She barely avoided running into the wolf. The animal hesitated, turning back toward her, and Amelia's heart rose in her throat. The animal bared its fangs and growled low. At one blessedly ignorant time, Amelia might have thought it was simply a wolf. She knew better now. She had a feeling she knew who this particular wolf was, as well.

"Mora?" she croaked.

The wolf lunged and knocked her to the ground. It was on top of her a moment later, snarling down into her face. The creature was going to kill her. The animal's breath didn't smell like raw meat, as had that of the man who had attacked Amelia at Collingsworth Manor. Oddly enough, the creature smelled like the perfume Amelia had once worn. Her mind still had trouble grasping that a person could shift their shape and become someone or something else.

Could Mora reason while in wolf form? If she could easily shift her form back and forth, Amelia had to assume Mora could think rationally even when she took on the guise of a wolf. Staring into the glowing eyes of the beast, Amelia could only do one thing. Appeal to the person she once knew as Mora.

"Let me go to him," she said. "Please, Mora. I know you really don't want to hurt either of us. Whatever you are, you are still human."

The wolf growled again, lowering its fangs dangerously close to Amelia's neck. She felt its breath, the warmth of saliva that dripped from its mouth. Amelia was mesmerized by the glittering gaze of the wolf. Mora's eyes, she realized.

"We were friends," Amelia whispered. "I cared about you. I trusted you."

She had no idea if the wolf understood her words, but she reasoned Mora surely understood her fear. Even an animal sensed that in a person. The wolf stared at her a moment longer; then it climbed down from on top of her. Amelia was afraid to move. Afraid Mora would reconsider. The wolf abruptly glanced up; then it was gone, like a wisp of smoke in the darkness.

Amelia scrambled up. She pressed a hand to her

pounding heart, then turned to run in the direction of the cottage. She only made it a step when she drew up short and screamed. A tall shadow stood among the trees.

"Amelia?"

"Gabriel," she said with a sigh of relief. Her first instinct was to rush toward him. To fling herself into his arms. She was never so happy to see anyone in her life.

"Don't," he said when she took a step toward him. "Run, Amelia. And keep running, no matter what you see or hear."

His voice sounded odd. Not quite like him. And how on earth had he managed to rise from bed, much less walk out into the woods? She thought he was dying when she left him.

"How—"

"Go now!"

"Not without you," she argued.

"I will follow," he said. "We are in the woods again. Do as I say."

She wanted to argue further. Amelia hadn't done all she'd done to leave him behind. There wasn't time to waste; she knew that and so did he. The others would be upon them at any moment. Either as men or as wolves.

"Promise me you'll follow," she said.

"Go!"

He almost growled the word at her. Amelia tugged up the hem of her skirt, tied it around her waist, and ran. She knew she couldn't return to the cottage. They wouldn't be safe there now. She hoped she was headed east. A glance over her shoulder and she saw the tall shadow following. At least he hadn't lied about that.

How he could follow at all was still not something she understood. There wasn't time to contemplate the matter. There was only time to run. It was dark, but the full moon overhead helped light her way, although the trees cast shadows and she still had to be careful.

Behind her, she heard the howls of wolves. They were close. Too close. Amelia glanced behind her again. She didn't see Gabriel. Had she moved too quickly for him? Had his leg given out? She stopped, dragging air into her lungs. Suddenly the sounds of animals fighting split the night. Or she thought it was the sound of animals fighting. Perhaps it was the sound of the wolves attacking Gabriel. Amelia went to the ground; she frantically searched for some type of weapon. The only thing she came up with was a large stick. Grasping it in her hand, she turned to retrace her steps.

A wolf suddenly appeared on the path behind her. A large wolf. Survival instincts came rushing to the surface, and Amelia ran. She doubted if the stick would ward off the beast. She also doubted that she could outrun it, but she pushed onward, fear driving her when her legs and lungs would have given out.

While she ran, she kept expecting the animal to lunge on her back and take her down, like felled prey. A glance over her shoulder told her the animal was still there. But it didn't seem to be chasing her. It seemed to be following her. And it was limping. She continued to run, jumping over fallen logs, tripping once when she stepped in a rabbit hole, but scrambling back up to run again.

She had a stitch in her side and her breathing sounded ragged a while later. Her legs were weak and shaky. She needed to stop and catch her breath, but she was afraid to. Where could she go where a wolf couldn't go? And if she did find somewhere to hide, would the wolf simply turn into a man and come after her? Where was Gabriel? Wherever he was, there was a wolf between her and him. She had to stop at least long enough for Gabriel to catch up. Maybe the two of them together could protect each other from the beast that trailed her.

It had been years since Amelia climbed a tree. Not since she was a young girl trying to steal her father's affection away from her younger brother. She'd thought if she could shoot and ride and climb trees as well as a boy, her father would consider her worthy of his much-needed attention. Of course later in life she understood that he loved her, cherished her in fact; he was just a busy man.

He had his duty. Her mother had her duty, and they both had expected Amelia to have hers, as well. "Duty," however, was sometimes a cold and unfeeling word. Love was warm and real, and her parents, if she survived this journey, would not be happy with any affiliation she might have with Gabriel Wulf. And she did plan to have an affiliation with him. She hoped it would be a very long one.

That Amelia would be thinking such thoughts at all strongly suggested she had gone insane since she had become wed and widowed. Perhaps her mind simply needed a break from the constant stress of running for her life. Her dress still hiked up, and thankful for the boots even if they were too big, Amelia chose a tall tree and proceeded to climb it. She hadn't gotten far when the wolf appeared below her. Sudden fear chased all other thoughts away. She climbed higher, then perched on a branch, staring down, waiting for the wolf to shift its shape and come after her.

The beast simply sat, staring up at her. She stared back, feeling far from safe and wondering if climbing the tree had been a good idea. She must come back down at some point. Squinting through the darkness, she used her higher vantage point to search the woods behind her. She saw no sign of Gabriel. God, had he fallen ill again? Had he been captured? She wanted to backtrack and find out, but she was in a sticky situation herself.

After a few moments of staring up at her, the wolf rose and limped off into the night. Amelia wouldn't breathe a sigh of relief just yet. She didn't feel safe and wondered if she'd ever feel safe again. Exhausted, she positioned her back against the thick trunk of the tree, allowing her legs to dangle on either side of the branch on which she sat. She closed her eyes for a moment. Just for a moment, then she would get up the nerve to climb back down and go in search of Gabriel.

CHAPTER TWENTY

Amelia came awake with a start. She tried to sit up straight, but the ground beneath her looked a long way off. She would have fallen had she not instinctively reached out and grasped a sturdy branch to stop herself. Morning had come, and once again, she was surprised to be alive to see it. She searched the ground below. No sign of a wolf. When she moved, her muscles put up a protest. She was stiff and sore from sleeping in a tree, but things could be much worse. Of course they could be much better, as well. Gabriel could be with her, and the fact that he wasn't was the only thing that motivated her to climb down from the tree and face the world again or, rather, the world as she'd come to know it.

Once she climbed down and dropped from the tree, she stood very still, listening, as Gabriel had often done on their trek to Wulfglen. Amelia was beginning to wonder if such a place really existed. If a world outside the forest, where normal people carried on about the business of their lives none the wiser that men and women could shift into animals and even other people, existed. She realized she could never go back to that world again and be who she was before. Not knowing what she now knew.

To her left she heard a twig snap. Her head swung in that direction. Her nostrils flared slightly, as if she might be an animal trying to catch the scent of danger. She was poised for flight when he appeared through the cover of thick foliage. Amelia's knees, weak to begin with, nearly buckled beneath her. He limped toward her, his green eyes blending with the forest. Gabriel needed a shave and his clothes were torn in several places. Still, he managed to somehow resemble the prince from her dreams.

"Gabriel," she breathed; then she raced toward him.

He limped faster and when they met, she threw herself into his arms. "I thought you were captured, or worse," she whispered, and suddenly she couldn't hold back the tears.

His strong arms went around her and he pulled her close. "Thank God you're all right."

Amelia clung to him. "What happened to you?" she asked. "Where did you go? I thought you were following me, then I didn't see you, and a wolf was there. I climbed a tree to escape it."

He ran his hand over her hair. "Did the wolf try to hurt you?"

She pulled back to look at him. "No. And that was the strange thing. It just stared at me, then limped off into the night."

"We must get moving," he said. "They're still behind us. We're not that far from Wulfglen. They know they must stop us before we reach the estate."

She wanted a moment longer in his arms. A moment

to simply feel him pressed against her. To know he was alive and there with her. She could face anything as long as he was beside her. Gently he pushed her away.

"We must go, Amelia," he repeated. "Now."

Her moment of heaven had ended. Hell waited for them and Amelia could face that, as well, as long as she wasn't alone. He took her hand in his and together they set off toward the east. They moved as quickly as his injury allowed, but he seemed better. Certainly he wasn't burning up with fever anymore. It must have broken at some point.

"Did Mora come to you?" Amelia asked. "Did she try to kill you?"

"Do you know what she is?"

"Yes," Amelia answered. "She is one of them. She's the reason we weren't attacked sooner than we were. She wanted time with me, to study me. She plans to take my place among society."

Gabriel frowned. "Well, she's not with us now, so they won't be holding back anymore. If we are confronted with them, I want you to run and not look back."

She squeezed his hand. "I know I'm supposed to follow your orders when we are in the woods, but I'm not leaving you again. I shouldn't have left you last night. I would have died had something happened to you."

He stopped, turning to face her. "You would have died had you not done exactly what you did. I know you have courage, Amelia. I also know you are smart. I don't want you to waste your life on me."

What a thing to say to her. Amelia was momentarily stunned. "You would waste yours on me," she said.

"My life is already wasted."

What was he saying? Did he not have the same dreams and hopes that she had? That they would manage to reach safety and spend the rest of their lives together, wiser than most for all that had happened to them but also stronger? Stronger together.

"You don't love me," she suddenly understood. Just because she loved him didn't mean he must love her in return. And that perhaps was what her mother had wished to spare her from. The pain that suddenly erupted inside of her heart.

"Now is not the time," he clipped, pulling her along behind him.

Amelia drew up, tugging her hand from his. "When is the time, Gabriel? We don't even know if we will see tomorrow. When if not now?"

His gaze softened for a moment. He swallowed. Then he glanced away and set his jaw. "Come on. I'm hoping we can reach Wulfglen before nightfall."

Amelia knew it would only prove how silly and spoiled she could still be to argue with him. She followed, not allowing him to hold her hand this time. What if they did manage to reach Wulfglen? Did he expect her to return to London, to society, and pretend they had never made love? They had never shared this adventure together? She couldn't return to that life. She wanted to stay with him. She wanted to wear men's trousers and boots and ride horses with him. She wanted to get to know him, and it suddenly struck her that she didn't know him, not really.

"Tell me your hopes and dreams," she said, because if she was going to die, she wanted to die at least knowing that about him.

He sighed. "Amelia, we can make better time if we don't use the energy to speak to one another."

"I need to know them," she insisted. "It won't hurt you to—"

"I don't have any," he interrupted. "Drop the matter, Amelia."

She would not drop the matter. "Why don't you have any hopes or dreams? Everyone does."

Gabriel stopped and turned to face her. "I don't. I don't because I have never allowed myself to have them. They are a foolish pastime for people who have nothing better to do. For those who cannot accept their lives as they are. For those who cannot accept themselves the way they are."

His bleak words stunned her. "By all means be forthright," she responded in the same dry tone he often used. "It isn't normal for you to feel this way," she added. "You do realize that, don't you?"

He glanced over his shoulder at her. "There are a good many things about me that aren't normal. You do realize that, don't you?"

Yes, she did. Besides the fact that his family was shunned by society—that he chose to hide himself away at the country estate, which made him different from most men Amelia associated with, he also had strange abilities. She knew at times he could hear things that she could not. See things that she could not. Even smell things that she could not. He had that intoxicating scent about him that drew her . . . that would draw any woman, she supposed.

His eyes didn't always look quite right, especially in the evenings. Amelia didn't count any of those things a reason not to love him. As a reason for him to set himself apart from the rest of society and give up having hopes and dreams.

"I told you that I like people who are not like everyone else," she said. "But everyone should have dreams and hopes to see them through the hard times in their lives."

Gabriel looked over his shoulder again and lifted a brow. "Have you had many hard times up until now, Amelia?"

He was being difficult today. She wondered if his leg was hurting again. They were moving at a brisk pace despite his limping. "Not many," she admitted.

"And I suppose you married Robert because he was different." He made a snorting noise. "He was as straight an arrow as you would ever find."

That was true. There hadn't been anything unique or interesting about Robert. Still, it wasn't polite to speak ill of the dead, and he had been her husband . . . for a day. "Vincent killed him," she said. "The creatures have a physician among them in London. He knew Robert's heart was weak. They left his body in the fields to go along with a story Mora planned to concoct when she showed up at Wulfglen upset about her missing husband. They have it all planned out, Gabriel."

In front of her, he stopped again. He took a moment to run his hands through his hair before turning to face her. "I'm sorry," he said. "I shouldn't have said that about him. He was a good man. At least he was once a good friend. I shouldn't have said what I did about you, either. You have been subjected to more than even most men could endure since your wedding night. You have held up better than most could have, as well. You are truly unique, Amelia, and you shouldn't be here. You should be in a London drawing room charming all around you, as you charm me."

He found her charming? Amelia supposed that was at least something. She would rather he love her, as she loved him. Maybe she had to finally resign herself to the fact that she could not always have exactly what she wanted. She certainly didn't want her current situation.

"We should get moving," Gabriel said. He took her hand again. Amelia allowed the contact, the feel of her smaller hand in his larger, stronger one.

Perhaps there were things about Gabriel Wulf she should question, and lord knew she had more she wanted to discuss with him. Such as how he could be dying yesterday and walking through the woods with her today? Where had he been last night? Why were his clothes torn? How had he escaped from Mora? They were all questions Amelia would ask him, if they did reach Wulfglen.

For now, he was right. She barely had the energy to put one foot in front of the other and move as quickly as he pushed her. Trying to pry more information from Gabriel when his mind was set on one thing and one thing only would merely exhaust her further.

*Gabriel knew Amelia had questions. He didn't have an*swers. None that he wanted to share with her. All he could concentrate on at the moment was getting her closer to Wulfglen. Getting her to safety. Then he would have to deal with his own problems. The leg was surprisingly better. His fever must have broken at some point, maybe when the change came upon him.

He'd battled the pain while he followed Amelia through the woods; then things became hazy. He didn't remember anything else until he woke this morning, again naked and shivering. He'd backtracked and found his clothing, ripped and luckily not too far off the path he knew Amelia had taken.

Once he'd dressed and his head began to clear, he realized he could have hurt her. Gabriel feared nothing as much as he had feared what he might have done to Amelia while he was in wolf form. And yet he would hurt her emotionally. He must, for her own good. He had nothing to offer her before the curse had come crashing down upon him. He certainly had nothing now. Searching his heart, he had to admit that what had happened to him embarrassed him more than anything.

He'd worked hard all of his life to make himself strong. He'd shut off his emotions; he'd kept his distance from society. And still, he was not strong enough to resist love, to fight down the beast inside of him. Both had defeated him. He wasn't angry at Amelia. She was simply irresistible to him. He was angry at himself.

And he was bracing himself for their inevitable separation should they reach Wulfglen alive. He didn't want her to know the truth. She loved him, or so she said. Why she would was beyond his understanding. He was nothing like the dandies who no doubt had chased after her in London. He was nothing like anyone she knew. Except for Mora, and now Amelia despised the girl she had once taken beneath her wing. Just as she would despise Gabriel if she learned the truth about him.

"Wait." Amelia suddenly halted.

"What is it?" he asked her.

"I thought I saw something from the corner of my eye," she whispered. "Shadows moving from tree to tree."

Gabriel pulled her behind him. He'd been lost in the turmoil of his thoughts and had lowered his guard. Again, not like him. He listened. The forest was quiet. Too quiet. His gaze scanned the surrounding area. Nothing moved, which was strange in itself. He closed his eyes and sniffed the air. At first he smelled nothing unusual; then a scent drifted to him on the slight breeze. Amelia's perfume.

Gabriel opened his eyes, turned to Amelia, and said, "Run!"

He didn't wait for her to react. Gabriel grabbed her hand and took off, pulling her behind him. She might not have been able to keep up, but although his leg was better, he wasn't completely healed. They heard the crush of boots behind them now. The shouts of one man to another. For whatever reason, the others did not come after them in the form of wolves but as men. Gabriel wondered if they were controlled by the night, the moon, as he was.

He didn't see the trap until it was too late: men in the trees above them. Two large nets dropped from the sky. Gabriel was forced to let go of Amelia's hand, hoping to keep the net from entangling him, but it was heavy and well-knit. Beside him, Amelia struggled with her own net. Her face was ashen, her eyes large with fear. Damn, he had failed her again. They were captives.

Chapter Twenty-One

The camp they were taken to wasn't far, which Gabriel was ironically glad of because the nets weighed them down and Amelia had stumbled and nearly fallen more than once. Their feet were free, but the nets drawn tight didn't allow for them to take anything but small steps. Their captors were not taking chances that Gabriel and Amelia would escape them again. He had a sick feeling in the pit of his stomach. He had vowed to protect Amelia, had thought he had done a good job of that, only to learn that because of Mora they were never being truly hunted . . . until now.

Why they didn't just kill Gabriel and Amelia when they had the chance, he didn't know. The men who had rounded them up and herded them to the camp had weapons. If Gabriel had been able to move his arms from his sides, he would have wrestled a weapon from at least one man and tried to shoot his and Amelia's way free.

A tent had been set up. It was a strange sight against the rugged backdrop of the forest. A few men milled around outside, stopping to stare as they neared. Gabriel studied the faces of the men. They looked like ordinary people. He supposed he would find that odd if he did not look like an ordinary man himself.

One of the men stepped forward. "They want to talk to him first," he told the others. "The woman stays outside."

Gabriel didn't like the fact that they were splitting him and Amelia up. He liked the fact less that she would be left on her own with these men, bound by the net around her, unable to defend herself. The thought filled him with rage and he tried to bring his hands up from his sides and free himself from the net. Two men were on him in an instant, holding his arms by his sides.

"No need to struggle," a female voice said. "It is pointless."

He glanced toward the tent. Mora stood there. She was dressed in what he had to assume was Amelia's finery, taken once they had fled Collingsworth Manor. Mora looked nothing like a servant. She did look every inch a lady, one who would blend in among the tonish set even if she did not take the form of Amelia Sinclair Collingsworth. Except for her eyes. There was a wildness there she could not disguise.

"Amelia won't be harmed," Mora said. "Not yet, anyway. Come peacefully or that will change."

It was worse that he and Amelia had been captured together. Gabriel knew they would use her against him if they wanted something, and they obviously did, or he and Amelia would have been killed upon capture. All he could do at the moment was go inside and see what Mora wanted. He tried to send Amelia a reassuring glance, although he did not feel assured of anything at the moment.

"Take the net off of her," he demanded. "She is not an animal."

Mora met his gaze, lifting a perfectly arched brow. A slight smile shaped her lips at his insinuation. "Tie her hands," she instructed the men. "Give her fresh water and find a comfortable spot for her to rest."

Although Mora spouted orders like a queen, a few of the men were clearly resentful of her authority and her instructions. There was no argument, however, and Gabriel was shoved forward and herded into the tent. There were cushions on the floor, a small table filled with food and wine. And there was another man inside the tent. He wasn't a guard, Gabriel quickly surmised. The man was too well dressed.

"You have led us on quite a chase, Lord Gabriel Wulf," the man said. He indicated a cushion on the floor. "Please join us."

Gabriel didn't have a choice. One of the guards had come inside with him and shoved him to the ground. "What do you want?" he cut to the point.

The man lifted a wineglass and took a drink. "I believe my sister has already informed you of our plans," he answered drily. He shot Mora a reproachful glance. "Mora sometimes takes too much for granted."

Gabriel cut his eyes toward Mora, who blushed slightly over the reprimand.

"And although she has great abilities, Mora isn't always the best judge of character, either." The man studied him from across the low table set with food and drink. "She should have known you were one of us. She should have sensed it, but she was too busy studying Lady Collingsworth and her mannerisms, as she was told to do, to question your own odd abilities."

"Get to the point, Raef," Mora interrupted. "I have been scolded enough for my oversight."

Raef, supposedly Mora's brother, looked nothing like her. Where Mora was light haired and fair skinned, her brother's hair was so black it was nearly blue. His skin was more olive. The only thing they shared was the color of their eyes.

The man took another drink of wine. "Mora has convinced me that you may be of more use to us alive than dead."

"I don't see how," Gabriel assured him.

When Mora's brother smiled, his teeth flashed white against his swarthy skin. "I think you do."

Of course Gabriel did. They wanted to use him, as they wanted to use everyone, to their advantage. "I have no standing among society," he pointed out. "Surely you are aware of that."

"Perhaps not now," the man agreed. He glanced toward Mora. "But with Lady Collingsworth as your wife, that could change."

Gabriel laughed. "Do you think I would marry your sister? Pretending to be Amelia or any other way?" He looked at Mora and narrowed his eyes. "I'd as soon sleep with a serpent every night. I'd trust the snake more."

He expected his insult to anger Mora; instead, she looked oddly hurt by it. What did she expect? He'd cared for her along their journey. He'd protected her, he thought. And truth be told, he was also angry that he hadn't picked up on her deception. He'd been naturally leery of her in the beginning. He should have paid attention to his first instincts.

"Mora does what she has been taught to do and what she is told to do," Raef said, and he no longer looked amused by the whole situation. "You are one of us, whether you wish to admit it or not. Why not join us?"

"I am not one of you!" Gabriel growled. "I am cursed. I do not embrace what I have become. I am shamed by it."

Raef set his wine aside and was in Gabriel's face so quickly, it took him by surprise. "If you'd been given nothing else in your cursed life but your extraordinary abilities, you would feel differently. If you watched your family starve, your brothers hunted like animals, you would feel differently. Mark my words on that."

"What are you going to do to Amelia?" Gabriel demanded.

The man sighed and reseated himself. "Beautiful Amelia is going to die. I'm sorry, but it must be that way. For the cause."

"Just like you murdered her husband for the cause?" Gabriel asked. "Just as you will murder anyone in your way and claim it is for the cause?"

Raef ran a hand over his rugged features, then stared at Gabriel for a moment, as if contemplating how to respond. Finally, he said, "From what I understand, it has been better for you that the husband was dead. He didn't love her, you know. He only married her for the large dowry her father had placed upon her. Every servant at Collingsworth Manor knew that. You saw his home. It was falling down around him. He hardly had the money to plant his fields. He was going to have to sell his precious horses if he didn't find a wealthy wife, and quickly. And he did have a bad heart. We simply sped him along his way."

Gabriel wondered if the man was telling the truth. Had Robert only married Amelia for her dowry? How sad if that was the case. Robert was an idiot if that was true. "Don't tell her that," Gabriel said quietly.

The man lifted a raven brow. "You are in love with her. It clouds your judgment. You should be thinking about your own skin right now, and saving it."

"I don't care about my own skin," he said. "I do care about hers."

Mora walked into view, standing behind her brother. "Does Lady Collingsworth know what you are?"

He couldn't look Mora in the eye.

"She will despise you," she assured him. "Just as she now despises me. I don't require you to love me, to even like me. Together, we can do a lot for our people."

He shook his head. "Our people? I've told you, I am not one of you. Whatever the hell it is you are."

"You are not like your lady love, either," Raef spoke up. "I think you need to be reminded of that. I think she needs to see exactly what you are. Mora believes the moon controls the change for you. Although we have learned to shift at will, the moon still has an effect on us, as well. It makes controlling the animal side of our nature more difficult. We will allow Amelia to watch you transform tonight. In the morning you can give us your decision."

There was nothing worse than the thought of Amelia watching him turn into a beast before her eyes. To know that she would understand he had deceived her. That he had made love to her without telling her what he was. That she had trusted him when he'd been lying to her from the moment he met her. He was no better than Mora, who had deceived them both.

"I would prefer that you just kill me now," he said.

Raef smiled, even if it was a rather sad one.

Amelia was terrified. After days of running from the creatures, she was among them now, at their mercy, and so was Gabriel. The creatures had kept them separated throughout the day. She'd been given water to drink, even offered food, although she refused, knowing it would not stay down with her stomach churning as it was. She sat in the shade at least. She was still alive at least. But she knew that wouldn't be for much longer.

Gabriel was across the camp. They hadn't removed the net from him as they had done for her. Her blond angel looked uncharacteristically defeated. She hoped it was simply a pretense on his part. She hoped while he sat brooding he was thinking of a way to get them out of this predicament. She'd exhausted her own mind upon the matter. They were well guarded. They were secured. They had no weapons. It was a bleak scenario.

She'd thought about throwing herself upon Mora's mercy, begging for her and Gabriel's lives, but knew it would do no good. Mora had her cause to love. She'd already proven it was more important to her than the lives of two people who had once befriended and protected her. And yet Mora had spared Amelia that night she'd escaped from the tavern. There might be a small hope of survival if their fate was left solely up to Mora, but obviously there were others in the camp of importance among these people.

Amelia had seen a tall, dark-headed man come and go from the tent. Those guarding them seemed to stand taller when he appeared, as if he were royalty. Amelia supposed under different circumstances she might have found him handsome. He'd barely glanced in her direction, as if she was of no importance to him. A means to an end.

Twice Amelia had been untied and allowed to attend to personal matters, but always with a guard standing within embarrassingly close distance. Did she have the strength to wrestle a weapon away from one of the men? Could she outrun them if she bolted? She'd have to leave Gabriel behind, which she could not do. Better to get a weapon and take a hostage. Someone they would easily exchange Gabriel for. Mora.

Amelia mulled the idea over as night drew nearer. She watched two men who had been curiously constructing something during the day, something made from thick branches lashed together by ropes. Only when they finally finished did Amelia realize it was a cage. A cage big enough to hold a man. Her gaze swung toward Gabriel. He was also looking at the cage, and his expression was so dark and dangerous she would be afraid of him if she didn't know him so well.

Mora and the dark man exited the tent. Amelia was more than annoyed that Mora looked better in her clothes than she did. Skinned rabbits were roasting over a spit in the middle of camp, and the smell of cooked meat made her stomach growl. Cushions were brought from the tent and placed on the ground around the fire. Mora nodded to the man guarding Amelia and he reached down and hauled her to her feet, pushing her toward where the other two were now seated.

"Sit," Mora instructed her.

Amelia would have disobeyed if she had a choice. The guard shoved her down.

Mora now glanced toward Gabriel. "Put him in the cage," she instructed.

Amelia's heart broke as she watched three burly men jerk Gabriel to his feet and drag him struggling toward the cage. One used a knife to slice the netting from Gabriel before he was shoved inside, the gate at one end secured so he couldn't get out. There wasn't room for him to stand. He had to draw his knees up to fit inside the cage. He glared at Amelia's companions, his eyes glowing blue in the coming dark.

"Would you like something to eat, Amelia?" Mora asked.

She couldn't eat now, even if the smell of meat was nearly torture. "No need to be civil," she said to Mora. "I know you're not, even if you suddenly like to put on airs."

The man smiled as if amused by Amelia's daring. "She's right, Sister. There is no need to offer comfort to the enemy."

"You know our own rules, Raef," Mora countered to the man. "As little suffering as possible. We should offer her what comforts we can until . . ."

The silence that followed might as well have rung loud in the night as a death toll. "What about Gabriel?" Amelia asked. "I haven't seen you offer him any comfort today. Why have you put him in a cage?"

"We had to secure him in some fashion," the man answered instead of Mora. He reached forward and tore a piece of juicy meat from a rabbit on one of the spits. "We thought seeing him thus might loosen your tongue. We could torture him if you don't provide Mora with information she needs concerning your background."

Perhaps that was the reason they had not killed Gabriel right away, Amelia reasoned. They wanted to use him to force information from her. She had sworn she would not talk, but she now had to reconsider. Amelia also had to face the fact that once they had what they wanted from her, they no longer needed her alive. As she'd told Mora once before, she wouldn't make it easy for them.

"I have a sister and two brothers," she lied. "My sister's name is Florence and my brothers' names are Michael and—"

"We know about your family and who they are," the man called Raef said drily. "Please give us credit for having the intelligence to learn those details quickly. We need private information. What is your favorite color?"

"Pink of course." Her favorite color was blue.

"What is your affiliation with the Dowager Duchess of Brayberry?" he asked next.

Amelia was surprised by the question. These people knew more than she suspected they might know about higher society. "We are acquaintances," she admitted. "Although Her Grace hardly tolerates me. She believes I'm too outspoken." Amelia doubted there was a more outspoken woman in the world than the duchess. She encouraged similar behavior among those she counted as friends.

"How is your relationship with your parents?" Mora asked.

It was too much suddenly for Amelia to realize this woman would try to make her parents believe she was their daughter. Tears choked her throat and she couldn't answer.

"We usually try to find those who have no close family left," Mora said quietly. "It's another reason Lord Collingsworth was chosen."

"Be quiet, Mora," Raef snapped. "You've told her too much already. You easily forget the ways taught to us. No need to pet the lamb before leading it to the slaughterhouse. Nothing you say will make her think better of you. Of any of us."

Amelia supposed it wasn't so bad to die for a cause, just not someone else's. Darkness had now fallen and it was harder to see Gabriel inside his cage. All she saw were his glowing eyes trained on her. She stared back, hoping to send him a message. Hoping he knew she truly did love him and if perhaps they would be together again after death she didn't mind dying so much. She would rather live. She would rather spend her days and nights with him. She would rather have his blond little boys. That possibility seemed far-fetched under current conditions.

Supper was removed from the spits and portions divided among the group. Amelia sat in silence as logs were added to the fire blazing before her. She was able to see Gabriel again in the orange glow cast by the flames, and for that she was grateful. She felt stronger when she could see him. Amelia knew she must help him. Refusal of food had been foolish when she might use it to her advantage.

"I find I am hungry," she said, glancing at Mora. "But I can't eat with my hands tied behind my back and don't wish to be further humiliated by being hand-fed. You can at least allow me my dignity."

Mora glanced toward her brother. "She's hardly a match for the rest of us," she said. "Shall we untie her hands so she can eat?"

Raef shook his head. "She's escaped us once already. You underestimated her, Mora. A mistake you should have already learned from."

Mora bowed her head submissively. Amelia mentally cursed that the brother was less trusting and less civil than his sister. How could she wrest a weapon away from anyone with her hands tied? Maybe Gabriel had a plan. She hoped he did.

"Can I speak to Gabriel?" she asked. "Can I take him food, water? You said your rules do not include torture, and what you've done to him looks like torture to me."

"The rules only apply to treatment of your kind," Raef said; then he smiled slightly in the firelight.

What did he mean by that? Amelia wondered. Women but not men would be treated with respect? "It is torture for me not to be able to speak to him. To say things to him that I feel should be said if we are to shortly be led to the slaughter."

She fully expected her request to be denied. Raef glanced up at the sky, glanced toward the cage, and shrugged. "Perhaps you should say your good-byes.

Go and have a closer look at him. You." He nodded toward one of the guards standing close. "Take her over to see him."

The man reached down and grabbed Amelia's arm and pulled her to her feet. Amelia was led to where the cage sat. Gabriel had his back to her. She bent before the cage.

"Gabriel," she said softly. "They have allowed me to speak to you for a moment."

He didn't turn to look at her. Was he blaming himself for their capture? He'd done all he could; she knew that. Amelia glanced at the guard. "Please, a moment of privacy?" she asked.

The man took a few steps back, but he didn't retreat as far as she would have wished. "Gabriel," Amelia tried again, keeping her voice to a whisper. "Talk to me."

"Can they hear us?" he asked softly.

Amelia glanced at the guard again. He seemed alert but not particularly interested in what they were saying. "Not if we keep our voices down," she answered. "Have you got a plan, Gabriel?"

"Yes."

She breathed a sigh of relief but wondered why he wouldn't turn and look at her; then she noticed he was shaking. "Are you ill again?" she whispered.

"That's not important," he said. He reached behind him and shoved something in her direction. The cage threw shadows inside and Amelia reached for the object. It was a knife.

She wondered how he had come by it; then she recalled the guard using a knife to cut the net away before they shoved Gabriel inside the cage. Somehow he had taken it from the guard, who obviously hadn't missed the weapon yet.

"Free your hands," Gabriel said.

Amelia wondered if she could, her wrists tied together as they were. "You may have to do it," she whispered.

He shook his head. "I'm shaking too badly. I might cut you. Use your knees. Slide the knife between them to hold it steady; then you can cut through the rope around your wrists."

Wondering what she was supposed to do once she had freed her hands, Amelia did as he instructed. She was thankful she wore a dress and could easily hide her actions within the folds of her skirt. The knife was sharp and it didn't take but a moment to free her hands.

"Now what?"

"Pretend you are trying to see me better and move toward the end of the cage," he instructed. "Use the knife on the ropes holding the gate together at the bottom. I should be able to kick it open. Appeal to me loudly to look at you before you reposition yourself."

So, this was why he kept his back to her. Very clever. "Gabriel, why won't you look at me?" Amelia raised her voice to ask. "Why won't you let me see you?" It now would seem a natural response for her to scoot to a position where she might better see him.

Once there, Amelia bent her knees, hiding the fact that her hands were free and going for the ropes that lashed the cage together on one end.

"How are we going to escape?" she whispered.

For a moment his shaking worsened. "I will create a diversion," he finally said, and she thought his voice sounded odd. "You are to run, Amelia, and keep running. I'll keep them off of you as long as I can."

She didn't like his plan. Not one bit. "No," she whispered. "We run together."

He shook his head. "That won't work, Amelia. They would be upon us before we made it past the camp perimeters. We have a better chance of escaping if you do as I say."

She had a better chance, Amelia wanted to argue. To her, it sounded as if he had no chance at all. "I've cut the ropes," she whispered. "Please look at me now."

Rather than do as she asked, he said, "Put the knife in your boot, Amelia. Can you use it if you are forced to? If it means your life at the cost of someone else's?"

Mora, she thought. He was asking her if she could use it against Mora if she must. Amelia wasn't sure. In self-defense, yes, she supposed she could. She wouldn't know unless tested. But that wasn't what Gabriel needed to hear.

"Yes," she answered.

"Promise me."

"Look at me," she insisted.

"Promise me first."

"I promise," she said, although she wasn't sure she wasn't lying to him, which she didn't want to do. A person shouldn't lie to someone they loved. Not without good cause. Amelia thought she had good enough reason at the moment.

He sat shaking for a moment; then slowly, he turned in the small confines of the cage to look at her.

She screamed.

Chapter Twenty-Two

Amelia scrambled back from Gabriel. His eyes glowed bright blue. In the orange hue cast by the fire, his features looked distorted, as if his face was rearranging itself. When he opened his mouth, fangs flashed white in the darkness. He held a hand out to her, beseeching, but his hands were misshapen, long claws jutting from his fingertips. This could not be happening. It was another dream. Another nightmare.

"Amelia." His voice came out garbled. "Forgive me."

All she could do was shake her head in denial.

"What do you think of your hero now?" She glanced up to see Mora standing above her. "He deceived you, just as I deceived you. Look at him and tell me that you still love him."

Amelia couldn't look. She didn't want to. She wanted to deny what she saw, deny the truth, deny that any of this was happening to her . . . to Gabriel. Had these people done something to him? Could they do something to a person to make him like they were? Could they do the same to her?

"What have you done to him?" she screamed at Mora.

Mora bent beside her. "We didn't do anything to him. This is his curse. He didn't tell you about this while he was wooing you into bed, did he? When he was stealing your heart away? Go ahead and tell him you love him regardless that he is a beast. Regardless that he has deceived you."

Amelia glanced toward Gabriel, who, oddly enough, seemed to be listening, waiting for her response, even as he changed forms. There were too many emotions running through her to examine any of them but one. She had to get away.

With a loud bellow, Gabriel suddenly kicked out and knocked the gate off of his cage. He was out in the bat of an eye. Just as quickly he was pounced upon by two of the closest guards. He fought like a madman. He fought like an animal. And with sudden dawning, Amelia realized he was fighting for her. This was the diversion that was supposed to allow her to escape.

Mora still stood beside her, but Amelia saw that she was caught up in the diversion. Amelia quickly glanced around the campsite. Even Mora's brother had risen from his cushion and stood ready to jump into the fray if the guards could not handle Gabriel. Amelia slipped the knife into her boot; then she began to inch away, slowly, so as not to draw attention to herself. Even with thoughts of escape on her mind, she couldn't take her eyes from Gabriel.

His fangs were more pronounced now, his nose longer, his body bent and misshapen, and yet he fought gallantly. She'd nearly scooted to the edge of the camp perimeters when he went down on all fours. Men stumbled away from him and she saw him clawing at his clothes.

It seemed to last forever, the transformation, although Amelia knew in truth only a few seconds had ticked past before he rose from the ground, no longer a man but a wolf. His coat was light colored. He was huge and she realized he had been the wolf that followed her the night she escaped from the tavern. The wolf that had sat below her while she sought safety in a tree, staring up at her. The wolf that had limped.

Gabriel, or, rather, the wolf that was once Gabriel, bolted in the opposite direction from Amelia. All around the camp, men's eyes began to glitter; fangs began to extract. They would hunt Gabriel in wolf form so that he had no advantage over them. And in a moment, someone would realize she was missing. Amelia scrambled to her feet. Although her knees were shaking, she ran into the woods. She ran as she had never run before, now more conditioned by her flight from Collingsworth Manor, from her journey through the woods toward Wulfglen.

Her mind wanted to think about Gabriel and what had just happened to him, but she would not allow it. She might easily snap if she did. Instead, she only thought about running, about staying ahead of the creatures she knew would soon come after her, if they hadn't already. A loud chorus of howls echoed around the forest behind her. Amelia swallowed down a scream and kept running.

There was no safety for her in the woods. No place that a wolf could not sniff her out. No possible way that she could outrun one if her captors were in pursuit of her. Those realizations nearly defeated her. She wanted to stop and rest. Part of her wanted to give up. Then she caught a whiff of smoke on the air. Could it be the night fires burning at Wulfglen? Was she that close? Or did she simply smell the campfire she'd left behind not long ago? Amelia did stop.

She took a moment to catch her breath; then she tried to figure out which way the wind blew. Toward her, she realized, which meant the smoke she smelled was not coming from the direction behind her but in front of her. But if she did manage to reach Wulfglen, would it be the safe harbor she once imagined it to be? Mora had said what happened to Gabriel was his curse. All of the Wulf brothers were supposedly cursed, by insanity, everyone thought.

Were Armond and Jackson like Gabriel? And if they were, did her friend Rosalind know about her husband? Did Lucinda know? Or had the Wulf brothers kept their secrets, the way Gabriel had kept his from Amelia? Would they want to kill her because she knew, like the others wanted her dead? Suddenly Amelia realized there was no one she could trust. No one who hadn't lied to her, deceived her.

But then, maybe that wasn't true. She was confused. Gabriel had lied to her, deceived her, but he'd also protected her. Even tonight he'd been willing to sacrifice himself for her. She had believed she loved him. Could she love a man cursed as he was?

Amelia had to make a decision. She couldn't stand around all night trying to sort through her thoughts and feelings. The only thoughts and feelings she should have at the moment were how to best survive the night. She had to take a chance on Wulfglen. Even if no one was home, servants would be about, wouldn't they? At least whoever was in charge of looking after the stable. Having made her decision, Amelia set off toward the direction where she still smelled the vague traces of smoke in the air. She didn't get far when she was attacked.

The wolf lunged at her from the shadows, knocking her to the ground. Amelia rolled in the dirt, then scrambled up. She knew the wolf now. It was Mora. She would have been the first to notice Amelia had escaped. She would have been the first to come after her.

"I will kill you," she said to the beast. "If you give me no choice, I will protect myself."

The wolf peeled back its lips and growled at her. Amelia was almost glad Mora had attacked her while in the shape of an animal. If she had to make good on her threat, it would be easier. Still, there was one thing these people could not change, and that was their eyes. It was Mora's eyes staring up at Amelia, not the eyes of a beast.

"Just let me go," she appealed to Mora. "No one would believe me if I told them about you and the others. They would think I had gone mad. I want the life you plan to steal from me. I will fight you to the very end to keep it."

The wolf inched closer. Amelia brought the knife up, her hand gripping the short hilt so that she could lash out with all her strength. The animal crouched, as if it meant to pounce, but from the shadows a larger wolf hurled itself at Mora and knocked her away. Amelia recognized this wolf, as well. It was Gabriel.

Wolf squared off against wolf. They circled each other, growling, hair down their backs raised. Amelia crawled away from them, her back pressed against a tree, the knife still held out in front of her. The beasts collided. They were a blur to Amelia's merely human eyes, but from the sounds of the fight, both were out for blood. In a battle of beasts, Gabriel clearly held the advantage. He was twice the size of Mora and quickly pinned her down. Amelia heard the smaller wolf yelp; then it was dragging itself away, crawling along the ground, bleeding at the shoulder.

Amelia expected Gabriel would finish Mora off, but instead his large head swung in her direction. He moved toward her. She swallowed loudly and brought the knife up before her again.

"Stay away, Gabriel," she whispered. "I don't want to hurt you, but I will."

The wolf stopped and stood regarding her. Amelia had no idea if Gabriel could understand her in wolf form, as she suspected Mora and her kind could. Mora had said he wasn't the same. He was cursed. His question came back to haunt her in that instant. When he'd asked if she could kill to defend herself, he hadn't just meant against Mora or one of her people. He'd meant against him.

Could she kill him if he attacked her? His eyes were the eyes of the man she loved, or thought she did. Whether he could understand her words, fathom who she was, he was still Gabriel beneath the fur and the fangs, wasn't he? Mora moved and the larger wolf immediately turned its head and growled at her. She stayed down.

Gabriel didn't want Mora to get too close to her, Amelia realized. Even as a wolf, he was protecting her. She lowered the knife. Whatever Gabriel Wulf was, he wouldn't hurt Amelia. She knew that with a certainty she'd never known about anything or anyone before. He had lied to her. He had deceived her, but she could still trust him with her life. But what about her heart?

Exhaustion set into her bones. She leaned her head back against the trunk of the tree and closed her eyes. For the moment, Gabriel wouldn't let anything happen to her. For the moment, she was safe.

*It was horrible. Coming awake naked and shivering, con-*fused, trying to figure out what had happened to him and where he was. Gabriel uncurled himself, his muscles putting up a protest, as if he'd been turned inside out. His leg was better. Either that or the rest of him felt so bad the leg seemed minor in comparison. He stretched in the cool morning light. Then he remembered.

Amelia. God, where was she? Had she escaped? Oddly, he had a blurry recollection of seeing her in the forest . . . a knife clutched in her hand. Odder still, he recalled what she'd said to him. She'd said she would hurt him if she had no choice. He wasn't dead. That left the horrifying possibility that she might be. Gabriel rose from the forest floor, naked. Then he spotted her a few feet away. She was asleep. He breathed a sigh of relief; then he spotted someone else.

Mora lay on the ground, human, her eyes closed. Leaves covered her like a blanket. One might mistake her for a fairy princess, if one didn't know better. The blade of the knife still clutched in Amelia's hand blinked at him when sunlight managed to penetrate the heavy canopy of trees overhead. Gabriel went to her; he bent and removed the knife from her hand. Her eyes opened. For a sweet moment, she smiled at him. Then, as dawning came to her, the smile faded and she pressed back against the tree, as if to get away from him. Gabriel had no time to offer her assurances that he was in his right head and she had no reason to be afraid of him.

He had to deal with the threat of Mora once and for all. Gabriel had never physically hurt a woman, but Mora would kill Amelia if she got another chance. He couldn't allow her to have another chance. He walked to where Mora lay, bent, and placed the knife against her throat. She opened her eyes, and for a moment, like he had felt earlier, she looked dazed. Her eyes widened upon seeing him leaning over her, naked and with a knife pressed against her throat. She tried to move, but the action brought a moan from her lips. The leaves fell away from her shoulder and Gabriel saw the nasty bite marks, the blood.

"You are my enemy, Mora," he said to her. "You are a danger to Amelia. It's time to end your threats."

He thought to make a clean, quick slash; regardless of what she'd done to him and Amelia, Gabriel did not want her to suffer. Suddenly a hand was upon his shoulder.

"Don't, Gabriel," Amelia breathed.

He glanced up at her. The sunlight danced around

her blond head like a halo. The compassion in her eyes pierced his heart.

"She could have killed me twice and she didn't. I don't think her duty is as simple as she was led to believe."

Gabriel glanced down at the woman pinned by his knife. Mora glanced up at Amelia. "They taught us how to speak, how to walk, how to fit into any setting, whether it be servant or superior. They did not tell us we would care. They did not teach us to kill without conscience. I'm not certain we are ready to take over the world yet."

Mora had deceived them before. Gabriel didn't feel as compassionate toward her as Amelia did. He damn sure didn't trust Mora. And he didn't have Amelia safely to Wulfglen. He had a decision to make, and it was not an easy one, regardless of Mora's deception. He had deceived, as well. Mora and her kind were only trying to survive. He should understand that, and maybe he would, if they held by their own rules.

"You talk of rules among your people and then discard them the moment things do not work out as planned," he said to Mora. "You have rogues among you, like Vincent, who would harm Amelia rather than woo her as he should have done. You are sometimes more beast than human. You will never survive among civilized society."

"Something to think about."

Gabriel turned his head to see Raef standing not far away, a pistol aimed at him.

"Now, get off of my sister."

Raef was not alone. His men stood behind him. Gabriel might end Mora's threat with the swipe of his knife, but there were still the others to deal with.

"I will trade her life to you for Amelia's," he said. "Let her go. You can do what you want with me."

"Gallant to the end," Raef said, the usual sarcasm flavoring his voice. "That is something that cannot be taught, unfortunately. I'm glad few of your station possess the trait."

"Raef," Mora called softly. "Do as he says. Let Amelia go. I could not fool this man when I took her form; I therefore doubt if I could fool others who know her well. Killing her is senseless and barbaric. She has shown me compassion, and I must do the same."

Mora's brother frowned. He did not lower the weapon. "They will tell others about us."

"Will they?" Mora challenged. She tried to struggle to a sitting position, recalled her naked state, and stayed as she was. "Even if they do, whoever they tell will think she's mad, and his family is already rumored to be insane. Why would he tell? He's no better than us. It would be to his advantage if society remains ignorant."

Raef didn't appear fully convinced. Gabriel pressed the knife to Mora's throat again to help convince him. If it were only one man he was dealing with, Gabriel would never use a woman as a bargaining tool, but for Amelia's safety he would. Raef seemed to sense Gabriel's dedication. Finally, he lowered the pistol.

"All right, Wulf. I will trade my sister's life for the life of your lady love. As for you, we have no use for a man who does not share our goals. Move away from Mora. Both you and the woman are free to go now."

Gabriel was still leery. These people had been pursuing them for days. They were dedicated to their cause. They had proven they would kill for it. He found it difficult to believe Mora's people would let him and Amelia walk away.

"He will keep his word," Mora said, as if sensing Gabriel's hesitation. "My brother and I are honor bound to the Wargs, but we do not always agree with their ways. It is time for us to slink back into the shadows. To think about this experience and evaluate it. And it is time for you to go home."

Home. Would it or could it be the same for Gabriel now? He was cursed. He had deceived the woman he loved. What was left for him? Survival alone? Was it enough anymore?

He felt Amelia's hand upon his shoulder again. "Let her go, Gabriel. It's over now."

Slowly, he slid the knife away from Mora's throat. "I never want to see you again," he said to her.

The smile that crossed her lips was both chilling and sad. "You will. But you won't know it's me."

Raef came forward, the pistol now shoved into the waistband of his trousers. He threw Amelia's valise on the ground, then snapped his fingers. One of his men appeared with a set of coarse clothing and a large pair of boots. He placed the items on the ground next to the valise. While Gabriel hurried into the trousers, the man handed Raef a blanket. Mora's brother bent beside her. A moment later he rose, carrying Mora's blanket-clad body in his arms.

He paused before Gabriel. "I gave my sister my word this time," Raef said. "If I cross paths with you again, I will not be so civil."

"Neither will I," Gabriel assured the man.

Their gazes held for a moment in silent challenge. Finally, Raef turned and walked away, his bearing that of a prince. Still wary, Gabriel watched Raef and his men move into the forest. A moment later, it swallowed them up, as if they had never been there. Gabriel stood staring, squinting into the shadows of the forest until he was certain they were truly gone. Then slowly he turned to face the woman he had deceived.

CHAPTER TWENTY-THREE

A barrage of emotions assaulted Amelia. Relief that Raef and his men were gone, that she was safe, that the nightmare had ended; only it was not over. Before her stood the man she loved, yet he had deceived her. He had lied to her. He was not what she thought he was. How was she supposed to feel about him? How was she supposed to take her life back when nothing about her life was the same anymore?

He stared at her now, waiting for her to say something, but what could she say? How could she understand what he had never explained to her?

"You deceived me," she finally said.

Gabriel could no longer hold her stare. He glanced away, bent his head, and studied the ground. "Yes," he responded. "I did."

"What is this curse that rests upon your family?" she asked. "Why didn't you tell me the truth from the beginning?"

He looked up at her with his forest green eyes. "In the beginning, if I'd told you the truth, you would have been afraid of me. You wouldn't have allowed me to help you. You wouldn't have trusted me."

That was true. After what had happened to her at Collingsworth Manor, had Gabriel told her he was different, that he could change his shape like the others, she would have been terrified of him. Still . . .

"Later, you could have told me," she said. "Later, you *should* have told me."

He glanced away from her again. "I know," was all he said.

She was tired of his secrets and wanted them exposed now. He owed her that much. "Tell me about your curse. Do your brothers suffer from it also? Do their wives know, or do they keep their secrets like you?"

Bending, Gabriel lifted the shirt left for him from the ground and slipped it over his head. "All who share our bloodline share our curse," he answered. "One of our ancestors was cursed by a witch long ago. But the curse must be set into motion. I have no idea if Armond suffers as I now suffer, or Jackson, although I had suspicions about him before he went missing."

Curious, Amelia stepped closer to him. "It must be set into motion? By what?"

He didn't answer. Instead, he pulled on the boots sitting next to her valise and adjusted his clothing.

"By what, Gabriel?" she repeated.

Finally, he glanced back up at her. "By a man's weaknesses."

His answer confused her. "Do you mean by sickness? Did it happen because your leg became infected?"

He shook his head. "No. I mean weakness. A character flaw—being unable to resist things a stronger man could resist. I lowered my defenses against the curse, and now it has taken me."

If the curse was simply tied to a man's weaknesses, Amelia wondered how it hadn't affected him before now. All men surely had weaknesses. "Did the curse just now come upon you? Or have you had the ability to shift your shape from the beginning?"

Gabriel walked to a fallen log and sat. He was still limping a little, she noted. "No, it just came upon me this full moon, and I do not have the ability to shift. I do not have a choice. But I have known about the curse for a long time. I have known I am different from other men."

She'd known he was different, too. But with the other threats aimed at her, she had never considered him one, as well. And she shouldn't have, Amelia realized. He'd never been a threat to her, not even when the moon changed him. He had still been her protector.

"What happens now?" she asked him.

Rising from the log, he walked over and picked up her valise. "Now I take you to Wulfglen. You go on with your life and I figure out how to go on with mine."

His words fell flat in the air around her. Was she supposed to forget what had happened to her? What had happened to him? That she loved him? Or did she? He wasn't her prince, he was a man cursed. A man who had deceived her, no matter how just he felt in doing so at the time. And still she wanted to believe in the dreams she once had about her life and his. In spite of all that had happened, she still had hope. Suddenly she understood why he did not have hopes and dreams.

"This is what happened to your father, isn't it?" she asked.

He kept walking. "Yes. He was weak, my mother as well. The curse destroyed them."

And, Amelia imagined, it destroyed their children in a way. Coddled and spoiled all of her life, she supposed she wasn't one to judge what Gabriel's father's suicide had done to him. Or his mother's quick passing upon the heels of what must have been a shock to him. Then the sons had been left with the fear embedded in them that their lives might end in a similar tragedy.

"You don't have to follow in their footsteps," she said. "You don't have to let this destroy you."

Drawing up, he turned to her again. "If you think I'm planning on fetching a pistol and blowing my brains out, you're wrong," he said. "If you think I can carry on a normal life like a normal man now, you're wrong in that, too. Come, Amelia," he added impatiently. "I'd think you'd be anxious to return to the life you've been forced to leave behind these many days. In two weeks' time you'll forget this even happened."

She was stunned he would say that to her. She did not fall into step behind him. "Do you still think so little of me?" she demanded. "That I am so shallow? That I will ever forget what happened to me, to us?"

He stopped ahead of her. For a moment he bowed his head, as if her questions shamed him. It was in that moment that Amelia realized that he did not trust her—that Gabriel Wulf had never trusted anyone. Perhaps not even himself.

"You won't hurt me," she said, "while in your wolf form. You protected me last night from Mora."

"I don't know that," he bit out, his voice bitter. "I cannot remember my thoughts or what happens to me while the night and the moon take control of my life. I can't know for certain that I would not hurt you. I could not live with myself if I did."

Her heart softened, and she knew then that she still loved him. She once thought she was too shallow to love, or too afraid, but now she knew that was not the case. She'd been given the greatest test of her love. Gabriel had been tested, too.

"You must learn to trust, Gabriel," she said. "If not in anyone else, at least in yourself. What you consider weaknesses are perhaps only human emotions."

His eyes bored into hers and he took a step toward her. "Do I disgust you now? Are you afraid of me? Are you wishing you had never given yourself to me?"

She was not disgusted by him. Nor was she afraid of him. And no, she would not take back the love she shared with him. The love they made to each other. But would words convince a man so mistrustful of the world and seemingly everyone in it?

Amelia closed the distance between them. Once she stood before him, she reached up, put her arms around his neck, and kissed him.

Gabriel had expected excuses, perhaps lies to spare his feelings; he didn't expect Amelia to kiss him. He breathed in her fresh scent, savored the feel of her soft lips pressed against his. Why didn't he disgust her? Why wasn't she afraid of him? Why hadn't she reacted to him as he had thought she would were she to learn the truth? Was she pretending? Did she fear if she let her true feelings toward him be known, he might not help her reach Wulfglen safely? And how far would she go with her pretense?

Gabriel cupped the back of her head and slanted his mouth against hers. She opened willingly to him and he tasted her, explored her for fear he would never be allowed the opportunity again. Her body melted against his, her ripe curves pressed against his hard muscles. He was on fire for her in a heartbeat. Perhaps the beast inside of him ruled him even when the sky was not dark, the moon was not full, or maybe it was just the man who couldn't resist her. The man who loved her but could not offer her a future, even if she was willing to share his cursed life.

With great effort, Gabriel ended the kiss, released her, and stepped away. "No need to whore yourself to me," he said. "I will make certain you reach Wulfglen safely. The beast only rules me at night."

Amelia did something else that surprised him. She slapped him. Her face suffused with color. "I'm not so sure of that," she snapped. "You're acting like one right now." She marched ahead of him. "Perhaps it has not occurred to you that I do not need your help to reach Wulfglen. Any idiot can figure out which way is east."

He stood staring after her, too stunned to respond for a moment; then he found himself laughing. She turned to him, placed her hands on her hips, and asked, "What do you find so funny?"

"You," he answered honestly. "You should be shaking in those god-awful boots you're wearing; instead you kiss me, then you slap me and put me in my place. It's no wonder I love you. There's no one like you."

Gabriel realized what he had just admitted to her when her cross expression faded and her eyes welled with tears. He wanted to take the words back, and yet he was glad to finally speak them. To finally admit them, even to himself.

She returned to him and reached up to touch his cheek softly. "Why is it so hard for you to say the words?" she asked. "Why do you consider your feelings for me to be a weakness?"

"Love is the curse," he answered without thought.

She blinked up at him. "What?"

He'd told her more than he intended. "Never mind; let's go."

Amelia grabbed his arm when he thought to forge ahead. "What do you mean, 'love is the curse'?"

He knew by her set expression she wouldn't budge without some type of explanation. And maybe she deserved the truth for once. " 'Love is the curse that binds you, but 'tis also the key.' It's a quote from the poem written by the first Wulf cursed." He had never understood that particular phrase of the riddle. How could love be both a curse and a key? A key to what?

"I am the reason you are now cursed by the moon. Is that what you're telling me?"

Gabriel didn't want her to feel guilt. He certainly didn't want her to feel beholden to him. Or, heaven forbid, pity. He could take nearly anything but that. Touching her cheek softly, as she had done to him, he said, "It is not your fault, Amelia." He assured her, "It is my own fault. I knew the consequences, and still, I allowed myself to be weak. To give my heart when I knew I should not. I traded everything for a chance to be only a man in your eyes. Even if only for one night."

As a tear slipped down her cheek, he brushed it away with his thumb. "I don't want you to cry," he said, her tears washing him in more guilt. "I want you to be happy. I want you to leave all this behind you and—"

"I told you once that I did not believe in love," she interrupted, her voice emotional. "I thought it was just a gentler word for lust, or duty. What I feel for you is beyond lust. I have no duty toward you. That is when I knew I did believe in love, and that I loved you. I need to know that I am more than a consequence to you, Gabriel. You need to understand that loving takes a stronger person than someone who hides their heart from the world. You need to understand compassion is not the same as pity. When you do learn these things, come and find me."

With that, she stepped away from him, picked up the valise he had dropped, and walked away from him. Gabriel started to go after her. To stop her, pull her around into his arms, and kiss her until she could not think straight. But he couldn't. She didn't understand the whole of what she would be forced to endure if she stayed with him. A solitary life for Amelia Sinclair Collingsworth? He could not imagine it, and did not want to.

There could be no children for them. He would have to take himself off when the curse visited him. He would have to leave her alone. In time, she might hate him. In time, she might leave him. Better to let her go now, although it tore at his insides to do so. He knew he would love her more with each day and the pain of losing her would be unbearable. Like the pain of losing his parents. The pain of realizing his life was cursed. The pain of letting all his hopes and dreams die on that night ten years ago when his father had turned into a wolf at the dinner table.

But for her he could sacrifice. Couldn't he? Gabriel watched her move ahead of him. He would not stop her. He would dog her heels all the way to Wulfglen to make certain she reached the estate safely; then he would stay in the woods until she was gone.

Chapter Twenty-Four

Gabriel stared at the lights burning in the windows of his family home, Wulfglen. Amelia must be inside now, surrounded, he hoped, by his brothers, hearing the tale of how she'd come to be there. He longed to be there, too, beside her. He longed to be an ordinary man who'd just had an extraordinary adventure. But of course he was not ordinary, nor had he ever been.

Even now, as darkness fell, he felt the wolf inside preparing to emerge. Gabriel would roam the woods of his home as a beast. For how long? How long until he could go home again?

"Tell me your hopes and dreams."

Startled, he turned to see Amelia standing a short distance from him. "I thought you would have gone on to the house. What are you doing out here?"

She shrugged, and for a moment she looked like a lost little girl with her valise sitting beside her on the ground. "It's odd, to travel for days, fearing for your life, only to find when your destination looms up before you, you cannot go."

Gabriel was confused and more than a little concerned that the beast would soon be upon him and

Amelia had not taken herself to a safe haven. "Of course you can go," he said. "It's just there." He nodded toward the house. "Someone is home or all the lights wouldn't be burning. I haven't seen the place lit up like that in years."

"Come with me," she said softly.

He longed to, but he could not. "You know I can't," he said. "Not now. Not when the night is nearly upon me. You shouldn't be here. I'm afraid I'll hurt you, Amelia."

"You already have," she said. "But I do not fear you when you become the beast. I told you, you won't hurt me. Besides, perhaps your brothers have found a way around the curse, since they are happily married."

"I do not know," he said. "But I do know I am not willing to take a chance that I might not hurt you. And neither should you."

She took a step toward him. "That is how we differ. I am willing to take chances. I am willing to trust."

Her stubbornness was a trait he might find endearing under different circumstances. "I do not want you here," he said more harshly than he wanted. He had to make her understand she should go. Even if a small part of him did not want her to go. Not ever.

She bowed her head and he hated having to be harsh with her. Amelia Sinclair Collingsworth could wrap him around her little finger with a pout or a tear. He knew that and wished he could spend the rest of his life spoiling her. Loving her and making love to her.

"I am afraid," she whispered.

Afraid? She shouldn't be afraid of anything now, except him. Mora and Raef had kept their word. Robert's death would be ruled an accident once Amelia reported him missing and his body was found in the fields. She would be a young widow, wealthy due to her own dowry, which Robert had not had time to spend. Collingsworth Manor would belong to her, since Robert had no living relatives and Amelia had been his wife, even if for only a night. Gabriel had made certain the consummation of her marriage could not be questioned. What did she have to fear?

Although he wanted to keep distance between them, he was drawn to her, standing in the coming dark, looking like a lost child. He walked to where she stood, reached out, and lifted her chin.

"What are you afraid of, Amelia?"

Her eyes shimmered with tears when she looked up at him. "I don't want to go back to my world without you. I would rather stay here in yours."

She couldn't mean what she'd just said. How could she trade the glittering life she had known for one in the shadows? Why would she want to? He didn't want her to; not even in his most selfish dreams could he deny her all that she deserved in life. That was when Gabriel realized he did have dreams, he did have hopes. Amelia had given them to him again.

"Let me tell you my hopes and dreams," he said. He reached out and gently took her shoulders between his hands, pulling her closer. "I hope that you will be happy. I hope that you will become the most shocking woman in London, because you will live your life as you choose, and not how others would have you live it. I hope you will savor each day, because now you know what it is like to fear that you have no tomorrows left.

And no matter what happens to me, I will dream of you. I will dream of seeing you dancing in a London ballroom, or riding in men's trousers and boots, and it will warm my heart. It will see me through whatever I must face."

She smiled softly at him. "And have you no dreams and hopes for yourself?"

He thought about it for a moment. And he realized that he did. "To be as brave as you are. To be as strong as you are. To love as you love, and trust as you trust. To feel compassion and know there is no shame in it. To understand that my weaknesses are what make me human, and to therefore cling to them."

Her eyes were the softest blue in the coming dark. "Oh, Gabriel," she whispered. "I do love you so."

He didn't resist when she rose on her tiptoes and kissed him. And somewhere in his jaded heart, he began to believe that she did love him. That neither of them could have escaped this moment in time no matter what paths their lives had taken. He had known from the moment he saw her on the streets of London months ago that she was special.

"I love you, too, Amelia," he said against her lips. "And no curse will stop me from loving you."

She pulled back to look at him. "Let me stay with you. Out here in the darkness tonight; then come morning, together, we will go to the house."

Doubt immediately returned. Allow Amelia to stay with him? While the curse took him? While he became a beast to roam the night? Could he do what she had asked and trust in himself? How could he when he would soon not be himself? And yet, staring down into her eyes, Gabriel thought that for her, he could do anything.

"Please," she whispered. "Trust in me; trust in yourself. Trust in our love."

Did he dare? God, he wanted to so badly. To cast off the dark cloud that had hovered over his head for ten years. Walk in the sunshine with her by his side. Feel whole. Feel loved. Be happy despite all the odds stacked against him. Live each moment with her as if it were his last. Her eyes told him he could . . . that his hopes and dreams were in reach. Could he hold out his hand to them?

"All right, Amelia," he said. "I will trust in myself and in my love for you. And pray to God that doing so is not a mistake."

He thought to bend and kiss her again before the darkness came to claim him, but the pain in his stomach hit him so quickly that it made him gasp and stumble back from her. He went to his knees.

"It's happening, Amelia," he said through clenched teeth.

She bent beside him. "I am here with you," she said. "I am not afraid."

He was. Not for himself, but for her. If Amelia could have courage in the face of the beast, so could he. It took all of his strength, all of his will, to trust as she asked him to do. He let the beast come. Challenged it to steal his dreams and hopes. Shouted out against the pain. Amelia was still there. He felt her cool hand against his forehead.

His eyes had started to blur, but he focused upon her beautiful face. "I love you, Amelia," he said.

"And I love you," she said in return.

Something boiled up inside of him. He thought he would become ill and tried to turn onto his stomach to retch, but it was not bile that spilled from his throat. It was a blue light. Wider and wider his mouth opened until he thought his jaws would crack. Amelia stumbled away from him, but she did not run. He saw her through a haze, felt pinned to the ground, unable to do anything but open his mouth wider for the blue light. It seemed to last forever, seemed to pull his very insides out with it as it spilled forth into the air. And as he watched it float above him, the light took shape. The shape of a wolf.

It now stood upon his chest and the pressure crushed him. It lowered its head and stared down into his eyes. Gabriel gasped for breath. Amelia appeared above him. Her face was pale.

"Get off of him!" she shouted.

The wolf raised its head and stared at her.

"Begone, beast!"

Helpless to do anything but lie there, for Gabriel felt as if he'd been beaten black-and-blue, he saw the beast flinch at her words; then it crawled off of him and slunk into the night. Gabriel's breath came back to him in a gasp. Amelia was kneeling beside him again.

"Gabriel!" Tears filled her eyes. "Gabriel, speak to me! Tell me you're all right!"

It took him a moment longer to catch his breath. A moment longer still to find the strength to reach up and pull her down to him. He held her pressed against him and felt her tears against his neck. And then the enormity of what had just happened struck him. The beast had left him. He felt its absence. In the coming dark, he had trouble making out the trees overhead. He couldn't hear anything but normal night sounds around him.

"It's gone," he said.

Amelia raised her head to look down at him. "What do you mean?"

"The curse, Amelia. It's broken."

Her eyes widened. "Are you certain?"

He was. And for the first time in ten years, he felt free. Truly free. He pulled her down so that he could kiss her. "Love is the curse, but 'tis also the key."

As their lips met, he understood the riddle. He understood his enemy had lain within himself. His inability to trust. Amelia's love had given him the strength to overcome his greatest enemy. And now, he was free to love her. Free to marry her. Free to have a life besides the solitary one he had chosen for himself. It was the greatest joy he had ever known, to dream again. To hope again.

While their lips lingered against each other, Gabriel felt his strength returning. His ardor returned just as quickly and he wanted to take her there on the ground. To make sweet love to her and know he was not deceiving her. He would never deceive her again.

"Don't you think we should go home?" she asked between kisses. "I'd love a hot bath and a soft bed. And you in both with me."

He laughed. "You are shocking, Amelia Sinclair Collingsworth . . . soon to be Wulf."

She pulled back and smiled down at him; then she frowned. "Not very soon. I must honor my mourning period of one year."

The thought made him groan. "A year? I doubt that society will approve of me sleeping in your bed every night up until the nuptials. And I fully intend to."

Amelia laughed. "I will suddenly develop a great love for spending time at my friend Rosalind's country estate. I cannot go back to Collingsworth Manor, Gabriel. Once we are wed, we will tear it down and use the land for the horses."

It was a good plan. A dream, a hope he would never let go. Gabriel eased Amelia off of him, rose, and offered her his hand. "I miss my brothers. I need to tell them what has happened to me. If I can break the curse, so can they."

She took his hand and he helped her rise, reached down and grabbed her valise, and together they walked toward the lights of Wulfglen. Gabriel suddenly wondered what his brothers would think of him showing up with a woman whose wedding they had attended only a week ago. He smiled over the mayhem sure to come.

CHAPTER TWENTY-FIVE

Gabriel couldn't have been more surprised when Hawkins answered his summons at the door. The man rarely visited the country estate but kept the home fires burning in London when the Wulfs were not in residence at the townhome. The man's cool expression never faltered upon seeing Gabriel standing at the door wearing coarse clothing and with a woman wearing outlandish boots with her torn and dirty gown.

"Lord Gabriel," Hawkins said formally. "Welcome home."

The man's gaze moved to Amelia. "Lady Collingsworth," he clipped, then bowed before he straightened and opened the door wider. Gabriel led Amelia inside. He heard voices coming from the front parlor. A man he did not recognize came down the hallway carrying a bottle of brandy. Both stopped and stared at each other.

"Who the hell are you?" Gabriel asked him.

"Merrick," the man answered. "Who the hell are you?"

It suddenly occurred to Gabriel that the man standing in his hallway was the spitting image of Jackson, only his hair was dark.

"Merrick, where's that brandy?" A man stepped into the hallway. Gabriel didn't recognize him, either . . . at least not for a moment. His eyes stung with tears when he finally did.

"Sterling," he rasped.

Sterling Wulf, his youngest brother, whom Gabriel had not seen in ten years, stared back at him. "Gabriel," he said. "We were just making plans about you, and wondering where the hell you were."

Gabriel set the valise down, released Amelia's hand, and stepped forward to hug his brother. Sterling had run away the day their mother died. None of them had seen him since. They had feared he was dead.

"Good God, man, where have you been?" Gabriel said against Sterling's shoulder.

"Traveling about with a circus troupe," he answered. "At least until my son was born. Then I thought it best to bring him home."

"Your son?" Gabriel found it shocking enough just to have Sterling home.

Sterling grinned, glanced at the man standing behind them, and said, "Have you met our half brother, Merrick?"

Gabriel could only nod dumbly.

"Where's the brandy?" Armond stepped into the hall. Upon seeing Gabriel, he breathed an obvious sigh of relief. "Gabriel, thank God you finally came home. We were planning to come and search for you."

Armond stepped forward and slapped Gabriel on the shoulder.

Jackson came into the hallway next. "Where the bloody hell did everyone go? Left me alone in there with all the ladies, not that I minded so much, but Lucinda and I wanted tea and I thought I'd tell Hawkins . . ." His voice trailed upon noticing Gabriel. "About time you came home, Brother," he grumbled. "I was actually starting to worry about your sorry hide."

Gabriel smiled and pulled Jackson into a hug. All the brothers, with the exception of Merrick, who hung back simply taking in the exchange, hugged. Then Gabriel saw Armond's eyes squint into the shadows.

"Lady Collingsworth? What are you doing here?"

Gabriel stepped away from his brothers and took her hand, pulling her into the light. "It's a long story," he said.

Armond glanced between the two of them. "Hawkins! Bring more brandy!" he shouted.

"And tea!" Jackson added.

An hour later, Amelia was soaking in a tub upstairs. Gabriel had not joined her, as was their original plan. Instead, she was surrounded by Rosalind, Armond's wife; Lucinda, Jackson's wife; Lady Anne Wulf, formally Baldwin, Merrick's wife; and Elise, who was married to Sterling, both of whom Amelia had never met.

After days of seclusion, running for her life, the room upstairs seemed overly bright and overly crowded. Amelia knew the men were cloistered in the study downstairs. She felt certain Gabriel was telling them about his and Amelia's extraordinary adventure and about his own. She, to the opposite, didn't even know where to begin explaining what had happened to her at Collingsworth Manor.

Rosalind helped Amelia wash her hair. She was comforted by her friend's presence but would have been more so by Gabriel's. It was odd, but for days Amelia had been hoping to awake from a nightmare and now she actually was afraid she would wake up in her room in London and discover she had dreamed it all. That Gabriel did not even know her, had never made love to her. That they had not vowed to marry in a year, when her mourning period had ended.

"When you feel like talking about what happened, I will be here for you," Rosalind said softly. "We are all here for you," she added, including the women stationed around the room like a small army. "We have all seen things no ordinary person has seen. We will understand what no one else ever will or can."

Emotion closed Amelia's throat. "Is the curse broken then?" she asked softly. "For all Wulf brothers?"

Rosalind smiled, although somewhat sadly. "For now," she answered, then unconsciously pressed a hand against the noticeable bulge beneath her dress. "Who knows what the future will bring? But together we will all stand strong against the bad and share each other's joys."

Having finished her bath, Amelia glanced around for a towel. Rosalind lifted a fluffy one from beside her and held it open. Amelia rose from the tub, immediately wrapped in the soft fabric. She was steered toward a vanity table where she sat while Rosalind brushed out her wet hair.

"Tell me, friend," Rosalind asked, "do you still not believe in love?"

Amelia's eyes met Rosalind's in the vanity glass. She smiled at her. "What do you think?"

Rosalind laughed, as did the other women gathered in the room. "I think you have been captured by a Wulf," Rosalind said. "We are all captives, very willing captives," she added.

"A word of warning," Lady Anne said. "The Wulf brothers seem to be highly fertile. There isn't a woman in this room who isn't currently breeding or already a mother. Well, except for you," she added. "Prepare to be a mostly-swollen-with-child captive."

It wasn't a horrible thought; in fact, it was a most pleasing thought, Amelia decided. Part of her dreams was to have little boys running around her skirts who favored their very handsome father.

"I hope I am not swollen before I am able to marry Gabriel next year," she said, then realized what she'd confessed. Her cheeks burned for a moment, but she saw no censuring in the warm gazes trained upon her. Instead, Lucinda, Jackson's wife, a beautiful redhead rumored to be a witch, walked over and placed a hand against Amelia's stomach.

Curious, Amelia stared at the woman as she closed her eyes, seemingly lost in a trance. A moment later, Lucinda opened her eyes and smiled down at Amelia. "You will not get your wish," she said softly.

Amelia hoped her mouth didn't drop open. Surely Lucinda couldn't know what Amelia couldn't possibly know until more time had passed, but she had a very strong feeling Lucinda was right. Just the thought made Amelia warm and tingly inside.

"You said you wanted to be the most shocking woman in London," Rosalind reminded her, then gave her shoulder a reassuring squeeze. "Be careful what you wish for, Amelia."

Gabriel had told his brothers the story that had led him and Amelia back to Wulfglen. He felt a little odd speaking in front of Merrick, who he did not know even existed, but the man was clearly one of them, and Gabriel knew he must accept him as the rest of his brothers obviously had done. Five men, all cursed, but now free. And all because of love.

"Mora and Raef," Armond spoke, swirling his brandy in his glass. "Do you think they will try again with their plans?"

Gabriel was sure of it. He just wasn't sure when they would try again. Or what they could now do about it if they did. "The curse has been broken for us, but along with it, we have lost our edge," he said. "We might have used it to our advantage if we someday felt it was necessary to sniff these others out. If they do not play by their own rules."

"True," Jackson said. "Now, we are like everyone else."

Gabriel was amused to see Jackson drinking tea when every other man in the room had a snifter of brandy. He was proud of his brother. He'd obviously fought his demons and emerged the victor, and his wife might be a witch, but she was the prettiest witch

Gabriel had ever seen. The babe, Sebastian, had been introduced to Gabriel before Lucinda took him upstairs for bed, and although Amelia had told him true and the boy did not in the least resemble Jackson, it was clear to Gabriel that his younger brother doted upon the child.

His nephew Trenton was a big strapping babe with blond curls and green eyes who resembled Gabriel more than Sterling, and so he'd immediately taken to the babe. It was all a bit overwhelming. To find Wulfglen, once so quiet and solitary a place, teeming with such life. They even had a housekeeper. Mary was her name and she'd once worked for Rosalind's stepmother. Hawkins, stuffy man that he was, had developed feelings for Sebastian's nurse, Martha. Jackson predicted the woman wouldn't be leaving, even when the babe was old enough to no longer need her plump breasts.

"Pardon, but I couldn't help but overhear." Lucinda, Jackson's wife, stepped into the study.

Gabriel was immediately struck by her beauty and the warmth in her eyes when she glanced at her husband. She clearly adored the scoundrel, and to Gabriel's surprise, Jackson in turn clearly adored her. Odd, but Gabriel recalled hearing certain rumors when Jackson returned from abroad over a year ago that he'd been chasing one Lady Anne Baldwin all over Europe. And now that same lady was in the house, married to a man who was Jackson's half brother.

There was no tension between either couple, so Gabriel assumed the past was not an issue between them. Lucinda walked across the room to stand beside her husband. Jackson, naughty as ever, pulled her playfully down into his lap.

"What is on your mind, Wife?" Jackson asked. "Besides when I'm coming up to bed."

Lucinda flushed and gave Jackson a halfhearted nudge to the ribs. "Behave," she said. "Gabriel, I heard your concerns about losing the gifts that went along with your curse. There is something you should know, something I have not even told Jackson."

"You tell me everything," Jackson argued, summoning an expression of mock hurt.

"This is serious," she said, and Jackson's expression immediately lost its playfulness.

Lucinda rose from Jackson's lap and walked to a large window that overlooked the front lawn of Wulfglen. "I'd like for you to all to come to the window for a moment."

Gabriel had no choice but to follow suit when his brothers rose and joined Lucinda. He was bone tired and he wanted to go upstairs and crawl into bed with Amelia. He joined them all by the window.

"Look out there, along the tree line," Lucinda instructed.

Gabriel realized in that moment that his gift of seeing easily in the dark was gone. He squinted in the direction she had instructed them to look and saw nothing . . . at first. Five sets of glowing eyes shone in the darkness. Gabriel tensed.

"The others, they lied. They are out there." He immediately thought to search for weapons to protect themselves, but Lucinda stopped him.

"No, it is not these others you spoke of. It is the spirit of the wolf that once dwelled in each of you."

"Why are they there?" Jackson asked his wife. "What are they waiting for?"

She glanced at each brother in turn. "For you to call them back."

"Call them back?" Armond repeated. "Why in bloody hell would we want to do that? Bring the curse upon ourselves again?"

Lucinda shook her head. "No, not a curse, because the choice is yours this time. They are only there in case you need them."

Gabriel was confused. "But how could they help us? When the wolf took me, I could not remember what I did or where I went. The gift is not a gift at all if it cannot be controlled."

"But it can be controlled," Jackson informed him. "Lucinda taught me how to think like a man, even in the form of a wolf. If need be, I'm certain she can teach all of you, as well."

Gabriel hadn't been normal long enough to know if he missed having the gifts that went along with the curse. "If need be," he agreed. "Until then, they can stay put."

The night got the best of him. He was tired, and he wanted to be with Amelia, regardless that he was filled with joy to be home, to have all of his brothers, even one he didn't know about, at home with him. Gabriel walked over and took what was left of the brandy and two glasses.

"I am retiring for the evening," he said to everyone. "We can catch up with one another in the morning."

It didn't escape his notice that each of his brothers took note of the second glass in his hand and raised their brows. Gabriel just smiled at them and moved toward the door leading from the study.

"I wouldn't share the brandy with Lady Collingsworth," Lucinda said at his back. "Tea would be better for the babe."

The bottle slipped from his hand. "What?" He turned to the lovely witch. "What did you just say?"

"Better listen to her," Jackson piped up, grinning like an idiot. "She knows these things. Our own babe is on the way and she knew long before she missed her first cycle."

"God, it's an epidemic," Armond remarked drily, and one by one, each brother began to laugh.

Always the serious one, the sensible one, Gabriel did not join them, at least not for a moment. He'd never dared to dream of children, of even having a wife. But Amelia had taught him to dream again, to laugh again, to have hope. How could a man cursed for so long suddenly be so blessed? It was as simple as finding love and surrendering to it.

EPILOGUE

LONDON, TWO YEARS LATER

The boy was the spitting image of his father; there was no doubt about that. He would break many a heart someday, but never his mother's, Amelia felt certain. His name was Treville, and all of society knew the child did not belong to Amelia's late husband. It caused talk to be certain, but Amelia didn't mind talk.

If she did, she would not that very moment be standing in the middle of Hyde Park wearing men's breeches and boots. She and Gabriel had ridden Rotten Row earlier. Her choice of clothing had caused quite a stir, but Amelia was used to causing a stir. Gabriel found it all very amusing. She watched him now, so full of love and pride that he belonged to her and she to him. He was speaking to her parents, who'd spread a blanket on the ground and brought little Treville with them. They doted upon the child, and finally, no matter what Amelia did wrong, they turned a blind eye.

All of the Wulfs were in London at the moment. The season had begun and the Dowager Duchess of Brayberry couldn't wait to host her first Wulf ball. Everyone would come simply out of curiosity. Amelia thought she might wear trousers and boots to the ball.

That would set everyone on their ear and please the old woman immensely.

"You're looking very fetching in those trousers, Wife," Gabriel teased, joining her. "I'm sure it will be all the rage tomorrow. Women wearing men's clothing."

"Well, maybe not tomorrow, but someday I imagine it will be," she said, leaning up to give him a quick kiss. "Are you nervous about attending your first social engagement in years?"

"I'd rather be at Wulfglen," he admitted.

Surprisingly enough, so would Amelia.

"Your parents are going to spoil that boy," he said, turning Amelia's gaze to the sight of her father hefting Treville into the air until he squealed with delight. Amelia smiled, watching them. Her smile faded a moment later.

"He will be all right, won't he?" she asked softly.

Gabriel put an arm around her shoulder and pulled her closer. "He will be all right because we will make certain that he is. If Treville is different, we will tell him why, and we will tell him it doesn't mean his life is cursed. It doesn't mean he can't have hopes and dreams, and a life like everyone else."

She took assurances from Gabriel. If he said things would be all right, then she knew they would be. Armond and Rosalind had a son, also. A very handsome boy. And Jackson's dimpled little boy would steal whatever hearts his older brother, Sebastian, didn't take for himself. Merrick and Anne had a daughter. A beauty she was, and as sweet natured as her mother. Sterling's son, although only toddling, seemed to have a gift with animals, like Sterling did himself.

The curse that had stolen their lives had given them back tenfold in the end. Perhaps that had been the witch's parting gift to Ivan Wulf, only he had never realized there could be a gift in a curse. Which reminded Amelia of the glittering eyes she saw every night in the shadows. The spirit of the wolf, waiting.

"You don't suppose we will see Mora or Raef this season do you?" she asked.

Gabriel frowned down at her. "I don't suppose we'd know we were seeing them if we did."

"Will you and your brothers hunt them?"

It was a subject they mostly avoided, but Amelia would know her husband's plans.

"Only if they give us cause," he answered. "They already force us to rejoin society's ranks whether we want to or not. Someone has to protect our race from theirs." He nodded toward Amelia's mother and father, who were laughing down at young Treville. "Who will protect those who have no idea what lives in the shadows?"

Amelia knew he was right. She might have once wished to remain blessedly ignorant. But not anymore. Only the strong could protect the weak, and only a strong woman could stand bravely by the side of a guardian. She was that woman. Gabriel's woman. His wife, his lover, his partner.

"Let's ride again while Mother and Father are entertaining Treville. I want to show off our horses so that everyone rushes to us to purchase one."

"Maybe we can find a secluded spot where I can steal a proper kiss," he said against her ear.

She giggled. "I'm sure you can steal more than that if just such a spot can be found."

"You are shocking," he said, smiling down at her.

"I do my best," she countered, then took his hand and led him toward their waiting horses. Today, if they were not simply an ordinary couple enjoying a day in the park, they were an extraordinary couple. She wouldn't worry that her husband might one day be forced to embrace the spirit of the wolf again and protect the country from invasion.

Lucinda had confided to her that such espionage should be handled by other men. Men without the responsibility of children and wives to worry over them. Men who would willingly accept a curse as a gift and do battle for those still blessedly ignorant. For if Lucinda said so, it usually came to pass.